Simple
Gifts
Pamela Browning

Harlequin Books

TORONTO • NEW YORK • LONDON
AMSTERDAM • PARIS • SYDNEY • HAMBURG
STOCKHOLM • ATHENS • TOKYO • MILAN

Published March 1988

First printing January 1988

ISBN 0-373-16237-5

The Heartland is its people

It is families like the Morrows and the Vogels, who have been neighbors and friends for generations. Together they've harvested the land and raised their children to respect and love the rich soil with its bounty of golden wheat.

Heartland chronicles the lives of those people whose memories, hopes and dreams are bound up in the acres they farm. Of Sarah Morrow, who must change if she is to preserve her way of life. Of Tim Vogel, who breaks with tradition and must find his own place in the world. Of Mark Sherrod, whose troubled heart leads him on a search for his family and for the home he's never known.

This is Sarah's story...

ABOUT THE AUTHOR

Pamela Browning is a native Midwesterner who grew up in Florida and now lives in South Carolina with her husband and her two teenage children.

Books by Pamela Browning

HARLEQUIN AMERICAN ROMANCE
101–CHERISHED BEGINNINGS
116–HANDYMAN SPECIAL
123–THROUGH EYES OF LOVE
131–INTERIOR DESIGNS
140–EVER SINCE EVE
150–FOREVER IS A LONG TIME*
170–TO TOUCH THE STARS
181–THE FLUTTERBY PRINCESS
194–ICE CRYSTALS
227–KISSES IN THE RAIN
237–SIMPLE GIFTS†
241–FLY AWAY†
245–HARVEST HOME†

*SPINOFF OF #123
†THE HEARTLAND SUBSERIES

HARLEQUIN ROMANCE
2659–TOUCH OF GOLD

SIMPLE GIFTS

'Tis the gift to be simple;
'Tis the gift to be free.
'Tis the gift to come down
Where we ought to be.
And when we find our-
selves
In the place just right,
It will be in the valley
Of love and delight.
            —SHAKER HYMN

Foreword

In North America, in the aftermath of the birth of the Rocky Mountains, ancient rivers gushed forth from the earth. They carried sand, gravel and rocks, scattering them across a wide expanse of wasteland that sloped toward the Mississippi River. Later, geologists tell us, mighty glaciers spread great sheets of ice over the northern parts of the region, leveling large areas into land well suited for farming.

After the glaciers retreated, strange toothed birds, huge turtles and the tiny early ancestor of the horse roamed here. The Kaw Indians, who called themselves the People of the South Wind, followed the mighty bison as he grazed the wild grasses of this gently rolling land that we now know as Kansas.

The Spanish explorer Coronado galloped across the wide plains pursuing his quest for gold, but to his disappointment, he never found it. Coronado didn't know that in order to harvest gold here, someone would have to plant it. And even after planting it, there could still be disappointment.

It was the squaws of the Kaw Indian tribe who first farmed this land. They stayed behind to plant corn while their men followed the hunt. They were strong, these women. But then, those who farm have always needed to be strong.

White women came to subdue the prairie with the husbands they loved, and life was hard. They raised their families in sod houses because wood was scarce. They braved searing hot summers and survived fierce cold winters and stood stalwart against the winds sweeping out of the wide sky. They suffered attacks from the displaced Indians, and they buried their children in plots of lonely prairie land, far from their loved ones in the East.

The women of Kansas gave their hearts' blood for the sake of the land, and in return, the land yielded to them its golden treasure—grain.

Today the state of Kansas is the nation's largest producer of wheat.

It is the nation's Heartland.

Chapter One

Sarah Morrow stood in the middle of a wind-ruffled wheat field and plucked three or four golden heads from their stalks. Expertly she broke them open and palmed the plump kernels, estimating their moisture content. Then she lifted her hand and touched the kernels to her tongue. They felt hard and not too moist.

"Good," she said when she had sifted the kernels into the wind. "Another week or so and we'll harvest. I had an idea harvest would come early this year, and it looks like I was right." She grinned triumphantly and set off at a rapid pace toward her pickup truck.

Her cousin Henry had to hurry to keep up with her as she strode through the field, which spread as far as the eye could see. The wheat rippled in shades of yellow, from saffron to topaz to palest buff. It was a glorious sight.

"Anything else you want me to do before I go home, Sarah?" Henry asked when they reached the dirt road.

"No, let's call it a day. We'll be busy enough for the next few weeks." Sarah smiled at him.

"See you tomorrow then," he said as she climbed into her big blue pickup truck.

Sarah watched him walk away through the waving wheat stalks, looking long and lanky in faded jeans and a T-shirt. Henry was not only a valuable farmhand; he was also a genius with machinery, which made him irreplaceable to her as an employee. She hoped Henry wouldn't get an incurable case of wanderlust like so many of the young men around here. She'd have to rely on his help even more heavily once Mama and Pop left the farm.

She drove home slowly, allowing herself to enjoy her own jubilation. She'd spent the past few weeks of the growing season steeped in anxiety. So many things could happen to the wheat before the harvest was safely in. Too much rain could fall. Or too little rain could fall. Disease or insects could inflict themselves upon the growing grain before it reached the proper state of ripeness.

Yes, worry had been her constant companion, but now the wheat was almost ready. All in all, it had been a superb growing season. Still, Sarah wouldn't feel totally at ease until the crop was safely harvested. Only then would she relax.

She paused at the top of the hill, easing her foot onto the brake of her pickup truck and warming to the inevitable thrill of anticipation she always felt before she saw the valley. It was silly. She felt sheepish about it, but she couldn't help the way her heart speeded up just to look at the farm—her farm now—spread out below her like a plump and well-loved patchwork quilt.

A fringe of green—those were the cottonwood trees bending their dense midsummer canopy of leaves over the lazy Bluestem River and its tributary, Oley's Creek. Between Lornbacher Hill and the river, orange roads unfurled dusty stripes between gently billowing fields of ripening wheat. Here and there amid the golds and yellows and greens a fallow field frothed at the edges with a border of black-eyed Susans, and all was domed by a shining blue sky.

Beyond, almost hidden among trees so tall that from the top of the hill she could see only shaded triangles of white clapboard and green-shingled roof, was the beloved house that was the center of her existence. It sheltered her family and had been doing so for generation upon generation. Sarah's family had farmed the Windrush Valley of Kansas since—well, since farming became a way of life on the plains, if you counted Mama's ancestors. Mama was part Kaw Indian.

Sarah let up on the brake as the pickup flew over the crest, spinning out dust behind. The hill swooped down, down—she pretended she was riding a roller coaster at the state fair—and then the road leveled out, and she was bumping rapidly over the ruts in front of the house.

She laughed out loud from the sheer fun of it and pulled to a scratching stop behind the corrugated metal barn, marveling that she still acted like a kid every time she drove over that hill. She'd have to stop pretending such things as riding roller coasters. More dignity was called for. She wasn't a kid anymore. She was a thirty-three-year-old mother. She was a daughter with responsibilities toward her parents. And she was the person in charge at Windrush Valley Farm.

Two towheaded dynamos erupted from the barn, followed by a grizzled black-and-white dog.

"Mom! Can I ride the three-wheeler? Please?"

"Mom! Ben tore up all the construction paper! We don't have any left!"

"Can I ride the three-wheeler? Pop said I'd have to ask you."

"I was going to make valentines. And now I can't."

"Wait a minute," Sarah said. All the exhilaration of the ripening wheat and her ride down the hill evaporated. Responsibility settled on her shoulders, weighing her down like the humidity on this hot summer's day. She drew a deep breath and slid out of the truck, slamming the door forcefully behind her. She assumed her no-nonsense pose, fixing her children, Ben and Lucy, with a stern eye.

"In the first place, Lucy, this is the fifth of June. You won't need to make valentines until February, which is eight months away."

"I just thought it sounded like fun," Lucy said, drawing a big *L* for Lucy in the dry dust with her bare big toe.

"Ben, you know I don't want you riding the three-wheeler ATV alone."

"Aw, Mom—"

"No exceptions."

"Just because of what happened to Dad? It was a freak accident, Mom. Everyone said so."

Sarah's stomach clenched at the memory of the accident that had claimed James's life, but she gave no sign to Ben.

"I need to help Grandma with dinner, so I can't go with you to supervise. Sorry."

Ben tried to hide his disappointment. "Okay," he said. He dodged a wasp hovering too close to his head, and it flitted away.

"Maybe tomorrow," Sarah said halfheartedly as Ben turned to walk back to the barn.

"You said that yesterday," her son reminded her pointedly over his shoulder. Spanky, the dog, scratched vigorously behind one floppy ear before loping after Ben.

Sarah watched Ben disappear into the barn, wishing she'd come home earlier. He loved to ride the Honda all-terrain vehicle she often used when she rode out to the fields, and Sarah was determined that Ben wouldn't develop a fear of the ATV because of what had happened to James. Two years ago the ATV James was riding had flipped over on uneven terrain as he'd ridden out to check the fields, and he had died instantly. Sarah still rode the ATV, and Ben was allowed to ride with her. Sarah believed that this was the way to teach Ben safe riding practices.

She rested her hand on her six-year-old daughter's head and turned her toward the house. "Come on, Lucy," she said. "It's so hot outside. Maybe you'd like to watch Mister Rogers on television."

"I think I'll ride my bike," Lucy said, twisting out from under Sarah's touch. Lucy ran nimbly on long legs to her red bike, once a Christmas present, and took off toward the hill, the faded skirt of one of last year's cotton summer dresses flapping far short of her knees.

Her mother was standing at the sink peeling potatoes when Sarah walked in, slamming the kitchen door behind her.

"If you think you could stand it, I'd be glad to help," she told her mother.

Charlotte Norquist laughed. "No, Sarah. Thanks, anyway. Maybe you'd like to take a nice cool shower before we eat."

"How am I ever going to overcome my reputation as a kitchen klutz if you never give me a chance?" Sarah asked playfully.

At a statuesque five feet nine inches, Sarah towered over her mother, who was almost a full twelve inches shorter. She grinned down at Charlotte.

"You'll have enough chances to refresh your cooking skills after your father and I move to the house in town," Charlotte responded.

Sarah pretended to shudder. "You're right," she said. She sat down on the kitchen chair and tugged off the heavy steel-toed work boots she always wore in the field. She didn't like to track the rich, black Windrush Valley dirt through the house.

"I think I will take that shower if you're sure you're okay." Her brown eyes searched Charlotte's face for signs of pain. Charlotte's arthritis had been growing steadily worse.

"Of course I'm okay. You can toss a salad together when you're through showering, if you like."

"That's a deal," Sarah agreed, hurrying off toward the stairs.

Her bedroom, which she and James had shared when he'd been alive, was at the back of the second story of the spacious farmhouse, and it had a private bath. Sarah shucked off her jeans and the pink cotton shirt, and she turned on the shower. She paused for a moment to unbraid her thick golden hair and remove her tiny pearl earrings. The earrings had been a long-ago birthday present from James.

She washed her hair, working the shampoo quickly through the long pale strands. James had once shampooed her hair for her, laughing as he'd rubbed her scalp with his strong, sure fingers. Before long, what had started out as a lark ended up in a session of passionate lovemaking.

He had been an impulsive man, James, a man who had infused her life with a kind of wild excitement she'd never found in anyone before or since. He'd encouraged her dreaming, her pretending. The two of them had loved to ride over the hill together in the pickup truck, squealing and laughing as though they really were riding a roller coaster at the state fair. James had been a good man, a kind man. A wonderful father. To see him cut down in the prime of his life by a senseless accident had almost broken her.

Yet now she was stronger, almost certainly because of what had happened to James. Living up to her responsibilities had brought out the steely side of Sarah's character. Not that she'd been prepared for the job she was doing. No, she had been prepared to be a farmer's wife. To be supportive. A helpmate. A partner.

Yet here she was, actually running Windrush Valley Farm and getting a charge out of doing it, despite the problems. Well, you never knew what you could do in life until you had to do it, she reflected as she towel-dried her hair and quickly braided it again into one long plait before hurrying downstairs.

Charlotte wasn't in the kitchen, but Sarah saw her in the garden picking peas for dinner. By the time Charlotte returned, Sarah was standing at the kitchen counter cutting lettuce for the salad. The warm summer evening flowed through the open kitchen window, bearing the scent of grass and roses.

"How long till the harvest?" Charlotte asked as she set the basket of peas on the table and paused to catch her breath.

"Another week at the most. The wheat looks good. I think we're going to have a record yield."

"What's that?" said Sarah's father, stumping in from the living room.

"I said I think we're going to have a record yield," Sarah said, raising her voice slightly. In the past year or so her father had become increasingly hard-of-hearing.

"That so?"

Sarah held her breath. It would be just like her father to contradict her. It was hard for him, this letting go of the farm. The transfer of responsibility to Sarah was already complete, but her father questioned almost everything she did, argued almost every decision she made. Well, Sarah did the best she could. Her brother, Duane, would have surely taken over the backbreaking job of running the farm—if he'd only survived Vietnam. But he hadn't, and so it had fallen to Sarah.

"Here, Elm," Charlotte said quickly before Elm could refute Sarah's statement. "Take these peas out on the back porch and shell them."

Elm clamped his mouth shut and took the peas out on the porch. He sat there shelling them while Sarah helped her mother set the table, using the old plates with the pictures of houses and trees painted in brown. The plates had been there as long as Sarah could remember. Like the walnut kitchen table beneath the blue-and-white checked tablecloth, like the oak-case clock that hung on the wall in the living room, with a swan and water lilies painted on its glass.

"I don't want any peas," Lucy said when she came in from playing.

"Of course you do," Sarah replied automatically, spooning them onto her daughter's plate anyway. She continued around the table, dishing a spoonful of fresh garden peas onto everyone's plate.

Lucy stuck out her lower lip, and Charlotte said just as automatically as Sarah had dished out the peas, "Just three bites, Lucy Anne." It was the rule. Everyone had to eat three bites of everything at dinner.

"Looks like it might be clouding up across the river," reported Elm, hurrying to the table and hitching up the legs of the denim overalls he wore every day but Sunday.

The weather in Kansas was changeable. They never knew what it would do next. A soft, warm wind could turn harsh in only a matter of minutes. With the wheat almost ready for harvest, the farmers in the valley didn't need weather problems.

"Does it look like rain?" Sarah asked anxiously. The last thing they needed was a storm. You couldn't harvest wet wheat.

"I dunno," Elm said, taking his place at the head of the table. "Charlotte, will you ask the blessing, please?"

They held hands as was their custom, and Charlotte bowed her head and murmured, "Bless this food, oh Lord, to the nourishment of our bodies," the way she began the blessing every evening at supper, but Sarah didn't hear a word of it. She was praying for something else. She was praying that nothing would ruin her harvest.

TEN MILES SOUTHWEST of Curtisville, Kansas, Cliff Oenbrink tugged at his tie and adjusted the air conditioner vent of the company car he drove so that the stream of cold air blew directly on him. He'd left Wichita an hour or so before, and the drive was boring. There were miles and miles of nothing except farmland stretched on either side of the road. He hardly ever saw another car.

At least the boredom gave Cliff a chance to think. A good place to think, Kansas. Here there was no crowding of his thoughts by the constant intrusion of billboards. If only it wasn't so hot! He'd never known any place as hot as Kansas in summer, but he hoped that the heat would hold off until after the harvest. He hated to think of the men working in the fields in this heat.

It was the kind of work he'd done himself when he was a boy. For three summers he'd followed the harvest with other men and boys who went custom cutting. They'd start with the first wheat harvests down in Texas, moving their big combines north on trucks as the wheat ripened, harvesting each field in turn and ending up somewhere in North Dakota in August. For a kid in college the pay had been pretty good, although the work was hard. He'd never minded hard work but he hadn't wanted to be a farmer.

Instead, now he was a consultant to farmers. Cliff worked for a Minneapolis-based farm management firm called Agritex. Farmers hired him to solve their crop problems, to recommend means of irrigation, to figure out where their cash was going and why. Cliff was a natural at it. He loved what he did.

He had arrived at this point in his life by a circuitous route that had included several years when he'd worked as a commodities broker, a job choice that had not been one of his wisest moves. It wasn't, however, his only blunder. The biggest mistake he'd made in his life, now that he had the benefit of hindsight, was marrying Devon. But his former marriage didn't matter anymore. That part of his life was over. It was all very painful, and he was sorry that it hadn't worked out, but now he was heading toward central Kansas from Oklahoma City, the last place he'd worked.

Everything he owned was stowed in the trunk of the company car. And he was ready to begin life anew. With the ink finally dry on the divorce papers, Cliff was desperately trying to be happy. It was a matter of attitude, he'd decided. A fresh beginning in a new environment would help a lot. Curtisville, the town where he would be living, offered a break with the past. It was a small town, and the idea of living in a small town again appealed to him.

He recognized one of his favorite tunes playing on the radio and turned up the volume. He glanced at the clouds piling up in the distance and pressed his foot on the accelerator. If he pushed it, he might be able to get to Curtisville before the storm hit.

CLIFF OENBRINK WAS not the only visitor to this area of the state. Another newcomer was a moist, warm air mass wandering in from the Gulf of Mexico, courtesy of a global jet stream meandering off course. The jet stream wafted a weak cold front across the state, and the cold front nudged the rising warm air, cooling it as it rose. Upon meeting the cool air, water vapor in the moist, warm air system condensed and formed clouds. Cool updrafts kept surging skyward, spinning the clouds ever higher into the atmosphere, where they cooled even more.

Microscopic water droplets in the clouds shivered and grew heavier, then larger. The cool winds from below tossed the water droplets higher and higher, freezing them into tight little ice crystals that began to drift toward the earth. But the strong updraft threw them aloft again so that they collected another thin coating of water, which then froze into yet another layer of ice.

The process repeated itself many times within the high, billowing rows of cirrocumulus clouds as it swept over the Kansas prairie, an anvil-shaped thunderhead dragging a ragged gray underskirt.

Below, people saw the storm building and shook their heads. They couldn't see the hailstones forming. But they knew enough to know that clouds that looked like fish scales meant rain.

"A mackerel sky never leaves the ground dry," said the old-timers, because it was what their fathers and grandfathers had said.

Still the storm brooded and bided its time, hulking over the land like some vengeful giant, and below, the golden wheat shimmered in the breeze, only days away from harvest.

AT WINDRUSH VALLEY FARM, the dishes were washed, and the adults were sitting on the back porch as was their custom after supper.

"My, it's hot," Charlotte said as she listlessly fanned her deeply lined face with a copy of the *High Plains Journal.*

"That's the truth," replied Elm. At seventy, he still had a full head of white hair. Smile lines fanned out around his faded blue eyes, and his skin was tan and firm. Though a slight paunch had begun to assert itself beneath his overalls, he was still a fine figure of a man, tall and strong as his name.

Sarah stood and went to one of the white wooden posts that held up the porch roof. She gazed across the river.

"I don't like the look of those clouds," she said.

"You can't do anything about them," Elm pointed out.

"I know, but they worry me."

"Half the things we worry about never happen," said Charlotte, regretting her chirpy tone almost immediately. Sarah was so serious. She was often serious these days. Charlotte supposed this was understandable under the circumstances, but she remembered Sarah the way she used to be. A dreamer. Not so practical.

Sarah batted at a fly humming around her face. "I guess I'll walk over to the barn. I want to check and see if I need to order more feed for Ben's lambs."

"Don't be too long. I made fresh peach cobbler this afternoon."

Sarah ran down the porch steps, and a plump cardinal swooped in front of her to land on the small patch of grass nearby. It pecked at something in the grass, then took flight again, disappearing over the house.

"You know what they say," Charlotte said playfully, brushing a stray strand of salt-and-pepper hair behind her ear, "Redbird fly above your head, first man you see in the morn you'll wed."

Sarah only laughed, but Charlotte was glad to hear the sound.

"Mama, I hope not. I'm far too busy to pay attention to any man. If he shows up, you'll have to send him away."

And Sarah headed toward the barn, her single braid swinging down the middle of her back, her mind on more important things than old superstitions and talk of such nonsense.

Chapter Two

The children were settled for the night, and her parents were watching television when the wind started.

Sarah looked up in alarm from the bookkeeping that had absorbed her attention for the past hour. The curtain at the window of her bedroom undulated inward, then whipped angrily at the corner of her chair. Thunder rumbled out of the sagging underbelly of the sky, and its reverberations shook the wooden floor.

The sound of the thunder sent Sarah flying downstairs. She couldn't see the thunderhead advancing across the darkened fields of wheat, but she could certainly imagine it. The tremendous clouds would roll across the land, cracking steely whips of rain, slashing the sky with lightning, battering the land with hailstones and leaving devastation in its wake. And now, her wheat was vulnerable. *Her* wheat. The crop she had planted, cultivated, sprayed and worried over. Her wheat, and no one else's.

"Pop?" She paused in the entrance to the living room.

Her father stood at the living room window, her mother at his side.

"It looks like a real thunderboomer," her father said, trying not to sound concerned.

"Better unplug the television set, Elm," Charlotte said. "We don't want lightning to strike it."

"Wait! Let's see if there's a weather warning," Sarah said. Sure enough, a crawler slid across the bottom of the television screen. The message warned of severe thunderstorms in Catalpa County—their county. Elm unplugged the set, and it went dark with a crackle.

"Mom?" called a tremulous little voice from the top of the stairs. Sarah looked up to see Lucy standing there, hugging her stuffed panda bear for dear life.

"It's just a storm," she told Lucy, running upstairs and taking the child by the hand. Lucy, still half-asleep, only wanted reassurance. Sarah tucked her snugly under her sheet and waited until Lucy's eyes drifted shut.

After she went downstairs again, Sarah stepped outside and stood on the back porch where windblown dust stung her flushed cheeks. She shivered with rage. How dare the weather threaten her beautiful crop. For she knew what Charlotte and Elm also knew: a storm could destroy the wheat.

Well, maybe it wouldn't be so bad, Sarah thought, sick in the pit of her stomach as she turned back toward the house. Maybe—

Then the first hard raindrops fell. They exploded little hollows in the dust at the bottom of the porch stairs and sent up a steamy smell peculiar to rain on a hot night. The rain pelted down in earnest from the dark sky, a sky churning with clouds. Jagged streaks of lightning rent the clouds. The porch light switched on suddenly, spiking the rain with silver, and Charlotte called, "Sarah?" through the screen door.

"I'll be there in a minute," Sarah said, choking out the words. She thought about her fields, about the amber perfection of the heads of wheat. She had invested the crop with the same energy she spent on her children. She had sowed it, and she had cared for it, and yes, she had loved it. She reacted to the storm's threat no less than she would have reacted to anything that would harm Ben or Lucy. And yet she knew that there was nothing she could do but wait.

As she turned to go back inside, a flash of lightning lit up the yard, illuminating the two big combines waiting over by the barn, ready for the harvest. The thunder crashed in her ears, but Sarah barely heard it.

Maybe it won't be so bad, she told herself. *Maybe there won't be any damage to my crop.*

But when the first hailstones fell from the sky, she knew. She'd seen what hail could do to a crop. She knew how the delicate heads of wheat, the all-important heads that carried the nutritious kernels, could be slashed from their stalks. She knew how the hail would push and beat and scuffle the wheat, utterly destroying the crop she had so lovingly tended. And when she thought of it, Sarah hung her head and wept.

"It might not be such a big storm," Elm comforted, sliding his arm around Sarah's shoulders. "With almost two thousand acres in wheat, some of it's bound to be spared. The Inman place, for instance. It's twenty miles away."

Yes, there was always the Inman place. Maybe it would escape the storm. Still, she farmed only four hundred acres there. She calculated rapidly in her head, trying to figure out, if she got a record yield at the Inman place, would she make enough money to cover the payments on the loans she had taken out to plant her wheat? To cover the loss of the rest of the crop? No. There was no way. Her stomach tightened, and she fought nausea.

"Go to bed, Sarah," her mother said softly. "There's nothing you can do until morning."

And so Sarah moved heavily up the stairs and lay down on her big lonely bed. The rain and hail drummed angrily on the roof over her head, and the inescapable sound echoed in her brain.

Sometimes when she was in bed at night, she imagined that James was there. She liked to think that if she'd only turn her head, she'd see his head resting on the pillow beside hers. Tonight Sarah wished more than ever that James was there to talk with her. To comfort her.

But James wasn't there, and there was no comfort. Sarah lay awake in the dark, long after the storm had passed and the hail had ended. She never did fall asleep.

BEFORE THE PINK CRESCENT of the new day's sun had slipped up from the horizon, Sarah was in the kitchen quietly making coffee.

"You going out to the fields?" her father asked, yawning as he tiptoed out of the downstairs bedroom he shared with Charlotte. He wore his bathrobe, and he didn't look as though he'd slept any better than his daughter.

Sarah nodded and sipped her coffee. Her eyes were puffy; there were blue half-moon shadows beneath them.

"I'll go with you," Elm said, moving to go back into the bedroom.

"No, Pop," Sarah said. "I'd rather go alone."

"You're sure? Want me to call Henry to go with you?"

"No." She set her unfinished coffee on the counter and lifted the keys to her pickup truck off their hook.

Sarah slipped out the back door just before Charlotte appeared in the kitchen.

"You didn't let Sarah go out by herself, did you, Elm?" Charlotte asked anxiously.

"That's the way she wanted it," Elm grunted.

"You should have gone anyway," Charlotte told him as she poured herself a cup of coffee and gazed pensively out the window at Sarah backing her pickup truck away from the barn.

"You know how Sarah is. Remember when James died? I offered to take care of the unpleasant details at the funeral home, but no, Sarah insisted on doing everything herself." Even now, remembering it two years later, Elm sounded indignant.

"Well, that's an independent daughter we've raised, Elm. I sometimes wish she was a little more docile." Charlotte squeezed Elm's arm in passing.

"It doesn't surprise me that Sarah wants to ride out to the fields by herself to see what damage the storm did to the crop. Losing a crop *is* like someone dying, after all," Elm said. He turned his back to her and stood staring out the screen door, and Charlotte knew not to interrupt his thoughts.

The loss of the crop was a death, and death requires a period of mourning. That was what Elm was doing, and Sarah, too. Charlotte understood. She had been a farmer's wife for a long, long time.

WHEN SHE LEFT THE FARMHOUSE that morning in her pickup, for once Sarah took it easy over Lornbacher Hill. She had a good overview of her fields from the crest, and she only fixed her lips in a grim line. She didn't stop to see what damage had been done to the home farm. She could see it from the seat of the pickup.

All around her, the wheat was battered and broken, the proud stalks chopped off as if by some huge scythe. The ground shone slick with water. It hadn't seeped completely into the rich, black soil yet, but lay in shiny, metallic puddles. The vegetation—sunflowers, the white fragile blossoms of the bindweed and the Indian grass alongside the road—was mushy where it had been trampled down by the force of the wind, rain and hail. It would begin to rot quickly in the hot sun. She fancied that she could smell the decay already.

She checked her fields at the Parker tract, once the Parker farm, which Elm had bought in his youth. Here a dank mist rose from the trees around the river. The wheat in these fields looked no better than the wheat at the home farm. With a sinking heart she drove twenty miles through the limp and lifeless wheat fields of her neighbors to the Inman place, her last hope. Maybe the storm's fury hadn't reached that far.

At the Inman fields she stepped out of the truck. Here the ground didn't squish beneath her boots. Here the wheat was wet, but not bedraggled or broken. Her spirits rose. At last she had found salvageable grain! Not much, but it was something.

She reached over and plucked one stalk of wheat. She held it in her hand. With thumb and forefinger she expertly explored the head. She felt a thrill of hope. She would be able to harvest this batch, thank goodness.

If the storm had done this much damage to her crop, what had it done to the other farmers? Sarah jumped back in her truck and drove the rest of the way into Curtisville. If she stopped in for coffee at the Chatterbox Café, she could find out if the other farmers were in better shape than she was—or worse.

When she parked under the unfinished mural in the parking lot of the small Main Street restaurant, the general gathering spot for local farmers, she saw that there was only one person inside. It was Ida Rae, who did everything from waiting on tables to cooking food.

"Where is everyone?" Sarah asked Ida Rae. Usually the place was crowded at this time of day with people stopping in for a cup of coffee while in town to run errands at the bank or the farmers' co-op.

"They're all out looking over the storm damage, I guess," Ida Rae said. "Did you notice how the Vogels' wheat fared?"

"Not very well, I'm afraid," Sarah replied. She took one of the heavy white Iroquois coffee cups from a tray, went behind the counter and filled it with coffee.

"They're going to be in trouble then," Ida Rae said with certainty. "Mina and Frank needed a good crop to make the payments on their loans."

"I know," Sarah said. Her family and the Vogels had been friends for years, helping each other over the hard times, sharing the good. The oldest Vogel child, Norrie, had been her brother Duane's sweetheart and Sarah's baby-sitter. Sarah was close to Tim, the youngest Vogel son.

"How about your crop?" Ida Rae asked.

Sarah just shrugged her shoulders helplessly, and after a searching look, Ida Rae sighed and went into the kitchen.

Ida Rae looked out a few minutes later and said, "Hey, see that guy coming out of the Country Inn across the street?"

Sarah, who had her mind on other things, looked up.

"I see him," she said.

"We've got this new arrangement with the Country Inn. They provide the bed and we provide the breakfast for their guests. Marlene, the desk clerk, called me up last night and said he'd be over. She says he's real good-looking. What do you think?"

"I think he's okay," Sarah said, still preoccupied. She hadn't really studied him.

Ida Rae came out of the kitchen, drying her hands on a towel. The newcomer was buying a newspaper from the rack outside the Chatterbox's door.

"I'd say he was more than okay," Ida Rae said. "How do you think he likes his eggs?"

"Oh, Ida Rae, I don't know."

"It's kind of a game I play. Bet you a quarter he likes them scrambled. What do you think?"

Sarah, whose head was filled with visions of wheat stalks, battered and broken, said without interest, "Over light, I guess."

"We'll soon find out," Ida Rae said as she hustled back to the kitchen.

The man came inside and walked to the counter, where Ida Rae, favoring him with a curious once-over, asked him how he wanted his eggs. He told her scrambled.

"Told you so, Sarah," Ida Rae called. Sarah ignored her. And him.

Cliff Oenbrink cast a cursory look around the Chatterbox, picked up the coffee cup Ida Rae had filled for him and sauntered over to the table where Sarah was brooding. She was alone at the far end of the long table, and she was gazing out the window. Her back was to him, her long, thick blond braid gleaming in the beam of light angling through the glass. He took in the blue jeans and the mud-spattered work boots, and he wondered who she was.

"Mind if I join you?" he said.

She appeared startled, and then she looked as though she was going to say no. Finally she nodded, so he sat down across from her.

"I'm Cliff Oenbrink," he said when she made no move to introduce herself.

"Sarah Morrow," she said abruptly.

"Some storm we had last night," he ventured conversationally.

She shot him a keen look. "That's right," she said. There was a long pause, and he wondered what to talk about. If everyone around here was so reluctant to speak with a stranger, he'd never build up his accounts. He'd been prepared for rebuffs, allowing for the clannishness of people living in a small town. But to fill in silences, he'd figured on falling back on the natural ease of man-to-man camaraderie. Women, with him, did not usually find it hard to converse.

"Are you staying at the inn?" he asked, although he was sure she wasn't. If she'd recently left the inn for breakfast, she wouldn't be wearing muddy boots.

"No," she said.

"I just arrived in town last night." He waited to see if she'd ask where he'd come from. She didn't.

Sarah stood up and went to refill her cup from the coffepot. With more than a casual interest, he watched her slim hips shape her faded blue denim jeans into curves that seemed more purposeful than decorative. She was tall and built with broad shoulders and long arms. Her neck was as sleek as a swan's, and her skin seemed sun-washed with a golden tint. He'd have liked to see her with her hair loose from that braid of hers.

"You owe me a quarter, Sarah," Ida Rae said as she glanced meaningfully at Cliff.

Wordlessly Sarah dug a quarter out of her pocket and slapped it down on the counter.

"You want anything to eat, Sarah?" Ida Rae called over the sound of frying bacon.

"No, thanks," Sarah called. "I couldn't." She went back to the table.

Two men wearing baseball caps, one of them green and bearing a John Deere logo, stomped in. They paused inside the door, shaking their heads in commiseration. Sarah only caught brief phrases, like "lost my whole wheat crop," and "the wind knocked out a couple of power lines." She strained to hear more, but this fellow, this Cliff, kept talking.

"This must be the community gathering place," Cliff said.

Distracted, Sarah spared him only a brief word. "Yes," she said.

"Ah," Cliff said. He studied her carefully. She looked tired. She sounded snappish.

He glanced at the men who had just come into the restaurant. He realized that when they sat down at the table, he would no longer be alone with Sarah.

"Look," he said. "I'm new in town. I hardly know anyone. But I'm here to stay for a while."

Sarah set down her coffee cup in her saucer with a clatter. She strugggled to recall his name. "Um, Cliff," she said, "I know you mean well. I just don't feel like making polite small talk right now. I lost most of my wheat in that storm last night. I feel like I lost not only a crop but a member of my family. So please excuse me if I don't respond enthusiastically."

Her eyes burned with a kind of naked pain, and suddenly he understood. He was, after all, a farmer's son. He knew how much the storm last night could have damaged a crop.

"I'm sorry," he said. He regarded her quietly, levelly, not making a big flap about her loss but not belittling it, either.

She studied him. He really *was* sorry, she thought in surprise. She took in his neat tan sport shirt, his wavy dark brown hair, the sympathetic dark eyes with wrinkles crinkling the corners.

"I don't know why you should be sorry, but I do believe you are," she said in a surprised tone.

He smiled and shrugged. "I was a farmer once, too. Farming is still my busines."

"What do you do? Are you here for the harvest?"

"I'm a farm manager. I work for Agritex."

While she absorbed this information, Bud Olsen sat down beside her and asked her about the damage at her place. Another guy ambled over, acknowledged that Cliff didn't belong there with a flick of his eyes and paid absolutely no attention to Cliff from that moment on. Neither did Sarah. Neither did anyone else, for that matter. As the farmers trooped in from the street and sat down at the table, Cliff was increasingly enveloped in weather-and-crop talk, in conversations that sounded bewildered, confused, angry and sad.

As he ate his eggs, Cliff listened and watched, picking up a lot of information that might help him later. Bud Olsen intended to stick out farming one more year. Frank Vogel said his son Bernie had quit the farm, had found a job in an auto parts store in McPherson and wasn't coming home.

Ed Wilson said he'd be lucky to get one-third of what he got for his wheat last year at market, but that he considered himself fortunate not to have lost more of his crop. There was a silence while everyone considered this.

Then, her words falling on dead air, Sarah informed everyone that she was considering planting Ar-Kan wheat next year.

"Your father won't go along with it," Bud Olsen said, not without kindness.

"I'm the person running Windrush Valley Farm now," Sarah said, and there was a sudden hush at the table before the men pushed back their chairs in flurry of movement and went to settle their bills with Ida Rae, suddenly leaving Cliff alone with Sarah again.

"Did you say something wrong?" Cliff asked.

Sarah's mouth quirked. "Only that I'm in charge of the farm."

"They didn't seem to like the idea."

"This group doesn't. Some of the men around here think it's pretty terrific that I'm farming almost two thousand acres, but unfortunately they weren't here this morning. These guys feel threatened that a woman farms the land."

"I don't meet many women farmers. How'd you get into it?"

"My father isn't well, and my husband died. There wasn't anyone else." She stirred her coffee and avoided his eyes, which lit up with frank admiration.

"So it really was *your* crop that you lost last night," he said.

She lifted her eyes to his. "Yes," she said. "And now I've got to go home and tell Mama and Pop and my two kids that we're in trouble. Serious trouble."

Cliff drew a deep breath. "Sarah," he said, "maybe I can help."

She laughed, but it was a bitter sound. "Sure. And I believe in Santa Claus, too."

"Oh, I don't mean you can save what's lost this time. It's too late for that. But you can plan for the future. You can do something about your cash flow, and—"

"My cash, Cliff whoever-you-are, is strictly going to be flowing *out*. That's O-U-T. Which is where I'm going right now."

She drained her cup and walked to the cash register, where she tossed a few pieces of change down. "See you later, Ida Rae," she called. "I put the money right here."

"Okay," Ida Rae replied from the kitchen.

Sarah wheeled and strode out the door. Cliff didn't catch up with her until she had reached her pickup truck and was about to climb into the cab.

"Hey, Sarah," he said. "I know you've had a tough break, but please don't take it out on me. I didn't send the storm, you know. I can help you. I really can."

Sarah closed her eyes, fighting for patience with the earnest stranger who didn't look as if he'd ever scraped a line of dirt from beneath his neat, well-shaped fingernails. When she opened her eyes, he was staring at her with an expression of such seriousness that she couldn't turn away. He believed he could help her, obviously. Why didn't she listen to what he had to say? Hadn't he told her he was a farm manager? One of those guys her father disdained because they only knew farming from reading about it in a book and then tried to tell farmers how to run things?

She wavered for a moment. She ought to go home. She ought to be making arrangements for harvesting what little wheat she had left. But something about him made her want to talk with him. She wanted to hear what he had to say.

"All right," she said heavily.

"Where can we talk?" he asked. "Inside the Chatterbox?"

She thought of Ida Rae. Ida Rae would hear every word they said to each other if they went back there. Before long their conversation would be repeated all over town. Sarah couldn't bear to have the other farmers laughing at her on top of everything else. She knew what they'd think. They'd think she was a fool to consider paying someone to teach her what they'd all grown up knowing. Except that some of them, Frank Vogel for one, were in worse financial shape than she was.

"No," she said abruptly. "And it's too hot to sit in my truck. Let's walk down to the park. It'll be quiet there except for a few kids playing, and there won't be many of them 'cause it's still so early."

"Okay," he said.

Sarah stepped onto the sidewalk and began to walk down Main Street. She was tall, and Cliff liked that. In high heels, she'd be about at his eye level. He'd like that, too.

She tucked her hands into the pockets of her jeans, drawing them snugly across her stomach. Her abdomen was slightly rounded, womanly. He didn't like the hollow emaciated fashion-model look. He liked to feel something substantial when he took a woman in his arms. Sarah, though trim, looked solid.

They reached the park, ducked past a willow tree and stopped to get a drink at a water fountain.

"Let's sit in the band shell," suggested Sarah. "It won't be as wet there as it is everywhere else." She inclined her head toward the blue-painted structure at the end of the path.

Once they reached the band shell, they hiked themselves up on the edge of the stage and let their feet hang over the edge. It was not the way Cliff was used to doing business. He didn't feel comfortable with his feet dangling in space like that. He needed to feel anchored. He drew his feet up and looped his arms loosely around his knees.

"Now what is it that you propose to do for me?" asked Sarah in her straightforward manner. The shape of the band shell amplified her voice, and self-consciously she lowered it at the end of her sentence.

"Show you how to manage your farm so that you're running it more efficiently."

"I'm doing it as efficiently as I know how," she said, her voice rising defensively.

Unfortunately this was often the reaction. Farmers had been doing what they did for years, and they resented any meddling by outsiders. Sometimes they didn't hire Cliff until it was too late and they were well on the way to losing everything. He hoped that it wasn't too late for Sarah.

"You need to diversify, you know," Cliff said gently. "You should plant more than one crop."

Her shoulders heaved in a giant sigh. "I've thought about it. But—" and she stopped. She stared straight ahead at the heart-shaped leaves and clustered flowers of a catalpa tree planted beyond the surrounding wooden bleachers.

"But you've always farmed wheat, right?"

"Right. Pop always farmed wheat, and his father before him farmed wheat."

"And then along comes a lollapalooza of a storm at the worst possible time, and there goes all of the crop. If you were planting soybeans and sorghum and alfalfa, they wouldn't have been at a crucial point in their growth. You'd have had something left."

"I know. But I've always done what Pop said to do. He said to plant Turkey Red wheat, and I planted it." A cascade of bird song sprang from the lush green oak trees sheltering the band shell.

"Sarah, how long have you been farming on your own?"

"I never have until now," she admitted reluctantly. "Pop's always been there. But he and Mama are planning to move to town soon, and then I'll be by myself."

"If you're going to be by yourself, you'll need to think for yourself," Cliff said, and Sarah's head whipped around.

"I think for myself now," Sarah replied defensively.

"I don't doubt that," he said. "What you need to do is revitalize your farm with new ideas."

"And I suppose you have these new ideas?" She regarded him through narrowed eyes.

"I have a lot of experience in helping farmers get their business practices on track. I'll look over your books, help you decide where to put the money you have so that it will do you the most good. I'll consult with you about what crops to plant, what fields to leave fallow. I'd like to see you make it, Sarah."

Sarah swallowed the lump in her throat. He was very nice, and he had happened along at a time when she was vulnerable. She needed his expertise, but she didn't have the money to pay for it.

"Sarah, what kind of crop insurance did you have on your wheat?"

Her jaw tightened. "None," she said. She had no insurance because she'd thought she couldn't afford it.

Cliff felt a pang of anguish on her behalf. She looked so noble, so brave. And she was in worse trouble than he thought.

"I was going to suggest you put in a crop of soybeans or sorghum to recoup your losses," he said. He knew now that Sarah didn't have the money to do this.

"I'll have to go see Ken Shumaker at the bank," she said, lifting her chin. "Maybe he'll loan me more money." *Maybe he won't,* she thought to herself. Ken had never been one to believe that Sarah could succeed at farming on her own.

"You'd better make an appointment soon," Cliff cautioned. "Ken Shumaker is going to be very busy seeing farmers after this storm, with all the damage it's done."

"I'll mortgage the house and the home farm if I have to," Sarah said suddenly. It was the first time the thought had occurred to her.

Cliff's face registered his shock.

"Don't," he said.

She shot him a quick look. "I didn't ask for advice," she reminded him.

"I know, but you'd better take it anyway. I'd never advise my clients to mortgage the house. There are other things you can do first.

Sarah felt abysmally ignorant. She might know a lot about growing a bumper crop of Turkey Red, but farm finance was beyond her. Pop could possibly advise her, but with his heart condition, she hated to bother him. And if she did, she'd be signaling that Windrush Valley Farm was Elm Norquist's farm, not Sarah Morrow's. She buried her face in her hands, trying to think.

"I'm going to give a seminar about Agritex and what we can do to help farmers," Cliff said gently. "Why don't you come? That way you can see what we're all about, and without any obligation."

Sarah lowered her hands from her face and struggled to maintain her control. She was scared, but she didn't like showing it. "When is it?" she asked.

"I'd planned to wait until after the harvest, but now that the storm has done so much damage, I'd better present it as soon as possible."

"Which would be when?"

"In a couple of days. I'll need to find a room where such a group can meet. Do you know of a good place?"

"You could try the town council chamber. And there's a meeting room at the library."

"Good. I'll check them out today. If you'd like, I'll call you as soon as I've set the meeting up."

If she didn't explore every opportunity available to her, if she made unsound decisions and if she lost the farm as a result of those uninformed decisions, she'd hate herself for the rest of her life. As much as it went against her grain to take Cliff Oenbrink's advice, she'd better take heed of it.

"I'd appreciate that," she said quietly.

"You're in the telephone book?"

"Sarah Morrow. On the Windrush Valley Road," she said.

"Come on," Cliff said, jumping down from the band shell. "I'll walk you back to your truck. I have a few calls to make this morning, and I need to get a move on." He held out his hand.

Suddenly conscious of her mud-spattered boots, she accepted his hand and steadied herself with it as she jumped down beside him. His palm was cool and smooth, and his brown eyes met her brown eyes, and she gazed up at him for a long moment, admitting her attraction to him.

And then they were walking back toward her truck, and Cliff was asking her interested questions about where to eat and what to do in Curtisville, and finally he was seeing her off with a friendly wave in front of the Chatterbox.

She drove home slowly. She was not at all eager to tell Pop how extensive the storm damage was in this area. And she knew she couldn't mention to her father that she intended to go to a seminar given by an employee of Agritex. Of that her father would definitely not approve.

But her current problems were not all she thought about. She thought about smiling brown eyes in a face shining with interest, and then she told herself that she was merely imagining things. She did have an active imagination, after all.

Better to restrict her imaginings to pretending she was riding a roller coaster over Lornbacher Hill. Although, come to think of it, both a fast ride in her pickup over the hill and talking with Cliff Oenbrink made her feel like the bottom had dropped out of her stomach.

Chapter Three

Pee Wee Wilson, age ten, of the Bluestem Farm Equipment team, hit a home run, and the ball disappeared over the tops of the willow trees beside the river. Pee Wee's short legs pumped around the bases, sending up short spurts of yellow dust. The crowd in the bleachers stomped their feet and cheered. Sarah cheered, too. Pee Wee was one of Ben's teammates.

After Pee Wee slid onto home plate, Sarah took a long drink of water to clear the dust from her throat and completed a transaction with Ham Severin, who was buying his son an ice-cream sandwich.

"That was some home run," Ham said, shaking his head in admiration. "That Wilson boy may end up in the major leagues."

"He might," Sarah agreed. Pee Wee had always been good at baseball. He and Ben had known each other since kindergarten when the two of them used to toss baseballs back and forth for hours at a time.

It was two days after the hailstorm, and Sarah was running the concession stand at the park's baseball diamond single-handedly because her co-worker had failed to show up. She looked around the ballpark for Janice Booth, figuring that she'd appear sooner or later. Janice was usually reliable, but she was the town veterinarian and sometimes had to tend to emergencies.

As she was looking for Janice, Sarah spied a tall man leaning against one of the bleachers, his foot propped casually on the first riser. She recognized him immediately. It was Cliff Oenbrink.

She had been expecting to hear from him about the Agritex seminar, but he hadn't called. He glanced in the direction of the concession stand, caught her eye and seemed startled to see her there. Then he smiled a slow genial smile. He began to saunter toward her as Tammy O'Duff arrived in the midst of a pack of kids who were running and pushing in their haste to buy refreshments.

By the time Cliff reached the flat-roofed shed, Sarah was feverishly scooping crushed ice into paper Pepsi cups. He towered over the kids who were shoving each other good-naturedly out of the way.

Sarah spared Cliff a harried glance and inadvertently dumped a scoop of ice on her foot. She jumped aside, but not before slivers of ice slid into her sneaker. She twisted her foot out of the shoe and stood on one leg, pouring Pepsi.

"I want *three* Pepsis, Mrs. Morrow," said Tammy. "And *two* Mountain Dews. You poured two Pepsis and three Mountain Dews."

Sarah quickly poured one more Pepsi and sent Tammy and friends on their way.

"I'll buy that extra Mountain Dew. Is it always this busy at the concession stand?" Cliff said as Tammy and her group disappeared into the milling crowd.

"Yes. And it'll get worse once this game is over. It's a doubleheader, and during the lull between games, I'll be swamped." She bent over, dumped the ice out of her shoe and put it back on.

A cheer went up from the bleachers, signaling the end of the game. "It looks to me as though you're about to be overrun by thirsty baseball fans right now," Cliff observed. "Let me help you."

"Oh, but—"

Cliff walked around to the side of the concession stand and let himself in the door. "Show me where things are," he said.

With people abandoning the bleachers and heading her way in droves, Sarah wasn't about to turn down an extra pair of hands.

"Drinks are in this cooler," she said, showing him. "And a new batch of popcorn is almost ready."

"I'll take care of pouring drinks if you'll handle the popcorn," he told her.

"Great," she said. She looked up at him, really looked at him for the first time, and saw that his eyes expressed a ready interest in her and in what she was doing. She turned away quickly and saw with relief that her friend Janice was hurrying toward them.

Janice arrived barely ahead of the crowd.

"I'm so sorry, Sarah, but my emergency pager went off as I left the house to meet you here. Marion Buchan's Foxy was hit by a car, and I had to rush over to my clinic and patch Foxy up. I tried to let you know, but you'd already left the house." Janice gave Cliff a friendly once-over while she waited to be introduced.

Sarah quickly introduced Janice and Cliff, and feeling that some explanation of Cliff's presence was necessary, she said, "Cliff offered to help me out. Cliff, Janice is our local veterinarian. By the way, Janice, how is Foxy?" Sarah knew both Marion and Foxy, her collie.

"Foxy will be all right. She was lucky. I think she'll have a healthy respect for the highway from now on, and Marion will be more careful about keeping Foxy in her pen."

"Are you here to stay? Or do you have to get back to the clinic?" Sarah asked.

"If there's room for me, I'd like to help. I feel guilty for not showing up."

"If you'll take people's money and make change, Cliff and I will do the rest," Sarah said, and then the rush began.

Sarah must have sold a hundred boxes of popcorn and Cliff probably filled more than two hundred cups with ice and soft drinks. Sarah noticed that Cliff was the object of much curiosity from the customers, especially Ben, who arrived hot and thirsty from the game in which he'd played first base.

"Did you see the triple I hit tonight, Mom?" Ben wanted to know as she handed him a box of popcorn over the counter.

"I certainly did. It was super," Sarah said fondly. Ben had run the bases so fast he had reminded her of his father, who certainly would have been proud of him.

"Who's that?" Ben said, pointing at Cliff, who was carefully transferring three Pepsis to the outstretched hands of a small child.

"Shh, he'll hear you," Sarah said in mortification. "And don't point, Ben, it's rude."

"Well, who is he?" Ben whispered.

"I'll tell you later. Go sit on the bleachers with Lucy and your grandparents. The second game is about to start."

With one last dubious look over his shoulder at Cliff, Ben gathered up his drink and his popcorn and hurried to seek the rest of the family.

Sarah barely had enough time to melt more butter before popcorn started to spew out of the machine. Boxing it and selling it kept her busy for the next twenty minutes. Then the second game started so that people headed back to the bleachers. At last Sarah, Janice and Cliff were able to relax for a few minutes.

"Whew!" Janice said, leaning against the counter and fanning her flushed face. "I apologize again for leaving you in the lurch earlier, Sarah. What a job this is!"

"I'll forgive you. Anyway, you were only taking over this job for Debby Howell out of the goodness of your heart."

"Yes, but this is the last summer I'll do anything of the sort. I've filled in for her at this concession stand for three years in a row because she always gets pregnant in time for baseball season. Enough is enough!"

"Janice doesn't even have a child in Little League, so she isn't really required to take her turn at this, like I am," Sarah explained to Cliff.

"As the mayor of Curtisville I have to do a bit of politicking, and the best place to do it is at a Little League game because everyone in town turns out for them," Janice said with a little laugh.

Cliff smiled. "I ended up here by mistake. I was going for my evening walk, and I saw people heading toward the park with lawn chairs tucked under their arms. I followed the crowd, and that's how I happened along."

"You're new in town, aren't you?" Janice asked.

"I arrived the night of the storm. I work for Agritex as a farm manager."

"Did you ever set that seminar up?" Sarah wanted to know.

"Yes. In fact, Janice isn't the only one who tried to call you tonight. I did, too. The seminar is scheduled for tomorrow night at the library. Will you be able to come?"

"I think so," Sarah said.

"Good. Please tell all your friends about it. I want to let them know about the many services Agritex offers."

"If you want to get a good turnout, you should put a poster on the community bulletin board outside the police station," Janice suggested.

"I will. Thanks for the idea. The Curtisville *Chronicle* is going to run a notice in tomorrow's paper, too," Cliff replied.

A spate of requests for drinks kept Cliff busy after that, and by the time the Andrews Hardware team had soundly trounced the Chatterbox Café team by a score of ten to one, the concession stand had run out of both Pepsi and popcorn.

As the tired players straggled off the field, Janice counted the money in the cash box.

"We made a good haul tonight," she said, flipping the box closed and locking it.

"What happens to the money?" Cliff asked.

"We're going to use it to build new bleachers—that is, when we get enough of it," Sarah told him.

"Money is hard to come by for such improvements. That's why the concession stand is so important at these games. There's not much money in Curtisville these days with the farmers in such dire financial straits," Janice said.

Sarah unplugged the popcorn machine and swept a few stray kernels into the trash basket. "I'd better go," she said. "I saw my family walking toward the parking lot, where they'll be waiting for me. Cliff, can I give you a lift back to the inn?" It was the least she could do after he'd pitched in so willingly when she'd needed help.

Cliff always enjoyed his evening walk, but he had developed an unbridled curiosity about Sarah and her family. He had noticed the little boy whispering to her earlier. The child looked so much like Sarah that Cliff had concluded that he must be her son.

So Cliff said, "Sure, I'd like a ride if you've got enough room and if you're sure it's not any trouble."

"You two go ahead," Janice said briskly. "I'll finish closing up here." She began packing away the popcorn and other supplies, and Sarah and Cliff set out through the rapidly thickening twilight toward the parking lot.

"Does your son play Little League ball?" he asked.

"Yes," she said. "He seems to be pretty good at it."

"Keep on encouraging him. It's good for him," Cliff said. He didn't know why he was offering advice. She hadn't exactly welcomed any of his previous counsel.

But Sarah smiled gently and said, "I know. His father was a Little League star."

Cliff wasn't sure how to proceed after that. Sarah made it easy, however. She glanced over at him and asked, "Did you play baseball when you were a kid?"

"Of course," he told her, and then, not knowing why he was confiding this to her, he said diffidently, "I've always wanted to coach a Little League team."

"Why don't you?" she asked.

Cliff shrugged. "I never seem to be in the right place at the right time."

"Coaches are always in demand. *Good* coaches, that is. Our local parents' group insists on Little League coaches who stress the positive rather than the negative. You'd be good at that."

He flicked his gaze toward her, but she was walking beside him looking straight ahead, and she didn't acknowledge that she'd said anything personal at all. Still, he appreciated the compliment. "Thank you," he said. "Maybe I'll try it sometime."

They were strolling past a grassy knoll, and suddenly they heard a warning shout. A baseball plummeted out of the sky, hit the ground with a thump several feet away and rolled to a stop in front of Cliff.

He picked it up and looked quizzically toward the trees.

"That's mine, mister," called a voice, and Ben ran down the incline.

"Cliff," Sarah said, "this is my son, Ben Morrow. Ben, this is Mr. Oenbrink."

Cliff extended a firm handshake. He liked the way Ben looked him right in the eye as they shook hands. "Call me Cliff," he told the boy.

Sarah seemed to want to keep walking, but Cliff noticed Ben's baseball glove. It reminded him of his favorite glove, the one he'd saved his money all one summer to buy.

"That's a nice glove," he told Ben as he adjusted himself to the boy's slower gait.

"It used to be my father's," Ben said proudly.

"Mind if I look at it?"

Silently Ben slipped the glove off his hand.

"It's real leather," Cliff said. "And it's an Early Wynn Professional Model, just like mine was."

"You had one like that? Honest?"

"I sure did," Cliff said.

"Wow," Ben said, clearly impressed.

"Come along, Ben, everyone is waiting," Sarah said over her shoulder.

Cliff and Ben didn't walk fast enough to suit her. They remained several paces behind, discussing the merits of baseball gloves.

"What you need to do to condition the glove, Ben, is to rub some neat's-foot oil on it," Cliff said.

"*Neat's-foot?* What kind of animal is a *neat*?"

Cliff chuckled. "Tell you what, why don't you look it up in the encyclopedia? It's always puzzled me, too. And you can tell me what you've found out in return for my getting the oil. Deal?"

"Deal!" Ben said enthusiastically.

This kind of man-to-man talk was probably good for Ben, Sarah thought as she resisted the urge to ask them to hurry up. Ben missed his father very much, and Pop wasn't interested in baseball. Sarah wasn't sure if there was such an animal as a neat, either, although she had heard of neat's-foot oil.

As Sarah approached the station wagon with Cliff and Ben trailing behind, Charlotte leaned forward from the back seat where she sat beside Elm to get a better look at Cliff.

"Who is that man with Sarah and Ben?" she asked.

"Danged if I know," Elm replied.

"Danged if I know, either," said Lucy, removing her shoes and socks.

"Don't say danged, Lucy Anne," Charlotte said automatically.

"Grandpa did," Lucy said.

"Well, you shouldn't. Sarah hasn't mentioned anybody, has she, Elm?"

"She mentions a lot of people," Elm said without patience as he settled more comfortably into the seat and closed his eyes.

"But I mean—you know what I mean," Charlotte sighed.

Elm said nothing, and Charlotte peered out the window at the approaching threesome. The stranger was a tall man, taller even than Sarah, who had inherited her father's height. He was nice looking, too. Not as handsome as Elm, of course, but then, to Charlotte few men were.

When the three of them reached the parking lot, Charlotte rolled the window all the way down, and Sarah introduced Cliff to her parents and Lucy. Cliff reached across the back of the front seat of the station wagon to shake Elm's hand. Elm eyed him skeptically, and Charlotte pinned Elm with a meaningful look. She didn't want Elm to make one of his tactless remarks and embarrass Sarah.

Fortunately he wasn't given the chance.

"And guess what, Grandpa—Cliff had a baseball glove exactly like mine when he was a kid!" Ben said as he clambered noisily over the tailgate into the back of the station wagon.

"Amazing," muttered Elm under his breath. He closed his eyes again, and Charlotte poked him in the ribs. She had no intention of letting Elm take a nap on the way home. He slept enough as it was.

"Lucy, move over to the middle of the front seat so that there'll be room for Cliff," Sarah was saying. "We're going to drop him off at the inn." Elm's eyes flew open at this, but he closed them when he saw the warning expression on Charlotte's face.

"I can't move, I just took my shoes off," Lucy protested illogically.

"That doesn't have anything to do with it. Come over here next to me." With an apologetic glance toward Cliff, Sarah slid behind the wheel. Cliff got in beside Lucy and slammed the door.

"Did you ever go barefoot when you were a kid?" Lucy asked Cliff.

"All the time," Cliff assured her with a twinkle in his eyes.

"Even in *winter*?" Lucy said in shrill disbelief.

"Lucy," warned Sarah.

"Well, he said all the time," Lucy pointed out.

"All the time inside the house, even in winter," Cliff assured her. "I never liked to wear shoes."

"Really?" Lucy said. Her eyes were wide.

"Nope. I still don't. I go barefoot every chance I get."

"So do I," Lucy said, grinning from ear to ear.

By this time, they had covered the short distance between the park and the Country Inn. Sarah pulled the station wagon over to the curb.

"Thanks for the ride," Cliff said as he got out.

"Thank *you*," Sarah said. "I couldn't have managed the concession stand without your help."

Cliff stood for a moment, leaning on the door. Charlotte, with some surprise, took note of the gleam in his eyes when he looked at her daughter.

"I'll see you tomorrow," he said before he slammed the door, and then he stepped back. Sarah drove away, hoping that neither of her parents had heard that last remark of Cliff's. It was a futile hope, however.

"*Where* will he see you tomorrow?" Charlotte asked when they were on their way down Main Street.

"At a seminar," Sarah said, and then she could have bitten her tongue. She'd had no intention of telling her father about the Agritex seminar, much less that she was going. She held her breath and prayed that he was asleep.

"What kind of seminar?" Charlotte asked.

"Just a—a seminar about farming," Sarah said, keeping an eye on Elm in her rearview mirror.

"Farming," Elm said, opening his eyes abruptly. "He's going to a seminar on farming, and you're going to meet him there?"

Sarah longed to tell her parents that it was none of their business, but she couldn't think of a tactful way to get her point across.

"I'm not going to meet him there," she corrected reluctantly. "He's sponsoring it. Cliff works for Agritex, the farm management company, and he's putting on the seminar to give local people some pointers."

"Local people could give *him* pointers if you ask me," Elm said with a snort.

"Well, no one did ask you, Elm," Charlotte informed him.

"I bet Cliff's a pretty good ball player if he had a glove like Dad's," Ben said from the back seat, and no one contradicted him. In fact, they rode the rest of the way home in silence.

Sarah was slightly late for the Agritex seminar, letting herself into the meeting room in the library as Cliff stood up to speak. He smiled at her as she slipped into a folding chair in the back of the room.

She was pleased, for Cliff's sake, that the room was almost full. Frank Vogel was there as well as Bud Olsen. Ed Wilson sat near the front of the room. All in all, Curtisville farmers seemed well represented, but Sarah was the only woman there.

Cliff had attached charts to easels placed strategically around the room, and she eyed them curiously. One was a chart on wheat performance. Another was a comparison of herbicides.

She turned her attention from the charts to Cliff, who had already warmed up to his audience.

He was an arresting speaker, but he wasn't overbearing. One of Cliff's biggest challenges in expanding Agritex's offerings into a new area was to win the confidence of the people whose business he wanted. Cliff seemed to understand this, and Sarah noticed right away that he did not talk down to them, nor did he talk over their heads.

First he tackled the subject many of them had been resisting, which was the comparatively new notion of putting their business records on computers. Although this idea was greeted with open skepticism by many in the group, a few, such as Abe Waterford, leaned forward with interest. After telling them the many advantages of computerized records, Cliff eased into a short discussion about tax management.

When he had touched on all the business aspects of farming, Cliff spoke of Agritex's modern labs and how they obtain accurate data for making fertilizer recommendations, so that farmers could maintain their crop yields while saving money on fertilizer bills. He mentioned how he could take up the slack when overworked county extension agents were too busy to pay farm visits. Bud Olsen and Ham Severin nodded approvingly.

Cliff told them about the Agritex workshops they could attend to learn how to increase production. He explained integrated pest management, a program by which farmers could cut their use of pesticides by forty percent. Finally he showed a short video about his company, Agritex.

After the video, Cliff passed brochures out to the attendees.

"Any of you who need to reach me can find me most mornings at the Chatterbox," he said with an easy grin. "If that doesn't work, leave a message for me at the Country Inn."

With that, he dismissed the meeting. He was immediately besieged by farmers eager to ask questions.

Cliff caught Sarah's eye briefly before bending over to hear what old Abe Waterford was saying. Sarah, who found herself intrigued by the freedom a farm management program would give her to concentrate her attention on her main concern—growing crops—walked slowly around the room, looking over the charts and graphs. She couldn't help hearing other farmers talk about Cliff's presentation.

"I don't know, Ed," Bud Olsen said. "It doesn't sound to me like hiring a farm manager is worth the money. These Agritex people don't offer any more than the county extension agent does."

"When was the last time you saw our extension agent?" Ed Wilson shot back. "I don't even remember the guy's name."

"It's Dan Robbins as you very well know," Abe Waterford said huffily. "And he's got a heavy work load. He doesn't have time to stop in and say 'how de do' whenever you get lonesome."

"You talked to this Oenbrink fellow, Abe. What did you think?"

"He's coming out to my place to tell me about setting up a computer system."

"Computer system! What would you want with one of those?" scoffed Bud.

"I want my son to be well-informed about new developments," Abe said. "He'll take over the farm one day, and I don't want him to have to spend a lot of money on it at that point to catch up with what the rest of the world is doing. Everybody has computers these days, Bud. It's a sign of the times." With that, Abe turned on his heel and walked away.

"What did you think about the guy's presentation, Sarah?" Ham Severin asked her, turning toward her and making room for her in their tight little circle.

"Well, I—"

"You haven't decided to hire him, have you?" demanded Ed.

Sarah recalled serving popcorn to Ed at the Little League game. He had seen her working side by side with Cliff.

She felt wings of color rising in her cheeks. "No, of course not. I believe in having an open mind, that's all," she said before escaping from the group.

At the front of the room, Sarah paused to examine the stacks of booklets on the table beside the lectern, walking around to the back of it to select several of the most interesting ones to take with her. She leafed through one about Ar-Kan wheat, the strain she wanted to plant instead of her father's old favorite, Turkey Red.

"Sarah," Cliff said. The room was almost empty now, and he walked toward her, carrying an armload of charts. She swallowed, feeling hemmed in by the table and the easel standing at right angles to it.

"So what did you think?" he asked. He folded up the easel, stood it in a corner, and sat down on the table.

"It was a—skillfully presented lecture," she said.

"Was it too long? Too boring?"

"Not too long. And definitely not too boring."

"So do you think they've accepted me?"

Sarah decided that the best thing to do was to be candid. "Let's just say that you've stirred up a few interesting topics of discussion," she said.

"Such as?"

"Such as, are Agritex's services worth the money?"

Cliff raised his eyebrows reflectively. "That's always a concern, I guess. Except that if they don't spend the money for good advice now, they may always regret it. Well, several people asked me to pay them a visit and explain exactly what I can do for them. That's a good start, at least. I'm glad you stayed, Sarah. I've been wanting to talk to you."

"About what?"

"Your plans. Have you made an appointment with your banker yet?"

"We're meeting tomorrow," she said.

"Tomorrow? That's good."

"I'm not so sure. Ken Shumaker didn't exactly sound delighted to hear from me when I called to make the appointment."

"He's running himself ragged talking to farmers who need help. I met him the other day at the Chatterbox, and he was telling me about all the loan requests he's had since the storm," Cliff said.

"Then I doubt that he's looking forward to talking with me, especially when he hears what I want to do," Sarah said with a sigh.

"What *do* you want to do?" he asked.

Her head shot up. "I want to plant another crop, like you suggested. Sorghum, probably."

"So you're going to double-crop, are you?" He was pleased that she was taking his advice.

"I don't know much about double-cropping, but I'm trying to learn," she said. "Pop always said, 'Wheat's a lazy man's crop. You put it in the ground, and you don't do any cultivation, and you don't have to irrigate it, either.' That's why he's in favor of growing only wheat. If I plant sorghum, it's a whole new ball game."

Sarah always planted wheat in October. It slumbered through the long prairie winter, bursting forth with new growth in the spring, heading out in May and ripe for the harvest in June. Sorghum would be a whole lot more work, that was certain.

"You must be worried about this new direction you want to take," Cliff said.

"I can't talk about double-cropping with Pop because every time we discuss the farm, we end up annoyed with one another. And even though once I might have gone to Frank Vogel for friendly advice, I can't add my problems to the ones he already has."

"So you need a sounding board," he said. "I'm glad to be that." He smiled encouragingly.

Sarah drew a deep breath and plunged on. She longed to talk to someone about these things. Her plans had been festering inside her all week.

"I want to plant sorghum in rows only twelve to eighteen inches apart," she told him. "I think this method will produce higher yields and conserve my soil better than planting in wider rows."

"Here are a couple of booklets about double-cropping and about the superthick sorghum management program you're thinking about," Cliff said, reaching into his briefcase and pulling out a handful of pamphlets. "You could plant a medium-maturing sorghum hybrid if it's suited to your particular soil management plan. Have you talked to your county extension agent about your plans?"

Sarah shook her head. Her eyes were dark and brooding. "No, I can't. He and Pop had some ridiculous feud years ago, and I haven't tried to reopen the relationship. I could, I suppose," but she thought of how hard it would be to justify her action to Pop, and again she rejected this idea.

"You'll need to be well-informed and prepared to discuss this new idea with Ken Shumaker," Cliff said.

"That's another thing," Sarah said grimly. "I'll only be able to double-crop if I can borrow the money for seed and fertilizer."

"You'll need lots of seed," Cliff said, his mind moving ahead quickly. "I've recommended a similar program for a farmer outside Lindsborg. He's going to rely on a heavy fertilizer program, too."

Sarah's excitement grew. "That's what I want to do, Cliff. Superthick sorghum is a good bet for my farm, I'm sure of it!" Then her face fell. "The amount of seed and fertilizer I need may take more money than Ken Shumaker wants to lend."

Cliff didn't like to see Sarah downhearted, especially when she had shown so much enthusiasm over her new plan. He could well imagine how overwhelmed she must be feeling at this point.

"Personally, I think you've got a good chance of getting the money you need from Ken. If you're forced into bankruptcy, the bank would only lose because I assume that you, like other farmers, have outstanding loans with them. Banks have enough problems without losing money. In fact, I've never met a banker yet who enjoyed foreclosing on a farmer who is honestly trying his or her best."

"Still," Sarah said. She felt at a disadvantage in dealing with First Farmer's Federal because even though she was learning all she could about farm finance, she still didn't feel well-grounded enough in the subject to persuade Ken Shumaker that she, farming on her own, was a good risk.

Then Cliff made a surprising offer.

"If you think it would help, I'll go with you to see your banker," he said.

Her eyes were startled for a moment, and then she veiled them with her lashes.

"I couldn't ask you to do that," she murmured.

"Sarah, you're in serious trouble right now, aren't you?"

Slowly she nodded.

"Well then," he said as though no further discussion was necessary.

"I can't afford to pay you," she said in a tight voice.

"I'll go with you on my own time," he said. "What time is your appointment?"

"At three o'clock," she said reluctantly.

"I'm meeting with a man in Marquette at one-thirty," he said. "I should be back in Curtisville by three tomorrow."

Her face softened with gratitude.

"If you can make it, that would be wonderful," she said.

Wonderful, he thought as she bade him goodbye and left.

He had found plenty of reasons to admire her, and he hoped that after tomorrow, when he would help her face Ken Shumaker, Sarah would find something to admire in him.

Chapter Four

The next day, when she was getting ready for her appointment with her banker, Sarah dug in the back of closet and found a five-year-old suit that she hadn't worn in ages. She decided to wear it.

"Why do you keep doing that?" Charlotte asked as she watched Sarah flit around her room getting ready to leave.

"Doing what?"

"Tugging at your skirt like that."

Sarah surveyed her image in the mirror on the back of the door of the adjoining bathroom. "It feels too tight," she said, pulling at it again.

"Don't be silly. It's a perfect fit."

"I don't know," Sarah said dubiously, looking over her shoulder to get a full back view.

"You ought to make yourself a new suit," observed Charlotte.

"I don't have time to sew," Sarah said.

"I'd make it for you, but my fingers have been so stiff lately."

"I should make Lucy some clothes, but little girls don't like to wear anything but jeans these days," Sarah said. She pinned her hair up quickly, forsaking her usual braid for a swirl atop her head.

"It's a good thing, I think. I always resented the way skirts restricted my movements when I was a child. Sarah, you act for all the world like you're running off to meet a man. Are you?"

Sarah blushed. "'Running off' is hardly a term I would use to describe a meeting at the bank with Ken Shumaker."

Charlotte narrowed her eyes speculatively. "If it weren't that old poot Ken Shumaker, I'd be suspicious. You haven't worn cologne in months, and now you reek of it."

"Mama, don't try to make something out of nothing," Sarah chided. She stooped to drop a kiss on her mother's cheek, and then she was out the door, leaving Charlotte staring after her in perplexity.

At the bank Sarah had to wait in an anteroom for Ken to finish with a previous appointment. She sat on the couch indicated by the receptionist, and she kept glancing nervously out the window. There was no sign of Cliff Oenbrink. What if he didn't come?

Sarah had little confidence in her ability to stand up to Ken Shumaker. He'd always been willing to work with her in the past, but it was a known fact that up until recently, Elm had helped Sarah make decisions concerning the farm. It was also a known fact that Elm's doctor had cautioned him against being too active in the work or management of the farm and that Elm would soon be moving into town. Sarah wasn't sure where that left her in Ken's eyes.

It was ten minutes past three, and there was still no sign of Cliff. She kept glancing at her watch, and she wondered if his appointment in Marquette had taken longer than he'd figured. She tried to read a magazine but found it impossible to concentrate. *Where is Cliff, anyway?* she thought with despair.

She twisted the strap handle of her purse nervously, realized what she was doing and tried to stop. When she looked down again a few minutes later, she had contorted the handle into a corkscrew again. Annoyed with herself, she pushed the purse to the other end of the couch.

She heard a stirring inside Ken's office, and then Ken showed Frank Vogel out. Sarah was surprised. She hadn't realized that Frank had the appointment before hers.

"How did it go?" she managed to whisper as Frank paused briefly to greet her.

Frank shook his head. He looked tired and beat, and his usually ruddy complexion had an ashen tone to it. He didn't say a word but walked out of the waiting room like a man who had just received a harsh prison sentence. Sarah stared after him, her pulse pounding in her ears.

"Mrs. Morrow?" Ken's secretary beckoned.

Sarah walked gingerly across the plush green carpet into Ken Shumaker's office.

"Sarah? Good to see you again. Have a seat." And Ken Shumaker stood long enough to reach across his cluttered desk to shake her hand.

She heard a conversation in the anteroom and swiveled her head. She expelled a sigh of relief when she saw that the newcomer was Cliff.

He spoke a few words to a receptionist, who waved him toward Ken's office.

"I'm not too late, I hope?" Cliff said anxiously.

Sarah could have thrown her arms around him in her relief. Instead she said, "We've just started, Cliff. Ken, you remember Cliff, don't you? You met him in the Chatterbox."

Ken came around his desk to shake Cliff's hand. "Are you advising Sarah about her farm?" he asked with some surprise.

Cliff smiled at Sarah encouragingly. "Yes, I am," he said.

"Then join us, please," Ken said, indicating the chair beside Sarah. He massaged his eyes for a moment, and in that moment Sarah suddenly had an insight into how hard a banker's job must be in these trying times.

Cliff sat down and shot her a reassuring glance.

"Well, Sarah," Ken said after a moment. "What can I do for you?"

"I lost over a thousand acres of wheat in the hailstorm, Ken," she said, regarding him levelly.

"That's a familiar story," Ken said.

"I know. I need to know if the bank will back me while I try to recoup my losses."

"What do you have in mind?"

"I want to plant a second crop on the land where my wheat was ruined," Sarah said.

Ken greeted this idea with silence.

"I think she's made a good decision, Ken," Cliff told him.

"Sarah, you've never planted anything but Turkey Red wheat," Ken said.

"I can make a go of sorghum. It's good, rich farmland, Ken, you know that." Sarah was beginning to feel desperate. Ken sounded so negative.

"What do you think of this, Cliff?" Ken asked skeptically.

"Sarah has a good chance of recouping her loss with sorghum—*if* we have a rainy summer."

"That's a big if," Ken said. He leaned back in his chair, folded his hands behind his head, and stared at the ceiling.

It was silent for a long time, and Cliff cleared his throat. "She could use a good, heavy fertilizer program," he suggested.

Ken let himself be sprung upright by his squeaky chair. "A fertilizer program like the one you must have in mind costs even more money," he said abruptly.

"It would be worth it," Sarah said. "I'd want to apply it at planting. I'm aiming for a one-hundred-bushel-an-acre crop, Ken."

Ken let out a long, low whistle. "You'd need a lot of rain," he said. "What if we have another summer like the last one? We only got about an inch of precipitation a month."

Sarah pushed herself up to the edge of her seat. "So far it's been a wet summer," she argued. "The soil has a good moisture content."

"We don't know what's going to happen in the future," Ken shot back. "We may have had all the rain we're going to get."

"That's a gamble I'd be willing to take," Sarah countered. She stood her ground, knowing that she had no choice.

Ken stared at her. "I admire your determination," he said after a long pause. He ran his fingers through his hair. Then he looked through her folder. "Let's see. You have several outstanding notes. There's the one for seed, and yes, here's the mortgage on the Inman tract."

"She won't mortgage her house or the home farm," Cliff interjected.

Ken raised his head. "I have no desire to force Sarah or anyone else into bankruptcy. I've been dealing with desperate farmers all week, and it leaves a bad taste in my mouth. I want to work something out with Sarah," he told Cliff.

To Sarah he said gently, "You won't need to mortgage your house or home farm. That's a mistake some farmers make. Your house and a hundred and sixty contiguous acres are an exempt asset according to Kansas law. What we can do is lend you money to buy the seed and fertilizer to double-crop. I know you, Sarah, and I realize that you'll do the best you can."

Sarah closed her eyes and gripped the arms of her chair. So he was going to let her have the money. And unlike the Vogels, whom she knew had taken this desperate step, she wouldn't have to mortgage the house or home farm.

"I think the interest you've been charging me is too high," she said boldly before she lost her nerve.

"We can give a lower rate of interest right now," Ken said.

"If you could put me on a different payment schedule," suggested Sarah, figuring that she might as well shoot for the moon.

"We can work that out, I think."

Sarah swallowed and shot Cliff a grateful look. He was smiling at her, and she smiled back.

The three of them argued the fine points of Sarah's loan package, and then Ken walked them to the door of his office.

"I've seldom met anyone more dedicated than you are, Sarah," he said, shaking her hand.

"I'll get a good crop," she promised. She felt excited just thinking about planting something new. When she walked out of the bank into the humid afternoon heat, she felt like dancing all the way.

Outside, she and Cliff exchanged triumphant grins. "Cliff, thank you from the bottom of my heart. I couldn't have managed without you," she said.

"Can I buy you a drink to celebrate your victory?" he asked before he thought. He'd forgotten that it was impossible to buy a drink here unless it was in a private club. There were no such clubs in Curtisville.

Sarah laughed. "I can tell you're a city slicker," she teased. She felt so lighthearted. It was good for her soul to be able to laugh out loud after the past week of stress and worry. She was overcome with gratitude to Cliff.

"Failing going for a drink, maybe we could—well, I don't know. Don't you have any suggestions?"

"I thought you had to go back to work," she said.

He shrugged. "I've been working a lot of overtime since I came here. Agritex can afford to let me have a couple of hours off."

Without realizing it, they had begun to walk toward the park. The entrance was straight ahead. "Let's stroll through here," Sarah said impulsively when she heard strains of folk music. She took off her suit jacket as they walked and slung it over her shoulder. Once she even skipped a few steps in time to the music.

"Do that again," Cliff said.

"No," she said, wishing that she hadn't.

A group of teenage folk dancers was rehearsing in the grassy area in front of the band shell. Bleacher seats were available, and they perched on the bottom row to watch the gracefully swirling dancers.

"Does it frighten you now that you've got your loan? Now you'll have to grow the crop."

"It gives me the willies to think about planting a crop I've never grown before," confessed Sarah.

"Still, it's worth a try," Cliff assured her.

"Thanks again for your help in there. If it hadn't been for your moral support, I might have caved in."

"I doubt that," he said, recalling how firm Sarah had been. He had been impressed.

"I wish I could repay you in some way."

"I won't take any money," he said. "There is something I'd like, however."

She turned puzzled eyes to him, only to be tantalized by his teasing smile.

"What's that?"

"A home-cooked meal."

Of all things. He *would* name the one thing she hated to do. Charlotte was the cook in the family. Charlotte was the one who would have to provide the home-cooked meal. In a way, she was relieved. This meant that Cliff would have to eat with her whole family.

"Come out to the farm for supper," she said, sliding off the bleacher seat. Cliff stood up, too.

"When?" he asked.

"Oh, one time is as good as another," Sarah said offhandedly. "Supper's always good. My mother cooks it."

They began to walk toward Main Street, and Cliff attempted to pin her down. He didn't want to show up for supper at a time when Sarah was away from the farm. "Are you sure any day is okay? And what time?"

"We usually eat around six," she said.

Cliff wished she wouldn't be so vague about it, but he didn't want to press her. When they reached the parking space in front of the bank he told her goodbye, smiling to himself as he watched Sarah struggle to climb into the high cab of her pickup truck, unaccustomed as she was to wearing a straight skirt. She had to hike it well above her knees to accomplish this. He got a long glimpse of a shapely leg, but it wasn't nearly enough.

SARAH THOUGHT ABOUT Cliff Oenbrink more than she wanted to during the next couple of weeks, and it wasn't merely out of gratitude. Something about him had captured her attention. His all-around friendliness, perhaps, or the way he had known how to speak to the farmers at the seminar without putting them down. Or maybe it was the solid support he had given her at the meeting with Ken.

Cliff seemed like someone Sarah could trust, and she needed someone like that. In the past week, she had had to do some serious thinking, and what she had thought about was that despite her best friend, Janice, whom she didn't see all that often because of her farm responsibilities, and despite her parents, she was more or less alone when it came to making decisions.

What it boiled down to, she supposed, was that she thought of Cliff as an equal, someone she could respect. She had been drifting away from Janice's friendship since taking over the farm, and to her parents she was still, in some ways, their little girl. The other farmers either patronized her or ignored her; that is, when they weren't being downright defensive. She felt that she could speak her mind and be herself with Cliff Oenbrink. He had no preconceived ideas about her.

Soon the wheat harvest was in full swing around Curtisville with the help of harvest crews who briefly overran their small town. Though Sarah concentrated on the harvesting of her remaining wheat, Cliff was never far from her mind. She wondered if he was succeeding in building up his accounts, and if he was entirely comfortable at Curtisville's only hotel, the tiny Country Inn. And one day when she drove one of the big red-and-green farm trucks heaped with grain to the farmer's co-op elevator, she held her breath when she spied someone who stood like Cliff, who walked like Cliff. But then he turned around, and it wasn't Cliff, she felt as if all the air had rushed out of her lungs.

Even though he'd pressed her for an invitation, he didn't show up for supper at the farm after she invited him, and she thought he had forgotten. She was amazed at how disappointed she was. She told herself that Cliff had found something more interesting to do and someone more interesting with whom to do it. After all, he was a carefree bachelor and new in town.

Therefore, she was surprised when Cliff appeared suddenly one day, two weeks after her appointment with Ken Shumaker, while she was floating in spring-fed Oley's Creek where it widened into a quiet pool before joining the river.

It was a peaceful spot, perhaps the most peaceful place on the whole farm. Sarah didn't come here often, and usually when she did, Ben and Lucy were with her. Today Ben was at baseball practice, and Lucy was visiting in town with a friend. Sarah had just told Pop that she was going to plant sorghum, and he had railed at her unmercifully about her decision. He'd finally subsided in the face of her obstinacy, and they had reached an uneasy truce when she had told him what a good loan package she'd wrested from Ken Shumaker.

Now she just wanted to be by herself for a while, to celebrate the end of the harvest and to distract herself from worries about planting a new crop. Playing helped. Sarah splashed sheets of water high into the air with the palm of one hand, watching with delight as they momentarily turned the sunbeams penetrating the surrounding trees into rainbows. She filled her mouth with water, floated on her back and squirted a stream of it into the air, pretending she was a whale. She was wholeheartedly enjoying her aloneness when Cliff Oenbrink stepped out of the surrounding shrubbery. She was startled and emitted a squeaky "Oh," embarrassed that he had caught her at her games.

"It's only me—Cliff," he said, smiling at her.

Sarah remained submerged in the cool water all the way to her neck. She wasn't floating anymore. Instead, her bare feet rested on the sandy creek bottom.

"What are you doing here?" she asked. He was different from the way she'd remembered him. How could it be possible that she had forgotten what he really looked like? In the flesh, he was bigger. More substantial. And absolutely real.

"I came out to call on the Vogels and realized that I'd been putting off that home-cooked meal for too long. How was your harvest?"

"My wheat yielded fifty-five bushels to the acre," Sarah said, reluctant to be drawn into any conversation with him at the moment.

"That's pretty good. Above average, in fact."

"I know. It's just that there wasn't much of it." She felt ridiculous discussing farm business with him while lolling up to her chin in creek water. Furthermore, she wasn't about to come out. Her swimsuit was several years old and much too skimpy.

"You look mighty cool in there," he said.

"Too bad you didn't bring a suit," she flung at him, wondering why she said it.

"Oh, but I did," he said. "It's in the trunk of my car. Was that an invitation?"

She opened her mouth, and closed it quickly. Then she said feebly, "I suppose so."

He towered over her on the creek bank, and she couldn't help wondering how he'd look without his clothes. With a quick nod he disappeared through the tangle of elderberry and grapevine to the road, where he had presumably parked his car.

Sarah submerged momentarily, blowing bubbles out her nose toward the silvery surface of the water. She'd have to caution Charlotte about sending men down here to the creek when she swam alone. Besides her embarrassment at being caught in the middle of pretending she was Moby Dick, there was another reason why it wasn't such a good idea. Sometimes, on days like today when there wasn't anyone around, Sarah didn't bother to put on her suit.

Cliff reappeared wearing blue swim trunks. Sarah was not surprised to see that his body was tight and fit. His legs were softly pelted with fine, dark hair, and the muscles in his arms were thick but well proportioned. He smiled at her. It seemed as if he was always smiling. She shivered suddenly. It had been a long time since she'd seen a man in so few clothes. It had been a long time since she'd seen a man as a man.

He waded in, barely flinching at the sting of the icy water. "We used to have an old swimming hole at home," he said. "It was a lot like this." He cupped his hands and scooped up some of the clear water. He ducked his face in it and came up sputtering. "Feels good," he said.

Sarah kept her distance. Ordinarily she would be performing a sedate breaststroke across the width of the creek and back again. Newly aware of Cliff's sheer male vitality, she was so self-conscious that she didn't feel like swimming now.

"So you really lived on a farm?" she said for lack of something more interesting to talk about.

"Sure. In Illinois."

"Why did you leave?"

"I decided I wasn't the small-town type at the time. I wanted to sample another kind of life. Anyway, I watched my dad grow corn, hogs and tired. He sold his farm and moved to town a few years ago." Cliff's skin glistened with water. It spiked his eyelashes into little points.

"A familiar story," said Sarah with a hint of irony.

"Dad said that it used to be that if you put hard work into the farm, you'd get something out of the farm. The day he figured out that it wasn't true anymore, he decided to sell."

Sarah dog-paddled downstream, her long braid floating out behind her. Her feet found the sandy bottom, and she turned to face Cliff. "It's still true," she said.

"Oh, Sarah, if you'd only admit it to yourself, you'd see that there's more to it these days. A good farmer can't just grow crops. He—or she—must be a good business person as well."

"I *am* a good business person," she said, flipping her braid over her shoulder with such force that tiny water droplets went flying across the creek.

"I'm not saying you're not," Cliff said reasonably. "I'm simply saying that you could be a better one."

"I thought this was a social call. You're trying to drum up business, aren't you?"

Cliff was quiet for a long moment. Insects chittered in the shrubbery.

"No, Sarah," he said finally. "The reason I really came here was for the home-cooked meal you promised. And I wanted to see you again."

Suddenly the whirring of the insects increased to a cacophony of buzzing, but the sound was all inside her head.

"I admire you, both as a woman and as a farmer. I'd like to get to know you better," Cliff said.

Wasn't this the same way she felt about him? Then why didn't she feel more accommodating? He was talking, after all, of an interest in her that might very well grow past the platonic.

Sorting it all out in her mind, she admitted to herself that she didn't know if she could handle that. First of all, there were her children. How would they accept the idea of a man in their mother's life? And then there was Pop. He had made it clear what he thought about farm managers.

"That's nice of you, but all it looks like to me is another problem," Sarah blurted.

He thought about this for a moment. In her tight-knit little world, he could see how it might be true. "I don't want to be a problem," he said earnestly.

"It seems," said Sarah, moving swiftly toward the shore, "that you already *are*. I—"

"Don't leave," he said in a louder tone, and it stopped her where she was.

She turned to him. The water was so shallow here that it came only to her waist. Her breasts were round beneath the swimsuit, and he tried not to let his eyes drop to where they swelled above the edge of the fabric, gleaming white and wet.

"I like your mother," Cliff said into the stillness. When Sarah only gaped at him, he said, "I arrived when she was working in her garden. She was having some trouble with the hoe, and I obliged by hoeing the weeds between the rows of beans. She's a very nice lady, your mother."

Sarah raised her hands to her face and pressed her cold wet fingers to her eyes. A dragonfly's wings brushed her cheek as it flew too near. She tried to think, but couldn't. She had the inevitable feeling that something major was happening in her life.

It was abundantly clear that the combination of Cliff and Charlotte spelled defeat, in this instance at least. "Supper will be ready in about half an hour," she said in resignation, and then she turned and waded out of the creek, knowing full well that Cliff Oenbrink's eyes were upon her every step of the way.

In order not to blush, she pretended she was invisible.

Chapter Five

"I don't want any peas," Lucy said, half an hour later.

"Of course you do," Sarah said, spooning them onto Lucy's plate anyway.

"*He* doesn't want any peas, either," Lucy said, pointing at Cliff.

Sarah straightened, embarrassed. Cliff stood in the doorway to the kitchen, watching her as she moved around the table serving everyone's plate. It was too late, of course. She'd already heaped Cliff's plate with a large spoonful of peas.

"I'm sorry," she said. "You don't have to eat them if you don't want."

"It's the family rule," piped Lucy. "You have to eat three bites *or else*."

"Or else what?" Cliff teased. It seemed best to focus his attention on Lucy. Sarah seemed distracted and preoccupied.

"Or else...or else..." Lucy said uncertainly. "Well, I don't know. I've always eaten the three bites."

"Then I will, too," Cliff said. "Since it's the family rule."

"If you're not family, you might not have to," Ben opined from the corner of the living room where he was gluing together a stack of wooden Popsicle sticks.

"Well, let's pretend I am," Cliff suggested. He was enjoying this. He'd eaten too many lonely meals at the Chatterbox, and it was fun to be part of a congenial group again. These people reminded him of his own family. Except for Sarah, of course. She still hadn't loosened up around him in the presence of her family. He could tell, though, that Charlotte liked him wholeheartedly.

He wasn't too sure how Elm felt about him. Sarah's father raised his eyebrows every time Cliff spoke, as though he was skeptical about the things Cliff said. Cliff could have clammed up, but he chose not to. He decided to treat Elm's reactions to him the way he would treat those of any farmer whose business he was courting and who was doubtful about Cliff's qualifications.

After they sat down at the table, they all joined hands for the blessing. As they ate, Cliff savored the delicious corn muffins fresh from the oven, the fluffy mashed potatoes, and even the peas from Charlotte's garden.

Their table talk dealt with farming, mostly. Elm mentioned the Vogels' trouble.

"Frank Vogel bought up a lot of land back in the seventies when it cost a whopping two thousand dollars an acre," Elm said, shaking his head. "He wanted his three boys to come into farming with him. Well, now the Vogels aren't making enough money on their crops to pay the payments on all that expensive land. The Vogels are deeply in debt and likely to lose it all. Why, two of the boys have quit. Bernie got him a job over in McPherson, and Tim never did like to farm. All Tim thinks about is airplanes."

"There's nothing wrong with that," Sarah said.

"I know you and Tim are friends," Elm conceded. "But he's breaking his father's heart. Frank and Mina Vogel always dreamed of building a farming empire for their sons, and Bernie and Tim want none of it."

"Bernie has a family to support, and they weren't making it on their share of the profits from the farm. And Tim—well, Tim's just Tim, that's all." Sarah had always held a warm spot in her heart for Tim. As Tim's older sister Norrie had once been her baby-sitter, Sarah had once been Tim's.

While this discussion took place, Cliff concentrated on Sarah, the way she talked, her seriousness when discussing something that was of importance to her, like her defense of Tim Vogel. Later, when dinner-table talk ranged over other topics, such as Ben's description of his lambs' antics, her smile started slowly, then grew and grew until it lit up her round brown eyes and finally, her whole face. He had the idea that Sarah was playacting part of the time, pretending that she was more matter-of-fact, more practical than she actually felt. He sensed that underneath her calm demeanor she'd like to be much more spontaneous.

When dinner was over, Cliff offered to wash the dishes, but Sarah was firm about that. "It's Lucy's and my turn," she said.

"Oh, Mom," objected Lucy, only to be silenced by a stern look from Sarah.

Cliff wandered into the living room to talk to Elm. Elm lowered his newspaper to his lap when he saw Cliff, and he said, "Sit down."

Cliff sat, staring down at his hands and wondering if the older man intended to ignore him. But no, Elm merely finished reading the newspaper article Cliff had interrupted and tossed the paper into a wastebasket before regarding Cliff over the top of his bifocals.

"So you're from Agritex," Elm said.

"That's right," Cliff replied.

"What makes you think you know enough about farming to tell anybody how to do it?"

"My father was a farmer. I grew up on a farm. I studied—"

"I've never put much faith in what books teach about farming. The people who wrote the books never get their hands dirty."

"Agritex is prepared to teach farmers how to make the best use of their land. We can show a farmer how to use a computer to his benefit. There are lots of things Agritex can do for a farmer, Elm."

"Computers don't grow crops," Elm said, looking Cliff up and down.

Cliff smiled. "That's true," he admitted. "A computer is a tool, that's all."

"Believe me, young man, a computer will never replace a tractor." Elm picked up the remote control for the television set and turned it on, apparently unaware that comparing computers to tractors was like comparing apples to oranges. Or Apples with Caterpillars, as the case may be, Cliff thought in amusement.

"I'm going to watch the news. You can watch it with me if you like," Elm said.

Cliff could tell that there was no point in arguing with Elm, who apparently had closed his mind to what Cliff had to offer. He tried to figure out a way to escape from watching the news. The reason he had come here in the first place was to spend time with Sarah. And she was standing at the kitchen sink, vigorously washing dishes.

"I think I'll visit with Sarah and Lucy," Cliff said, a bit too casually, and was rewarded by a searching look from Elm.

Cliff ambled into the kitchen where Sarah was immersing a large pot in dishwater. Suds reached almost to her elbows. She had a funny double-jointed way of standing with her legs bowed backward. She wore a divided skirt which didn't quite reach her knees and a blouse with cap sleeves. Something about her stance struck straight to his heart. Although she was very methodically washing and instructing Lucy about drying and putting the dishes away, he knew she was aware of him as he watched her. Well, he'd just have to stick around and hope he had a chance to talk with her later.

Charlotte walked into the kitchen and picked up a newspaper filled with pea pods and potato peelings. "Guess I'll put these out on the compost heap," she said, heading for the back door.

Cliff hurried across the width of the room to hold the door for her.

"Mind if I come with you?" he asked.

She shot him a grateful glance. "I'd like that," she said.

They walked out into the fresh summer evening. The rows of Charlotte's garden were straight. Beans hung pendulous from the vines, and the sweet corn was almost as tall as Cliff.

"You have a beautiful garden," Cliff told Charlotte as she dumped the newspaper's contents into the nearby compost bin. The sight of well-tended garden plants always thrilled him. The thrill came from thinking about the nurturing of the earth's bounty and the remembered enjoyment of doing it himself.

"Oh, I'm going to miss my garden," said Charlotte, reaching out and letting a leaf from the nearest cornstalk slip through her fingers.

"Miss it?"

"Yes, Elm and I are going to move to a house in town soon."

"Sarah mentioned that you were leaving," he said.

"Elm has heart trouble, and my arthritis makes it hard for me to get around. We have a little house that used to belong to Elm's maiden aunt. When we move, Sarah will be alone here on the farm. I have to admit that the idea worries me a bit."

"Sarah seems very capable."

"Oh, she's *capable* enough," Charlotte said, but then she feared that she was revealing too much to this nice young man. She'd been about to say that she'd hoped Sarah would find a man to marry so she wouldn't have to worry about her being all alone in the world. All this women's lib stuff aside, a mother still liked to think of her daughter's being settled. *Married* and settled.

"Anyway," Charlotte said, moving on, "I suppose I'll just have to get used to—to everything. I mean, missing my garden and all."

"My mother always had a garden," said Cliff. "She used to can her own vegetables and preserves every summer. We ate out of that garden all year long."

"So do we," Charlotte said. "We always have. It seems silly to buy something you can grow yourself. Anyway, I'm sentimentally attached to this little plot of land."

Cliff glanced at her curiously. "How so?" he asked.

Charlotte laughed. "It was my garden that first won my mother-in-law over all those years ago. My mother-in-law was a big strapping woman who, at first, took a dim view of Elm's marrying me."

"Why?"

Charlotte shook her head in reminiscence, and she laughed a little. "Of what possible worth could a tiny woman like me be to the family farm? Norquist women weren't supposed to be slight and wispy. They were strong and robust. Besides, I wasn't from the Windrush Valley, nor was I from the nearby community of Curtisville where the Norquists studied and worshipped. To top it off, I'm one-eighth Kaw Indian.''

"You seem to have weathered farm life very well," Cliff observed, and Charlotte's dark eyes snapped with good humor.

"Well, in time Hulda learned to love me, even though I turned out be a slow breeder. I only produced two children. Duane was born in 1941 just before the attack on Pearl Harbor, and Sarah a full twelve years later. Hulda loved her grandchildren, but it was the garden that first won my acceptance in my mother-in-law's eyes." She smiled as she thought about it.

Hulda had admired Charlotte's big, fat green beans, stacked in clear glass mason jars on shelves that Elm had built in the cellar. Corn relish, packed in jars with tiny hot red peppers. Cool cucumber pickles, both sweet and dill. Glowing tomatoes, stewed in the middle of the steamy hot summers, then poured into jars to be decanted in winter when all of them at Windrush Valley Farm craved fresh vegetables.

"Remember when we all sat around on the porch and ate and ate Charlotte's tomatoes until we was way too full to move?" Charlotte's father-in-law would reminisce at supper some evenings when snow covered the ground and the biting prairie wind nipped at the corners of the old house.

And Hulda would smile and favor Charlotte with an approving look, and Elm would glance at her over the heads of their children, and she would know what he was thinking and how well he would express his love to her after everyone else in the house was asleep.

There had always been a lot of love in this house. All kinds of love—love between husband and wife, between parent and child, between in-laws.

As Charlotte and Cliff made their way out of the garden, Ben came running out of the house and, not the least bit shy, caught Cliff's hand.

"Want to come out to the barn to see my lambs? Their names are Tweedledum and Tweedledee," he said to Cliff.

Beyond Cliff, silhouetted in the frame of the back door, Cliff saw Sarah, watching. Could she have sent Ben to ask him to look at his lambs? Would Sarah, too, come to the barn?

"Sure," Cliff said easily. "I'd like to see your lambs."

He and Ben headed toward the barn, and Charlotte looked at Sarah and back again at Cliff's retreating back.

Cliff Oenbrink was such a personable fellow. He liked Sarah, Charlotte could tell. And now Sarah looked as though she was hanging back, as if she wanted to go out to the barn, too.

"Sarah," Charlotte said sharply. "I really think you need to take a look at the inside far corner of the barn. You know all those wasps we keep seeing? I think they're nesting in the barn. I really do."

Charlotte was immediately gratified when Sarah set off at a brisk walk toward the barn.

I handled that rather well, didn't I? Charlotte thought, and then she grinned. Maybe Sarah had been looking for an excuse to go out to the barn. Maybe Sarah liked this nice young man more than she was willing to let on.

There was lots of love in this house. Plenty to go around. Wouldn't it be wonderful if Cliff Oenbrink was the man who was meant to share that love with Sarah?

"IT'S CALLED LAMB *creep*," Ben said. "Isn't that a weird name for what you feed lambs?"

"It sure is," Cliff replied, bending over to scratch the top of a curious Tweedledum's head. "But I think what's in it sounds fairly normal. It's made of alfalfa and corn and other grains." The lambs, realizing that they were about to be fed, tried to climb up on the railing of their pen.

Ben carefully measured out a can of the feed pellets, then dumped it into a wooden feeding trough suspended from the fence.

When he climbed down from the fence he said suddenly, "Oh, Cliff. I almost forgot. I looked up neat's-foot oil and guess what it's made of?"

"You mean it's not made of oil of neat?"

"Nope, it's made by boiling cattle feet. There's such a thing as neat's tongue, too. It's the tongue of an ox. I found out about that on the next line in the dictionary."

"Well, that's very interesting, Ben. I'm glad you looked it up. I've been wondering what kind of exotic animal a neat was all my life, and now you tell me it's only a plain, ordinary old cow."

"Yeah, and there's nothing neat about *them*! My friend Pee Wee lives on a dairy farm, and I've helped him shovel out the stalls." Ben made a face, and Cliff laughed.

"I've tried to buy neat's-foot oil for you here in town, but I couldn't find any. I'll pick some up next time I go to Wichita," Cliff promised.

"Grandma says she thinks there's a wasp nest out here," Sarah said, unexpectedly behind them. Cliff turned and saw Sarah moving gracefully through the barn's gloom, picking her way through pieces of farm machinery scattered on the floor.

"I haven't seen one," replied Ben.

Sarah peered up into the dark corners of the barn. She didn't see any sign of a wasp nest either. There seemed to be no wasps in evidence. There was lots of other stuff in evidence, though. Much too much stuff.

"Someday I'm going to clean out this barn," she said. The place embarrassed her in front of a visitor. It was a jumble of farm equipment, toys and household objects that were no longer in use but were too good to throw away. The barn also housed the two three-wheeler all-terrain vehicles, which were kept in one corner.

"Don't clean it up," Cliff said with a wry look. "That would take away its atmosphere."

Ben was oblivious to them. He was jackknifed over the railing of the lamb pen, murmuring to his lambs. Tweedledum and Tweedledee were a 4-H project, and he had bought them himself. He was very proud of those lambs.

"Let's get out of here," said Sarah. "All this clutter makes me claustrophobic."

Cliff fell into step beside her, and they walked out of the dank, musty-smelling barn into the sweet fragrance of almost-dusk. Quite naturally, Sarah turned left onto the road up the hill instead of right toward the farmhouse. So he was going to be alone with her. Cliff could scarcely believe his luck.

"I enjoy going for a walk after I've cleaned up the kitchen," Sarah said. "You don't mind, do you?"

"I like it," Cliff said. All around them, things were settling down, preparing for twilight. Flocks of birds wheeled overhead, going, he presumed, to wherever they nested for the night. Even the ever-present prairie wind had died.

"Sometimes Tim Vogel comes over after supper and we walk to the top of the hill," said Sarah. "Have you met Tim yet?"

"He's the one who hangs out at the airport, right?"

"That's Tim."

"I met him briefly when I was talking with his father and older brothers."

"Are they going to make it, Cliff? Our family and the Vogels go back to when our parents were young married couples. Why, Norrie Vogel was my idol. I wanted to be just like her."

"Norrie? I've met Frank and Mina and the boys, but I don't remember any Norrie."

Sarah's eyes clouded momentarily. "Norrie was the Vogels' oldest child. She was exactly my brother Duane's age. She went away a long time ago, and no one knows what happened to her."

"How could that happen? Don't people around here keep pretty close track of their kinfolk?"

Sarah shrugged. "Norrie simply disappeared. She left one night and never came back. The Vogels searched and searched, but it was like she'd dropped off the ends of the earth. I cried for weeks, I remember. I loved Norrie. I didn't understand how she could go away without saying goodbye to me. And Tim— why Tim wasn't born until after Norrie left. He never even knew his big sister."

They had almost reached the top of the hill now. "Isn't that some of the Vogels' land over there?" Cliff asked Sarah. Below them, fields swept away in all directions. The horizon, flat as a floor, seemed infinitely far away.

"That's Vogel land to the west as far as we can see. They're not going to go bankrupt, are they, Cliff? You never did say."

Cliff took his time answering. "I hope not, Sarah," he said finally. "But it doesn't look good."

They walked on. Sarah's head was lowered, and she seemed lost in thought.

"Well, thanks for being honest," she said at last. "Tim seems to think that the farm is a lost cause, but I'd been hoping he was wrong. I can be of more help to him if I know how things really stand." She glanced at him curiously. "Tell me, how did you get into this business?"

"As I mentioned, I grew up on a farm in Illinois. I picked up a degree in agronomy at the state university, and then, after I saw that the future for farmers was less than promising, I left the family farm and moved to Kansas City where I worked as a commodities broker at the Board of Trade, working the trading pit."

"That's what I call a stressful job," Sarah said.

"When I realized that if I kept it up the stress would kill me, I found the job with Agritex in Minneapolis. I moved into consulting work, and I've been doing it ever since."

"You like it, don't you?"

"I love it," he assured her. "I like the feeling of helping people. I didn't want to farm the land, but I did want to stay connected to it, somehow. It's the perfect job for me. A perfect life, except—"

"Except?" She shot him a sidelong glance.

"Except, oh, I suppose I'm bothered by a sense of not feeling rooted. A lack of permanence. That's what I object to about my life right now. When I see someone like you, living in a house with three generations of your family on the land your ancestors farmed, it makes me feel rootless. And I guess I am."

"You never married?"

"I married, all right. If I'd stayed married, I would have felt even more at loose ends than I do now. My wife was a Bostonian pursuing a banking career in Kansas City. She was a high-powered, upwardly mobile type. At the time, so was I. It seemed the most natural thing in the world to marry each other.''

He paused, thinking how it had not seemed at all natural to Devon to move to Minneapolis after he'd quit the commodities brokerage, even though she'd found a job in Minneapolis right away. After the move from Kansas City, Devon itched to get back East, and their discussions on the matter had escalated into arguments.

Cliff didn't like the East. He was, he told Devon over and over, a Midwesterner with a Midwesterner's solid outlook. He hated cocktail parties, trendy discos, women with green goo smeared on their eyelids, and Boston accents. The latter hadn't occurred to him until he was in the middle of a fight with Devon one night and she told him to go to hell. He had only gone as far as the couch in the guest room, but after that it was clear that the marriage was over. Devon had departed for Boston soon afterward, and Cliff had been transferred to Oklahoma City, a place Devon would have hated even more than either Minneapolis or Kansas City.

"I'm sorry it didn't work out, Cliff," Sarah said softly, interrupting his thoughts.

He looked at her. Around her face her hair had escaped from its confining braid, and little wisps pale as corn silk feathered against her cheeks. Her eyes were wide and serious, and he sensed a softening toward him. He was elated to see that her expression shone with growing interest.

Had he finally made an impression on her? Had he, in telling her about his life, made himself a real person in her eyes?

"Don't be sorry," he said gently. "I'm not."

And for the first time, he really wasn't sorry that his marriage was over. He wasn't sorry in the least.

Chapter Six

The summer heat settled down upon Catalpa County with a stifling monotony. The sun flooded the land with a hot, lucent light. Frequent rain didn't dispel the heat, and the resulting humidity only made the heat more oppressive. Lucy and Ben fought more openly over little things, Charlotte more than occasionally snapped at Elm, and Elm retreated into silence more than was his wont. Preoccupied with farm matters, Sarah tried not to notice.

On the morning that Sarah started to plant sorghum seed, she first drove Lucy into town to spend the day with a friend. She dropped Lucy off and drove slowly out of town, drinking in the dappled cool shade of the city streets. Big leafy trees sheltered neat clapboard houses, and here and there, children played baseball on wide front lawns. It wasn't the kind of place where a man like Cliff Oenbrink would fit in.

But there was no time to worry about Cliff now. Once on the flat highway heading toward home, she pressed down hard on the accelerator. Henry would be waiting for her at the barn. He was filling the hoppers of the grain drill, the piece of machinery they used to distribute the seed in the fields.

To Sarah's dismay, her father was walking around the yard when she drove up. She had hoped that Charlotte would keep Elm busy in the house until Sarah got out to the fields, but apparently that had proved impossible. Sarah slid out of the pickup truck and, determined to hold her tongue, climbed into the tractor seat. She watched her father's approach out of the corner of her eye.

"The trouble with double-cropping," complained Elm as he worked his way around the big tractor to a point where Sarah would have to look at him, "is that it's too dependent on the weather."

"Pop, we've been through this again and again," Sarah said. She revved up the tractor engine so that she wouldn't hear Elm's objections and backed it up to the grain drill so that Henry could hitch it on.

"You'll have to worry about not having enough rain and getting a mess of chinch bugs," Elm shouted over the engine noise.

"Leave that to me, Pop," Sarah said after she cut off the tractor engine. She hopped down from the cab. Her father still looked perturbed, and her heart softened toward him. She slipped her hand through the crook of his elbow.

"Come on, Pop, let's see what new butterflies Ben has caught for his collection. He may need some help."

"You won't have enough moisture in the soil for that sorghum unless it rains a lot," said Elm stubbornly, refusing to budge either physically or mentally.

"Hey, it's going to rain enough, Pop. I'm going to have beautiful fields of sorghum this year." When Pop got in a mood like this, it was best to jolly him along.

"Beautiful! Sorghum? We've always planted wheat at Windrush Valley Farm. Only wheat. Is this sorghum business an idea you got from Cliff?"

"He gave me some booklets, that's all. I'm the one who decided on this particular soil management technique. I can't wait to try it."

"Never have heard of planting sorghum this late, anyhow," Elm grumbled.

"There's Ben now. Ben! Grandpa will help you with your butterflies."

"Butterflies," mumbled Elm, and with a last backward resentful glance at the tractor and a little push from Sarah, he went reluctantly to meet Ben, who was ambling around the corner of the house carrying a glass specimen jar.

"I guess Uncle Elm doesn't think much of your decision to double-crop this year," Henry observed, once Elm was out of hearing distance.

"It's the only choice I have after the hail destroyed my wheat. What am I supposed to do, let the fields lie fallow when they could be growing something that would pay?"

"Sarah, judging from what your father says, maybe I'd better do a rain dance," was all Henry said.

Sarah climbed into the cab of the tractor. "Getting the seed in the ground in late June the way we are lets the soil store up moisture prior to planting. Don't get out your dancing shoes, yet," she called down to him. Henry only laughed.

Out in the field, Sarah settled comfortably into the tractor seat and turned up the air conditioning and the radio, which was set on a classical music station. Sarah was convinced, despite Elm's objections, that she was doing the right thing by planting sorghum now.

Sarah was excited at the prospect of doing something new on her land, at inaugurating a program of her own choosing. She'd still grow wheat, of course. The fields planted in sorghum now would lie fallow before being planted in wheat again. And she was reading up on soybeans and lespedeza and other crops for the future.

Why was Elm so set against growing a variety of crops? He was used to the old way, the old days, when a farmer could grow wheat and nothing else and still make a decent living. Those days, though Elm refused to realize it, were gone forever. It was up to American farmers to use all the techniques at their disposal to make the best use of the land. As Sarah saw it, the land was a sacred trust, handed down from generation to generation. Sarah, in accepting the responsibility of farming the land, had committed herself to preserving that trust for future generations. For Lucy and Ben. She fervently hoped that they would farm the land after her.

All around her, she was seeing results of land and assets that had been poorly managed. The Vogels, for instance. Frank

Vogel had made some bad decisions. No one knew if the Vogels would, indeed, survive. Frank's dream of passing the land to his sons was all but shattered.

Sarah gritted her teeth. She might have bad luck, but she wouldn't be stupid. She would read, she would study, she would get good advice. She'd preserve Windrush Valley Farm for her children, and one way to do that was to do what she was doing now. To embark on a well-thought-out program of farm management, even if she had to take a lot of criticism from her own father.

One person who stood staunchly behind her was Cliff Oenbrink. He was a resource she intended to use to the fullest extent possible. She'd come to be thankful for his sharing of his expertise. And so far, his advice had been offered entirely on his own time. She hadn't had to pay him for it. In her current financial situation, that helped. That helped a lot.

A FEW DAYS AFTER Sarah finished planting, Cliff drove over the crest of Lornbacher Hill. He was glad to see that Lucy and Ben were in the yard near the barn playing with Lucy's bike. Cliff hoped that this meant that Sarah wouldn't be too far away.

"Lucy, you're making a mess of it," Ben said scornfully as Cliff got out of his car.

"I am not," said Lucy, who was struggling with long, stretchy ribbons of red, white and blue crepe paper. Cliff saw now that she was decorating her bike for the Fourth of July.

"Yours is gonna be the ugliest bicycle in the Fourth of July parade," Ben said.

"It is not."

"I'm going to win the Best Pet-Trick Contest, me and Spanky."

"You are not," Lucy said, true to her present negative mode. She poked a wad of crepe paper through the spokes in her bicycle wheel and bit her lip when the wad fell in the dust on the other side.

Ben abandoned Lucy for Cliff, running to his car and dancing around him like a gamboling puppy.

"Is your mother around?" Cliff asked.

"Nope. She and Henry are out at the Parker tract."

"Oh." Cliff tried not to show his disappointment. Instead he watched Lucy decorating her bicycle. He had to agree with Ben—privately, of course—that she wasn't doing a very good job of it.

Cliff strode over to where Lucy sat in the shade of the barn. Spanky, the family dog, flapped his tail against the wide trunk of the sycamore tree a few yards away.

Cliff knelt and inspected the bicycle wheel. "Need some help?" he asked.

"Oh, boy, does she ever!" exclaimed Ben.

"I do not," Lucy said, but it didn't sound as though her heart was in it.

"I used to decorate my bike every year for the Fourth. It won first place in the contest a couple of times," Cliff said.

"How'd you do it?" Lucy asked suspiciously.

"I used to wind crepe paper through the spokes like you're doing, but I fastened two small American flags to the handlebars, too. And I stuck a matchbook through the spokes, so it would make a buzzing sound when I rode it."

"I remember some bikes in last year's parade that made noise like that," Ben said. "But I've never seen any with American flags."

"Well, I don't have any flags for my bike," Lucy said in a quavering voice. "I thought this would be something like making valentines for Valentine Day, but it's not at all like that."

Cliff noticed that she was holding her right index finger in one hand.

"Did you hurt your hand?" he asked gently.

"I caught my finger between two spokes when my bike slipped off the kickstand. Look." She thrust a bruised finger at him.

"You got grease on your shorts," Ben pointed out.

"It's all over the bike wheels," she said, swiping at the grease stain. She stuck her bottom lip out. "I have a feeling that Mom isn't going to like that grease spot one bit," she said.

"I could get you some flags for your bike if you like," Cliff said.

"Could you?" Lucy perked up considerably at this suggestion.

"Sure. I could even help you get that crepe paper woven through the wheels."

"Oh, Cliff, please do. I'm having a *terrible* time," Lucy said. She edged over and hunkered on her heels as Cliff expertly wound the crepe paper through the bicycle spokes.

"Funny, when you do it, the crepe paper doesn't wrinkle or stretch or break," she said.

Cliff put Lucy to work cutting streamers to tie on the handlebars and to hang from the seat. Even Ben finally helped, pinching the edges of each streamer to make ruffles.

"There," Cliff said at last. He stood up and eyed the bike. Each wheel was woven from spoke to tire with a neat pattern of red, white and blue. Streamers hung from handlebars and seat, and he'd bring the flags over tomorrow.

"Take a ride, Lucy," he suggested. "Let us see how your bike looks in motion."

Lucy hopped on the seat and took off for a spin around the yard. Old Spanky, roused from his slumber by the resulting breeze, even struggled to his feet and ambled after her, although he gave up after only a few minutes.

Lucy crowed with glee. "I'm going to have the prettiest bike in the whole Fourth of July parade," she shouted as she whizzed past again with the red, white and blue streamers flowing.

"I'm going to enter Spanky in the Best Pet-Trick Contest at the Fourth of July celebration," Ben said importantly, trying to capture Cliff's attention for himself. "He's going to do a trick."

"What trick?"

"I can put a dog biscuit on his head, and he won't eat it until I say so. Sometimes he can flip it up in the air and catch it on the way down. Want to see?"

"Sure," Cliff said.

Ben ran into the barn and returned with a handful of dog biscuits before rousing Spanky from his snooze. Cliff dutifully watched as Ben put the biscuit on top of the dog's head, then made Spanky wait until he said, "Okay." Spanky tossed his head, ducked under the biscuit, and misjudged. The biscuit fell to the ground, but Spanky gobbled it up anyway.

"Usually he catches the biscuit," Ben explained. "It's just that he's getting a little old."

"Well, dogs get that way. How old is he?"

"I'm not sure. He belonged to Dad before he and Mom got married. Spanky's a lot older than I am. He used to roll over and run after his rubber ball and stuff. Now I guess he's too tired."

Cliff scratched Spanky beneath his ruff. The dog rolled his eyes blissfully and sank to the grass, where he soon fell asleep again.

"Did Mom tell you to come over today?" asked Ben.

"Well, I mentioned that I might."

"Can you stay for supper?"

"Oh, I don't know," said Cliff, wanting to. He didn't like to impose, though.

Charlotte came out on the porch. "Why Cliff, it's good to see you. I was wondering who would eat all the pot roast I'm cooking for supper. You'll stay, won't you?"

"Stay, Cliff," Ben begged. "Please stay. Anyway, here comes Mom."

Cliff saw the big John Deere tractor lumbering down the hill. His heart lightened considerably at the sight of Sarah inside the cab.

"I'd like to stay," he said, although he thought he might be wearing out his welcome. In the past week, he'd been invited for supper no less than four times.

Sarah pulled the tractor to a stop alongside the barn and jumped out. She tossed her single braid back over her shoulder. She hugged Lucy, slid an arm around Ben and smiled when she saw Cliff.

"What a day!" she exclaimed.

"Tell me about it," Cliff said, giving her his undivided attention. When Sarah was around, the others ceased to exist for him. Charlotte, even though he was fond of her, receded into the background. So did Ben and Lucy.

Realizing this, Charlotte elected to remove herself entirely. "Ben, Lucy Anne, come inside," Charlotte said. "It's time to help me set the table."

Although they complained about it, Ben and Lucy followed Charlotte into the kitchen. As she set about finishing dinner preparations Charlotte looked out the window to see Sarah talking to Cliff in an animated fashion. She didn't know what her daughter could be talking about, but Charlotte meant to see that Sarah had some uninterrupted time with Cliff.

The way the two of them went about courting, nothing would ever come of it. Either Elm would collar Cliff and keep him in the living room talking about the weather or the crops, or Ben would enlist Cliff's help with his latest Popsicle-stick construction project, or Lucy would hang around listening to everything that Sarah and Cliff said to each other. Well, maybe Sarah and Cliff weren't exactly courting. But they would be soon if Charlotte had anything to do with it. She opened the window a tad more so that she could unobtrusively tune in on their conversation.

"So what did you do then?" Cliff asked as Sarah threw herself down on the middle porch step.

"Well, after my pickup truck tire went flat on that bumpy dirt road, I walked a half mile to somebody's house and called my cousin Henry to come rescue me. Henry came out and we got the flat tire off my pickup, and after Henry put my spare on, he went back to his truck and said, 'Sarah, you aren't going to believe this, but a tire on *my* truck is going flat.'"

Cliff laughed. "Then what?"

"He didn't have a spare because he'd already had a flat tire *last* week and hadn't stopped by the garage where it was being fixed to pick it up. So I drove him into town and we got the tire, and then we changed the tire on his pickup and hurried back to the home farm. Henry walked into the barn, took one look at the chisel plow, and one of the two tires on *it* was flat."

"What did he do then?"

"Henry drove back into town to buy a new tire for the chisel plow, and on the way home he saw Frank Vogel's truck pulled over to the side of the highway, so Henry stopped, and guess what!"

"Frank's tire wasn't flat?"

"You bet it was! I don't know what's going on around here with all these flat tires, but we'd better warn Lucy. I wouldn't be a bit surprised if that bike of hers didn't turn up with a flat tire before supper."

Cliff smiled. "So I guess you didn't get as much of that field plowed as you thought you would."

"I didn't get out to the field until early afternoon, and then only after Pop hassled me about the kind of fertilizer I'm using. But I made up for lost time once I got out there."

Cliff noticed that Sarah sparkled today. She seemed young and more unself-conscious than she'd ever been around him. In her plaid cotton shirt and faded jeans, she was leaning back with her elbows on the top step and with her chin tilted back so that the light breeze could reach her neck. The top three buttons of her shirt were unbuttoned, and her skin was suntanned in a V beneath it. Below the tanned V swelled smooth white skin, white as gardenia blossoms.

She noticed him looking at her. "Well, I guess I'll go shower," she said abruptly. "You're staying for supper, aren't you?" She'd accepted Cliff's frequent presence at their table as though it wasn't unusual. Which it wasn't anymore.

"I'll be here," he said.

As his eyes followed Sarah into the house, Charlotte stepped outside. "Won't you come in, Cliff? It's a mite cooler in there."

"Just feel that breeze," he said. A whisper of a breeze wandered around the corner of the house, tarried on the porch and disappeared in a swelling of the curtain at the kitchen window.

"Mighty little breeze," Charlotte commented.

"Well, you've got to appreciate it when you feel it. There might not be another one for a long time."

Charlotte shaded her eyes against the tangerine light of the setting sun.

"Will you take a look at that Spanky," she said. "I don't believe he's moved from that spot underneath the sycamore tree all day long."

"Ben showed me Spanky's biscuit trick," Cliff said.

"Spanky used to do lots of tricks. I guess he's getting too old to do tricks anymore. Like lots of us."

Cliff shot a sharp look at Charlotte, but she revealed no expression other than placid acceptance. He had expected, perhaps, self-pity. He knew, by this time, how much her arthritis bothered her.

"May I help you with the supper?" he offered.

"Thank you, no. I've got everything under control, especially with Ben and Lucy Anne helping. Why don't you go talk to Elm? He gets lonely sometimes now that he can't go into town every day to visit with his pals at the Chatterbox."

"He used to go every day, did he?" asked Cliff as he followed Charlotte into the cool shadowed interior of the farmhouse.

"Every day, without fail. Now, with his heart condition, he's not supposed to drive. You go on in and talk to him, will you, Cliff? He likes you so much."

Cliff spent a good half hour listening to Elm expound on the topic of shrinking farm exports, and then Sarah came downstairs wafting a clean fresh soapy fragrance in her wake and with her pale hair piled on top of her head in a smooth topknot. After dinner, Sarah refused his offer to wash dishes, insisting that it was a good thing for the children to learn to help her. While Ben helped, Cliff sat on the porch with Charlotte, Elm and Lucy.

Charlotte's cat, a calico named Quilter, hopped up on the porch, and Charlotte leaned over to pet her. It was almost dark, with fireflies flashing on and off in the tall grass near the barn, when a figure appeared at the top of Lornbacher Hill. Charlotte straightened and spied the visitor approaching in the deepening dusk.

"Oh, it's Tim Vogel! He's back from Wisconsin! Sarah told me that he's been up there spraying crops. He's a flyer, you know," she informed Cliff. "Fell in love with airplanes and joined the Air Force. Now he does all kinds of flying."

"Tim, Tim!" cried Lucy, running toward him.

"Tim's here?" Sarah said, emerging from the house with Ben right behind her. Ben went charging after Lucy, and to Cliff's surprise, Sarah, without even stopping to hang up her dish towel, ran to meet Tim, too. Even Spanky, who had been lying in front of the door like a shaggy doormat, stood up, shook himself, and set off at a trot to greet Tim.

Cliff had been taught to judge a man by the firmness of his handshake, and he found nothing to criticize about Tim Vogel's. The one thing that did surprise him about Tim was that Tim was so much younger than he'd expected. He'd met Leonard and Bernie, Tim's brothers, and they were both in their late thirties. Tim seemed as if he might be only in his mid-twenties.

Tim was invited to visit. Sarah, suddenly finding a dish towel in her hand, hung it over the porch railing and sat down beside Cliff.

"Well, what's the news?" Tim asked. "What did I miss out on last week while I was out of town?"

"The Howells' baby was born," said Sarah. "It was a girl."

Charlotte rocked and tried to think of what else had happened around Curtisville. After she'd thought awhile, she said, "Thurmond Paulk died, finally. He'd been in intensive care for a couple of weeks after he took sick again."

"I'm sorry to hear that," said Tim.

"We had a committee meeting the other day," contributed Elm. "We're planning the biggest and best Pioneer Day yet." The town of Curtisville celebrated Pioneer Day every September in honor of the founding of the town. Elm had served as chairman for the past ten years.

"Maybe I'll enter the Pioneer Day beard-growing contest," Tim said, rubbing the blond stubble on his face. "Maybe I'll win this year."

Sarah grinned. "Looks to me like you'll have better luck this year than that first year you tried to enter. All you managed was a crop of peach fuzz."

"Well, I was only sixteen," Tim retorted, sounding aggrieved. "Anyway, I'd like to see *you* enter the beard-growing contest. *You* couldn't even grow peach fuzz!"

Ben laughed out loud, and Lucy giggled. Apparently this banter between Sarah and Tim was expected. Cliff felt relieved. Whatever their relationship was, it didn't seem to be a romantic one.

"How're your dad and mother doing, Tim?" asked Sarah. "They haven't been over to see us in a while."

"Oh, Ma stays busy with her flower garden and doing the bookkeeping for the farm. Pa—well, he's scrambling. Trying to keep his head above water. I wish he'd had the sense to quit farming a long time ago." Tim's voice was tinged with bitterness. As though he didn't want to be questioned about his family's situation anymore, Tim rose abruptly to his feet.

"Guess I'll be going," he said. He tweaked Lucy's ear. "I'm glad I got to meet you," he said, nodding in Cliff's direction. Then he took the porch steps two at a time and headed into the darkness, disappearing up Lornbacher Hill.

The adults were silent with unspoken thoughts. The blackness of the night seemed to crowd in upon them as insects throbbed in the shrubbery. At last Elm mopped his face with a handkerchief and lurched to his feet. "Time for my favorite TV program," he said. "You coming, Charlotte?"

"Time for bed, Ben and Lucy Anne," Charlotte said. She was bound and determined to get the children out of Cliff and Sarah's way again.

"Aw, Grandma," Lucy said, but she and Ben both marched obediently ahead of Charlotte into the house. The screen door slammed behind them.

Cliff and Sarah remained on the porch.

"I wish I could do something," Sarah said suddenly.

"For Tim, you mean?"

"For Tim and his family. We all grew up together, the Vogel kids and my brother Duane and me. I hate to see them in trouble now."

"Just because the Vogels are in trouble doesn't mean that they aren't good at what they do."

"Frank Vogel knows farming," said Sarah.

"Say, it's not just the Vogels you're worried about, is it? You're not in more serious trouble than you thought?"

"No, no," said Sarah. She stood at the porch railing, using her fingertip to trace little circles in the yellow dust settled there.

Cliff stood behind her and longed to put his hand on her shoulder. A simple gesture, but one that implied possession. How he wanted to touch her!

"What is it, Sarah?" he asked gently.

"I guess it's just everything." She slipped out of the space between Cliff and the porch railing and walked out into the darkness. Cliff followed her. She strolled slowly toward the road, her hands in the pockets of her wide gathered skirt.

"You can tell me what's bothering you," he said. "I'm guaranteed not to gossip."

She spared him an amused look. "From that statement I can guess that you know how things work in a small town."

"I grew up in Medallion, Illinois. It's about the size of Curtisville. A person couldn't turn over in bed without everyone in town knowing about it."

Sarah thought she detected a disparaging note in his voice. She smiled. "That's the way it is here, too. I have friends, Janice for instance, but—well, it's not the same as when my husband was alive. When I had James, I knew that someone was always on my side. We talked to one another freely about our deepest joys and sorrows without fear that our words would be repeated all over town. I miss that freedom and that very special trust."

"My marriage wasn't at all like that. I envy you and James for what you had together."

"It was too short," she said in a low voice. "Much too short. It's been very hard to accept that he's really gone."

She spoke calmly, but Cliff knew how much she must have grieved for him.

"He'd be proud of you for what you're doing with the farm," said Cliff.

"Yes. I know that. But the farm is exactly why I need him. It would be such a comfort to have his advice, his love—" Here her voice broke, but she couldn't help it. Suddenly she was filled with a vision of James: of his laughing eyes, his curly hair, of the sound of his booming voice. Her heart hammered inside her chest. It was as though she actually felt James and saw James and again walked beside James. For a moment she let her imagination fool her that it actually *was* James. But then the man walking beside her spoke. She turned to him, and he wasn't James. He was someone else entirely, and though his smile was warm, it was hesitant, and she felt a sudden sharp anger at him for not being James.

"Sarah," Cliff said. Her eyes haunted him. He found her very beautiful with her huge dark eyes and with her pale hair gleaming in the darkness. He wanted to reassure her, but he felt helpless. And she wasn't returning his smile. She was staring at him as though she didn't know him.

They had, almost without realizing it, reached the top of the hill. Sarah, to hide her confusion at finding Cliff beside her when her thoughts were filled with James, suddenly left the road and headed toward the Osage orange hedge bordering the farm's small fruit orchard.

"Sarah," Cliff said again as he hurried after her. Her tall figure slipped through an opening in the hedge, and at that moment the moon sailed out from behind a cloud. The leaves of the trees seemed cast in silver.

"You've never been to the orchard before, have you?" she asked, walking slowly between the rows of trees. The timothy grass was almost knee-high and stained the hem of Sarah's skirt with dew.

"No," he said, striding fast in order to keep up with her long legs, which seemed disinclined to stroll.

"I should do something about it," she said distractedly. "I shouldn't let weeds grow here." Patches of wild larkspur gleamed in the moonlight, and tangles of foxtail intermingled with spikes of horehound.

"You can't do everything," Cliff pointed out. "You have enough responsibility overseeing the paying crops."

"Well, Mama does set such store by her jams and jellies," Sarah said. "Cherry, apricot, plum, you name it. Every summer she—well, not every summer, I guess. She didn't make any jelly last summer. She didn't feel well enough."

"You take it all so seriously, don't you? The farm, your parents, the responsibility." He stuck his hands in his pockets so he wouldn't be so tempted to touch her. His fingers ached with the urge, but he sensed that it wasn't the proper time.

"I suppose I do," she said gravely. "Here I am, supposed to run this farm, and it isn't easy."

"Your father is proud of you for all that you do."

"Is he? I don't know. All I get is criticism from him. You should have heard him today. I feel as though I'm butting up against a stone wall whenever I get into a discussion about farming with him."

"He's finding it hard to let go of the farm. It was his life. I saw it happen with my father when he sold out. He kept going out there to see the new owner, hanging around and giving the new guy unwanted advice. Elm is like that, too."

"I try to be patient, but it's hard."

"Give Elm time. They'll be moving to town soon, won't they?"

"Yes, which may cause new problems altogether. I'll have to the farm to handle, plus the upbringing of my two kids. Sometimes I wonder how I'll manage it." Cliff noticed that she had knotted her hands in front of her.

"Well, Sarah Morrow," he said cheerfully, hoping to convey his confidence in her, "I think you'll manage very well."

She sighed, looked down at her hands and appeared surprised to see them clenched so tightly. They dropped to her sides. "That's what everyone says. Everyone expects me to be superwoman."

"I don't. I like you to be just Sarah."

She let her eyes meet his. They shone with gratitude. "I think that's one of the nicest things anyone's ever said to me," she told him.

"Is it? Then people don't appreciate you enough."

"I have to admit that I have felt that way at times." She walked on in silence. Then she said, "You know, I can really talk to you," she said in quiet surprise. "It means a lot to me."

How much? thought Cliff, but he only smiled at her and tore his gaze away. They had made a full circle of the orchard, and rounding the corner of the hedge, found themselves back on the road again. At the bottom of the hill, the house glowed with warm, welcoming light shining from the windows.

"What a pretty sight," he said under his breath, and Sarah nodded appreciatively.

"It is, isn't it? Sometimes I think of generation after generation of Norquists walking down this hill to the house, maybe my great-grandmother, or even my great-great-grandmother, and I think that nothing can harm me in the whole world as long as I have this place to come back to. I guess it's silly but it's comforting to know that whatever happens to the people in my life, the house and the land will always be there for me. And for my children."

"I don't think that's silly at all," Cliff told her seriously. "In fact, I wish I had a place like that. A place that would always be home."

"You've traveled around a lot, haven't you?"

"It was what I thought I wanted to do when I was a kid. I couldn't wait to leave Medallion, Illinois, and find out what the rest of the world was made of."

"And did you?"

"Oh, I found the fast lane, all right. I've lived in Kansas City, Minneapolis, Oklahoma City."

"Was city life what you expected?"

Cliff chuckled. He was laughing at himself, though she didn't know that. "It was more than I ever expected," he said.

"I think about the world outside Curtisville sometimes," mused Sarah, walking more slowly now. She didn't want to reach the house too fast and cut this long conversation short. She had so few people to whom she was able to communicate the things on her mind. "Sometimes I wonder what it would be like to go to cocktail parties every weekend. To attend glamorous dinners and balls. To wear velvet gowns. To ride in fast cars and smoke brown cigarettes in diamond-studded holders and have my fortune told." She laughed at her fancifulness.

"I've done most of that, and Sarah, I don't think you'd like it much."

"Wouldn't I? Why?"

He thought about Sarah, about how fresh, wholesome and unspoiled she was. He couldn't imagine her among any of the people he had known when he and Devon were married. Cocktail parties, brown cigarettes—she might have been describing his ex-wife. Sarah would be sullied and tarnished by that kind of life.

"You're more real than that," he said shortly, and she didn't understand what he meant. But they had reached the yard now, and Sarah was afraid that he'd get in his car and drive away to his small room at the Country Inn.

"Come inside for a glass of lemonade, Cliff. Surely you don't have to leave yet." Her eyes were enormous, and her lips curved into an inviting smile.

"Thanks, I will." He was achingly aware that he wanted to touch her.

And so he went inside and listened to Ben and Lucy preparing for bed upstairs and watched Sarah as she mounted the stairs to shush them. He watched television with Charlotte and Elm, and he held out his glass to be refilled with lemonade by a Sarah who could not seem to sit still.

Finally, when the ice cubes in his glass had melted to the size of marbles, Charlotte and Elm turned off the television and said good-night. Sarah walked Cliff to the door.

"Lucy told me when I went upstairs that you helped her decorate her bike. Thank you, Cliff," she said.

He wondered what she would do if he simply put his arms around her and kissed her. But this he did not do. He merely forced himself to smile pleasantly before saying goodbye, hurrying to his car, and driving away in a cloud of dust.

He was making inroads, he knew. The advice he had given her about changing her methods of farming had been well-taken. She had learned to respect and trust him. He knew that it still wouldn't work if he tried to push her into seeing him alone, away from her family, but tonight he and Sarah had reached a new level of communication.

He wouldn't have traded their shared intimacy for anything.

Chapter Seven

That Sunday as Sarah was waiting to go inside the church for the service, Dottie Olsen, wife of Bud, made a point of seeking her out in the memorial rose garden where Sarah often went to think about her brother, one of the servicemen to whom the garden was dedicated.

Sarah was sitting on a marble bench listening to the splashing of the fountain when she saw Dottie approaching on the other side of the low iron fence separating the rose garden from the church.

"I hear that you've hired that man from Agritex to help you with your farm," Dottie said without preliminaries. She plunked herself down beside Sarah and smoothed the hem of her dress. Her two children saw Lucy standing beside the fountain and ran to greet her.

"Cliff Oenbrink. No, Dottie, I haven't. Where did you hear that?" Sarah put out a hand to restrain a rambunctious Lucy as she spun past.

"I guess I must have heard it from Bud," Dottie said, peering up at Sarah through her gold-rimmed glasses.

"I've thought about hiring him," Sarah said slowly. "I'm double-cropping, you know."

"Bud told me that, too. The reason I thought you'd hired Mr. Oenbrink is that Bud says he spends a lot of time at your house."

"He's only been there a few times, mostly to visit with Mama and the kids," Sarah said. This wasn't entirely true, she knew, but it was all Dottie Olsen needed to know.

"You know how much I admire you, Sarah, for running the farm and all. But why do you need Mr. Oenbrink? Why don't you pay attention to what your daddy tells you to do? He's farmed Windrush Valley Farm for years." Dottie's plain face was genuinely perplexed.

"Times change," Sarah said with the utmost patience. "Farming isn't the way it used to be."

"Oh, Lord, don't I know it," Dottie said in a heartfelt tone.

"Everything's okay with your farm, isn't it?" Sarah asked in concern.

Dottie patted Sarah's arm reassuringly. "Yes, but we know plenty of people who aren't having an easy time of it. Bud and I, we're all right. I hope you are, too. Just don't go doing anything foolish. Don't go hiring somebody to tell you what your own daddy could tell you about farming."

Suddenly the sweet scent of the roses seemed unbearably cloying. In the sanctuary, the organist began to play the prelude. Sarah was overwhelmingly relieved when Dottie stood up, gathered her children around her, and went looking for Bud. Sarah congratulated herself for hiding her annoyance from Dottie and took Lucy firmly by the hand before walking into the church by the side door.

All through the Invocation and Kyrie and the first hymn and the Prayer of the Day, it irked Sarah that Dottie would not—perhaps could not—accept Cliff and what he had to offer farmers in their community. She, Sarah, was apparently regarded by her friends and neighbors as even more of a rebel now that she had made Cliff welcome at Windrush Valley Farm. Otherwise, why would Dottie, who apparently thought she was being helpful, have sought her out to give her that unwelcome bit of advice? After planting a new crop of sorghum, Sarah felt even more strongly that she was the person in charge of the farm now. She would hire or fire whomever she pleased.

Besides, there was something else at work here—the locals' distrust of any stranger to the community. Sarah liked Cliff.

She sympathized with how he, as a newcomer in this close-knit community might feel.

No matter how easily Cliff persuaded farmers to trust Agritex, he'd have a hard time winning their personal approval. No one knew him. Unlike everyone else in Curtisville, his history wasn't known. Because of that, and because in Curtisville everyone knew everyone else, Cliff Oenbrink wasn't real to them. And he wouldn't be real to the people here until he had found a niche where he belonged, so that people could see where Cliff was in relation to them—socially, economically and psychologically.

The idea of inviting Cliff to Sunday dinner occurred to Sarah suddenly as they passed the inn on the way home after the service. She had an urge to defy public opinion, to do what she wanted to do despite what people like Dottie and Bud Olsen, well-meaning as they were, advised.

As for Cliff, for all Sarah knew he didn't care if people talked about him or not. Still, if he wanted to, he could casually mention around town that he'd been to Windrush Valley Farm for Sunday dinner. That would give people a point of reference for Cliff. Invitations to Sunday dinner were not taken lightly.

Sunday dinner was a Curtisville institution. It was a time for family and possibly very good friends, and it was considered several cuts above an ordinary weekday dinner, which was called supper by most people. A stranger wouldn't be invited to Sunday dinner. No, Sunday dinner was the time to set the table with good china and a lace tablecloth and to sit around catching up on family news and gossip. Even Charlotte hadn't yet gone so far as to include Cliff at their Sunday dinner.

When Sarah suddenly swung the Chevy station wagon into a diagonal parking place in front of the inn, Ben said, "Hey, what are you doing, Mom?"

"I'm going to ask Cliff to come to Sunday dinner," was all Sarah said before she stepped out of the car into a rising wind that all but whipped her words away.

As he watched his daughter disappear into the inn, Elm said, "I wonder what got into her all of a sudden, wanting to invite Cliff to Sunday dinner."

And Charlotte thought hopefully, *Now that's a new wrinkle.*

Sarah stopped at the desk in the lobby where the air conditioning provided a welcome relief from the sweltering heat outside. The lobby smelled of the accumulation of years of lemon oil applied religiously to the old furniture. A clock ticked behind the desk. Marlene, the desk clerk, wasn't there. Sarah cleared her throat and shifted her weight back and forth on the wide wooden flooring planks, hoping that the resulting creaks would summon Marlene out from wherever she was hiding.

They did. A door opened and Marlene stuck her head out.

"Oh, hi, Sarah. I'm in here trying to fix the ice machine. It's gone on the blink again." Marlene eased into full view and waved a pair of pliers in the air. "I guess I could call the repairman, but last time, they had to send someone all the way from Wichita, and it took the guy a week to get out here. What can I do for you?" Marlene's eyes were frankly curious.

"I came to see Cliff Oenbrink. Can you ring him on the phone and tell him I'm here?"

"Oh, our rooms don't have phones. You'll have to go up and knock on his door. Or I can carry a message up for you if you like."

"No, no, don't bother. I'll just run upstairs." Sarah started up the narrow staircase.

"It's room six," Marlene called after her.

Room six was marked by a paint-encrusted number on the door. Sarah self-consciously pushed a strand of stray hair behind her ear and knocked.

Cliff opened the door immediately. He greeted Sarah's appearance with an appreciative scrutiny of her Sunday finery.

"Cliff, I was thinking—I mean we were all thinking—that we'd like you to come out to the farm and eat Sunday dinner with us," Sarah said. To her embarrassment, she stumbled and stuttered in a way she hadn't stumbled and stuttered since she was a mere girl.

But Cliff smiled and said, "Your invitation is the best thing that could have happened to me today, Sarah. You have no idea how much I was dreading another empty Sunday afternoon."

Clearly he understood the underlying significance of being invited to Sunday dinner.

Sarah ran back down the inn stairs, almost bumping into an inquisitive Marlene. "Did you find him?" Marlene asked. "Was he in?"

"Yes," Sarah said, escaping out the door.

"Is he coming?" said Ben when Sarah slid back into the station wagon.

"When will he be there?" asked Lucy, who had removed her shoes and was in the process of removing her socks as well.

"I hope we'll have enough strawberry pie," said Charlotte, who was glad she didn't have to worry about stretching the main course: there was always plenty of food at their house, especially at Sunday dinner.

"He'll be there shortly after we get home," Sarah said blithely, her voice tripping over the words in happy anticipation.

"Good," said Elm in his own succinct way.

So Cliff had indeed come to Sunday dinner, and Sarah contrived to mention this fact to Ida Rae at the Chatterbox on Monday. Ida Rae's eyes had lit up at this news, and she had studied Sarah speculatively while Sarah nonchalantly ate an egg salad sandwich. *Let Ida Rae think what she will,* Sarah thought, and it seemed to Sarah that every time she heard Cliff's name mentioned during the following week, it was with more than the grudging acknowledgment of his presence that had been accorded him before.

His growing acceptance aside, Sarah didn't see Cliff all week. She just missed him at the Chatterbox a couple of mornings in a row when she stopped in for coffee as usual, and she heard that he had been ranging far and wide, giving Agritex seminars in the surrounding towns.

She wondered why she didn't hear from him. Had he decided, perchance, that he was getting too involved with her family, especially as evidenced by the invitation to Sunday dinner? That he wanted to lessen his involvement with them?

Cliff would know that tongues would wag about his spending so much time at the home of the widow Morrow. He might not like the talk around town to link him with any one woman. The best way to stop the gossip would be to avoid her. To spend time doing other things. This shouldn't surprise Sarah; in fact, it didn't. She had known all along that he wasn't the type to adopt the quiet, peaceful family-oriented way of life that prevailed in this corner of the world.

On the Fourth of July, Sarah waited for the phone to ring, thinking that maybe Cliff would call on this holiday. The phone remained silent all morning. Finally, giving up, Sarah packed her parents and children into the station wagon for the drive into town for Curtisville's annual Fourth of July celebration. With Spanky sandwiched into the back with Ben and Lucy's bicycle, it was a tight fit. They all sighed with relief when Sarah pulled the station wagon to a stop beneath the unfinished mural in the parking lot beside the Chatterbox.

Sarah shot several covert glances at the Country Inn across the street. She saw no sign of Cliff. She wondered how he planned to spend the Fourth.

"Looking for somebody?" asked a keen-eyed Ida Rae, who sauntered out of the Chatterbox to watch the parade preparations on Main Street. Sarah tried to figure out how to answer her.

"Here, Ben, let me help you drag that danged dog out of there," said Elm, unfolding himself from the front seat. "Sarah, can you give me a hand?"

This provided exactly the distraction Sarah needed at the moment. "I'm not looking for anybody, Ida Rae," Sarah said untruthfully. She immediately turned her attention to helping her father and Ben, wishing that she'd parked somewhere else besides across the street from where Cliff lived and where Ida Rae stood sentinel.

"I haven't seen Cliff all day," was Ida Rae's smug parting shot before she disappeared into the Chatterbox again.

Thanks partly to Ida Rae's astute observations, which she offered freely at the Chatterbox to anyone who would listen, Sarah had come to see that Cliff was the most exciting man to hit Curtisville since—well, since a traveling mural artist had blown into town five years ago and promised to paint a fabulous mural depicting the town's history. The artist had been flashy and fast-talking, and women had hung all over him.

The mural artist had gotten himself into so much hot water that he'd had to flee Curtisville before he ever finished the mural. The unfinished masterpiece still adorned a long building on the other side of the parking lot from the Chatterbox, and it was the only thing left to remind the residents of Curtisville and its environs that the artist had ever been there. Unless you counted Lana Lowman's four-year-old daughter Loretta, who had hair the same fiery shade of red as the long-gone artist.

Sarah and her family found places to sit at curbside on Main Street and awaited the start of the parade. Lucy rode off in the direction of the parade lineup to ride with other cyclists who had entered their bikes in the Bike Decorating Contest.

A hot July sun gleamed off brass polished to a brilliant shine as the Curtisville High School Marching Band played a rousing and only slightly off-key rendition of the "Washington Post March." Cymbals clashed, and Ben waved a brand-new American flag in time to the music. Charlotte, settled in a folding chair beneath an enormous bur oak, said tartly, "You make a better door than a window, Ben. I can't see through you. I wish you'd either move over or sit down." Beneath her chair, Spanky lifted his head and let his tongue roll out of his mouth.

Ben stepped to one side. "There's Cliff! Hey, Cliff! Cliff!" He waved his flag high in the air in hopes of attracting Cliff's attention.

Sarah, too, saw Cliff. In the spirit of the occasion, he wore blue jeans and a red, white and blue plaid cotton shirt. He dodged baby strollers and the clowns who were selling candy for the Lions Club at the curb, and he waved when he saw them.

He lost no time in joining them, and Sarah noticed that Cliff maneuvered so that he would stand next to her during the rest of the parade. He wasn't obvious about it, but his intent was clear to Sarah, who felt her heart speed up and her mouth go dry.

"When do the bikes go by?" Cliff asked Sarah as he craned his neck trying to see the end of the parade, which was nowhere in sight.

"They're usually next to the last. Just before the Bridle & Saddle Club."

"When is the judging of the bikes? I hope Lucy wins," said Cliff.

"There's a judges' stand down in front of the town government complex," Sarah replied.

"You're coming to the park, aren't you, Cliff?" asked Ben. "Spanky's going to be in the contest then."

"Sure I will. Your grandma invited me."

Sarah turned startled eyes on Charlotte. Since when did anyone need to be invited to the Fourth of July celebration at the municipal park? Charlotte had certainly never mentioned inviting Cliff. But Charlotte only blinked innocently at Sarah.

"There'll be fireworks at the park," Ben said.

"And bands and sing-alongs," Charlotte added. Charlotte always especially enjoyed the musical portion of the program.

"You'll be there, won't you, Sarah?" Cliff asked in an undertone.

"I'll be there, of course," she murmured, casting her eyes downward until they focused on a piece of litter just beyond the toe of her shoe. She bent to pick it up, mostly to hide the expression in her eyes, which, if Cliff saw it, would betray her vulnerability.

What was it about him that made every emotion rise to the surface when she was around him? She'd successfully hidden her softer side ever since James died. When she had been learning to run the farm, it had become clear to her that her vulnerability was a weakness, and emotion made it harder to deal with her given world. So, casting about for a way to adapt to her new circumstances, she had dug down deep into her psyche and found an innate practicality that had gradually replaced her true personality. A temporary measure, she thought when she had time to think about.

Around Cliff, she felt exposed. She had opened herself to him, let him see parts of the real Sarah, and now she found it impossible to be the manufactured Sarah around him.

"Look, the bikes are coming!" shouted Ben, and they all looked for Lucy among the wobbly ranks of the children who had entered the Bike Decorating Contest.

"There she is!" said Sarah, relieved to have her daughter provide a diversion.

Lucy rode bravely in the middle of the group of kids, most of whom were older than she. Lucy's bike was draped in an abundance of ruffled crepe-paper streamers, while some of the other bikes sported only a sparse two or three. And, thanks to four matchbook covers, two flapping against the spokes of each wheel, her bike made an awesome noise.

"Lucy's bike looks good," Elm said.

"I helped her fix it up," said Ben. "Didn't I, Cliff?"

"You sure did," said Cliff, gripping Ben's shoulder for a moment. Ben gazed up at Cliff adoringly.

Lucy was smart enough not to remove her hands from the handlebars in order to attempt a wave as she passed her family group. She rode staunchly on, mindful of the judges' stand ahead on the right.

"Well, Lucy Anne ought to win first place," declared Charlotte, settling back in her chair.

"Can we go now? It's almost time for the Best Pet-Trick Contest," Ben said.

They gathered up their belongings. Ben revived Spanky with the gift of a hot dog he'd saved from lunch. The old dog pranced alongside Ben as they walked.

"What did you think of the parade?" Sarah asked Cliff as they lagged behind the others.

"It was better than the ones we used to have in Medallion."

"Why?"

"Oh, I think Curtisville has more community spirit."

She glanced up at him curiously. "How so?"

He shrugged. "Just a feeling I get. A sort of enthusiasm. The number of kids who entered the Bike Decorating Contest. The big mural outside the Chatterbox. When is it going to be finished, by the way?''

Sarah sighed. "Maybe never. It's been in its present condition for several years now. Even the paint is starting to chip off in places. My guess is that they'll eventually paint over the whole thing, and no one will know it ever existed.''

Cliff looked thunderstruck. "Why, they can't do that! It's an impressive painting. It tells the history of the town, doesn't it?''

"It's supposed to. That is, when and if it's ever finished.''

"From what I saw, the mural depicts the Indians on the prairie before the white man arrived, and then the settlers crossing it in their covered wagons, and a pioneer woman holding her baby, and a tornado—what's the significance of the tornado, anyway?''

"A tornado destroyed the town," Sarah said. "That was back when it was still called Gopher Prairie. When they rebuilt the town, it was rechristened Curtisville after the first vice president of the United States from west of the Mississippi. He was part Kaw Indian, too, like Charlotte.''

"Curtisville has a rich history. It should be commemorated in that mural. Why doesn't the artist finish it?''

"The artist skipped town with the money for the mural. And there's never been enough money left over from the town budget to pay someone else to finish it. If there was someone else to do it, and there isn't.''

"Now that's a shame," said Cliff. They had reached the park, and had caught up with the rest of the family who were surrounded by milling people.

"There's Janice Booth. She's the one you should talk to about finishing the mural." Elm beckoned to Janice, who was helping set up chairs on the wooden platform where a microphone stood.

"Hi, Elm, Charlotte," she said. "Ben, how's old Spanky? Pretty good? Great. And Sarah. Where have you been hiding?''

"Out in the fields, mostly. Janice, I'm sure you remember Cliff Oenbrink from the time we all worked at the Little League concession stand.''

The two exchanged greetings, and then Sarah said, "Cliff's been asking about the Curtisville mural. He says he'd like to see it finished."

"So would I," replied Janice fervently. "But I can't seem to get money appropriated for it. And we need an artist. That's another small point."

"It's too bad. It seems as though with a little effort, somebody could get the money together."

Janice became more serious. "In better times, we probably could. But with the local economy in a tailspin because of the farmers getting such low prices for their crops, everyone has a hard time making ends meet. Local businesses suffer when the farmers suffer, and the businessmen who might push to get the mural completed in better times simply don't have the means. We have the complete plans, which the original artist left, but..." Janice shrugged and smiled ruefully.

"You have the plans? Could I see them?"

"Surely. Just drop by the town hall sometime and tell them that I sent you. Any ideas you have on the subject, I'll be glad to pass along to the town council." Someone called Janice from the platform. "I have to run. Nice seeing you again, Cliff. Bye, Sarah," and with that, Janice took off at a run.

Cliff and Sarah made their way slowly toward the bleachers where they could sit for the contests and upcoming entertainment.

"Seriously, Cliff, are you that interested in getting the mural finished?" Sarah asked.

"It seems like there ought to be something somebody could do," Cliff replied, but then a man in a white straw hat with a red, white and blue hatband began testing the microphone and thereafter announced the Best Pet-Trick Contest.

Cliff climbed the wooden bleachers and sat beside Sarah, fielding curious glances from people who, he realized, knew Sarah but didn't know him. More than one person elbowed another and asked, behind a cupped hand, who he was. He smiled to himself. Let them wonder. Let them envy his being here with Sarah.

For today Sarah was beautiful. She had done something different with her hair. Instead of fastening it in a braid or a bun she had parted it in the middle and turned its shimmering length up in some kind of roll, and it looked as though it was braided sideways. Cliff didn't know what this style was called, but it was softer than the styles Sarah usually favored.

"They're going to have the Best Pet-Trick Contest now," said Sarah, and when she turned to look at Cliff she realized that he was studying her and had probably been doing so for some time.

"There are other things I'd rather look at than the Best Pet-Trick Contest," he said.

Sarah looked away quickly. "Look, there's Ben with Spanky," she said.

Cliff realized he had been holding his breath, and now he let it go as slowly and as unobtrusively as possible. But the way Sarah had changed the subject so rapidly told him all he wanted to know.

Ben led Spanky through the biscuit trick. This time, too, Spanky missed catching the biscuit, but the dog had the smarts to scoop up the biscuit in his yellowed teeth and trot over to one of the judges, depositing his biscuit carefully in her broad lap. This provoked lots of laughter and undoubtedly won Spanky a few brownie points. Ben, his cheeks burning, led Spanky away to a huge round of applause.

A spotted dog turned a somersault, and a parrot in a cage refused to talk, and some wise guy had entered a pet rock, which when placed on an incline rolled over. Cliff, though he laughed and applauded in all the right places, wasn't paying attention. Sarah was the only thing on his mind, even when Spanky won the prize for Personality Plus.

"That's my boy," Sarah congratulated warmly when Ben climbed the bleachers to the place where they sat and proudly displayed Spanky's trophy. Ben wouldn't let Sarah hug him, but he seemed delighted when Cliff shook his hand.

And then the prizes for the Bike Decorating Contest were announced, and Lucy won first prize. She ran up to get her ribbon and flashed a V for victory with her second and third fingers before she, too, climbed up and sat in fidgeting excitement with Sarah and Cliff.

After a Dixieland band played lively jazz, and after a choir director from one of the churches led a group sing-along, the people slowly made their way to the bank of the Bluestem River to watch the fireworks. The Norquists and the Morrows spread blankets on a grassy knoll overlooking the bridge. Charlotte sat in her folding chair.

"They block off the bridge during the fireworks," Elm told Cliff. "The volunteer fire department sets the fireworks off from a remote area of the campground on the other side."

A few preliminary loud pops announced the bigger, more elaborate fireworks, and Cliff dutifully oohed and aahed with everyone else. The fireworks were pretty, but they couldn't outshine Sarah tonight. Cliff's attention wasn't fully captured by the display overhead. He preferred to watch Sarah. Her eyes shone with pleasure as each silvery waterfall fluttered toward the ground, as every new one flared against the sky. She sat, softly stroking Spanky's head, which rested in her lap. Tonight Sarah seemed young and unaware of her responsibilities; tonight Sarah was a girl again, wrapped up in the wonders of the Fourth of July.

In an hour or so, when the display had crackled to an end, Charlotte dug packets of sparklers out of her big tote bag.

"Kids have to have sparklers on the Fourth," Charlotte explained.

"I didn't know you'd brought those. If the kids light them here, it'll make it so late when we get home," Sarah said.

"That's what I always used to say when your father would bring them for you and Duane," Charlotte said with a smile. "And what did you always say, Elm?"

"It's only once a year. Let the kids have their fun." Elm grinned, producing a packet of matches.

Sarah sighed, but she really didn't mind if the kids lit the sparklers now. It was, after all, the Fourth of July.

She stood up and brushed a few burrs from her slacks. "I think I'll walk over to the Chatterbox, get the station wagon and drive back," she said. "That way we all won't have to walk to get it."

"I'll tag along with you on my way back to the Country Inn," Cliff said. He gave Sarah an inquiring look. "That is, if you don't mind," he added.

"No, of course not," she said a bit too quickly.

"Thanks for letting me celebrate the Fourth with all of you," Cliff told her family. They said goodbye, and then what he had hoped for all night happened: he and Sarah were walking alone, leaving the group behind.

People gathered in clumps along the riverbank, assuring each other how lucky they were that rain hadn't spoiled the holiday and that the fireworks had been prettier than ever, hadn't they? As they drew away from the others, Sarah felt encapsulated with Cliff, as though they had found their own world in the midst of the real world and were set apart by it. A cool breeze scented with water and damp rocks swept off the river, and Sarah inhaled deeply.

"I just found out that you can follow this river path all the way to the end of Main Street and walk up stairs by the bridge," Cliff said.

"It'll be a pretty walk tonight," Sarah said. "Most people will probably go back into town through the park. This'll be the quietest way."

The narrow path, barely wide enough for two people, led them around the willow trees fringing the river. Behind them they heard the laughter of townspeople heading away from the focus of the evening's celebration. But where they walked, only the purling water upon the stones along the shore broke the silence. That and the stifled giggles of two teenagers who had found a private place in a rocky hollow along the bank.

"This must be the local lovers' lane," observed Cliff in amusement.

"No, that's out on the Old Mill Road. This is merely a convenient trysting spot for kids who need a quiet place to go." Sarah smiled to herself, remembering how she and James used to meet here. For a moment, she keenly felt her lost youth. But only for a moment.

The amorous teenage couple hadn't given Cliff ideas that he didn't already have. He glanced sideways at Sarah, assessing her mood.

He hoped she knew that there was more to what he felt for her than the physical. He was attracted not only by her fresh-scrubbed beauty but by the aura of warmth and stability surrounding her. She had an unshakable inner fortitude; in fact, maybe that was her true appeal. She had made herself strong for others, and he wanted to be strong for her.

Sarah was in a turmoil. Should she have suggested that it would be better to walk through the throng in the park, where there would have been people around? Part of her wished she had, for then she would have been spared this breathless feeling.

On the other hand, usually when she was with Cliff there were other people present. She had had enough of wondering if he felt what she felt when they were together, or if he was only being kind to her because he acted that way with everyone. He had chosen to stay with her and her family tonight. It wouldn't have been too hard for him to find someone else to sit with at the small park. Cliff certainly knew some of the people there. But he hadn't sought them out, and he'd shown no eagerness to be anywhere else.

The bridge at the end of Main Street loomed in the shadows ahead as they rounded the curve in the river. Soon they would reach the steps, and when they did, she still wouldn't know if this shortness of breath, this rapid beating of pulse and heart, was something that she and Cliff Oenbrink shared.

Tonight she again felt like the carefree girl who used to sneak away from parties to meet her boyfriend on the riverbank. Oh, she'd changed, she'd grown up, and rightly so. But it didn't seem wrong to dream that someone could respond to her enough to kiss her, to make real her fantasy that at thirty-three, she was still pretty and still desirable.

"Careful," said Cliff, grasping her firmly by the hand when her foot struck a rock in the path. They stopped, and he nudged the rock out of the way with the side of his foot.

Then, before she realized what was happening, they were facing each other and he captured both her hands in his. His eyes were dark and lustrous in the dim light from the stars overhead.

"Sarah," he said softly, tenderly. "If only you knew."

"Knew what?" she whispered, feeling the world recede to a faraway blur. The stream beside them slipped over the rocks, bubbling and churning, ever moving, but she and Cliff were entirely still, staring into each other's eyes.

"If only you knew how long I've wanted to do this," and then, as if caught up by the motion of the river, he flowed toward her until she melted fluidly into his embrace.

Chapter Eight

The colors of Sarah's world took on a different hue after the Fourth of July. Green fields glowed with the intensity of emeralds; the blue sky seemed electric now; the clouds, great billowing white feather bolsters, dazzled her eyes.

And all because Cliff had walked with her beside the river, had taken her in his arms and kissed her.

She had kissed him back. Oh, she had been no shrinking violet. She had wanted it, and she had gloried in it.

It had been more than one kiss, and then, because they heard others whooping along the path and felt the heavy running footsteps vibrating in the soles of their feet, Cliff and Sarah had broken apart and walked hand in hand to the bridge and up the steps.

Yet it was enough. Or it was not enough. Sarah was confused by it and by the emotions she felt, but she knew one thing. She had certainly liked being held and being kissed gently, then not so gently, on the lips. And it wasn't just the kissing. It was the fact that Cliff Oenbrink, someone special, actually cared for her.

She was thinking about it when Elm stumped into the barn one day a week later. Sarah was leaning over Ben's lamb pen, absentmindedly rubbing Tweedledee on the top of his woolly head.

"Sarah," her father called through the gloom of the barn.

"Yes," she answered, loath to be interrupted in the midst of her daydreams.

"Sarah, your mother and I have been thinking about spending the weekend in town," he told her. "That won't inconvenience you, will it?"

"Why—why, no, Pop," Sarah answered. "But you don't have all your stuff moved into Aunt Millie's house."

"There's no problem with that. Cliff's going to help us move it."

"Cliff?"

"Sure. He offered and I took him up on it. Anyway, it's just a few boxes. Sheets, blankets, some food. Stuff like that."

"Oh. When is he going to do this?"

"Maybe tonight after supper. He'd like to use your pickup truck, and I told him you wouldn't mind."

"Of course I wouldn't."

"I don't think you need us for anything over the weekend, but your mother thinks you won't be able to survive without us."

Sarah smiled. "I'll manage. And I think it would be good for both of you to get used to living in town."

"On Saturday morning I'll be able to walk over to the Chatterbox," Elm said. "I can visit with my friends."

"Pop, I think it's a wonderful idea," Sarah said warmly. She did. And Cliff would be here again for supper, which now seemed like the perfect way for an ordinary day in the life of Sarah Morrow to end.

"JUST HAND THAT masking tape up to me, will you, Sarah?" Cliff said. Since shortly after supper, he'd been energetically taping cartons for Elm and Charlotte, who fluttered around the kitchen supervising the loading into the pickup, which Sarah had backed up to the porch steps.

Cliff taped the last box and grinned down at her from the bed of the truck.

"Okay, that looks like it. Do you want these boxes put anywhere in particular when I get them to the house, Charlotte?"

"In the kitchen," Charlotte said. "That would be the best place. I'll unpack them over the weekend when we're there."

"It'll give her something to do while I'm hanging out with the boys at the Chatterbox," Elm said with a wink.

"You'll drive into town with me, won't you, Sarah?" Cliff asked.

"Sure," she said.

Sarah handed over the keys and climbed into the cab of the pickup beside Cliff. He drove slowly to the top of the hill, and she said on impulse, "You're supposed to step on the gas right about here."

Of course he had seen the way Sarah flew over the hill when she drove, and so, grinning at her, he floored the gas pedal so that they swooped over the hill's crest and flew down the slope on the other side.

When the pickup slowed at the bottom, he looked at Sarah. Her eyes danced, and she laughed.

"Ben calls the hill Mr. Toad's Wild Ride in honor of the Disneyland attraction," she said, halfway apologetic for her childlike pleasure.

But Cliff liked to see her having fun. He ought to see that she had more of it. So he laughed too, and he made a mental note to find something that they could do together where Sarah could express the fun-loving side of her nature.

Today was so hot that the light shivered with the heat above the highway. They met no other cars on the way into town.

"Everyone must be staying inside because of the heat," Cliff said.

"Maybe so, but you know what they say," Sarah said. "If you don't like the weather, it'll change in a few minutes anyway."

Cliff knew what she meant. Kansas was known for its quick weather changes. He'd become accustomed to listening to his car radio for weather bulletins. It was important to his own safety to know the forecast when he was traveling lonely roads like this one where a tornado or severe thunderstorm might catch him unaware.

They passed the sign that announced, Curtisville, Population 2,019, and then the Pizza Palazzo loomed on their right just inside the town limits.

"Okay, now tell me where we're going," Cliff said when the highway intersected with Main Street.

"Turn right here, then down two blocks," Sarah directed. They pulled up in front of a little white frame cottage with a green-shingled roof.

"Cute place," Cliff said. It was surrounded by tall trees, and rose bushes on either side of the door spilled over in a fountain of bright blooms. Shutters folded back from the windows like cool green leaves.

"It's perfect for my parents' retirement. Pop can not only walk to the Chatterbox, but it's within walking distance to the family doctor's office, too."

Sarah jumped out of the pickup and began to tug cartons out of the back.

"Hey, let me do that," Cliff said.

Sarah, however, insisted on carrying many of the boxes in. When the cartons sat in a heap in the middle of the tiny kitchen, she leaned on the counter and exclaimed, "Whew! I never should have believed Pop when he said there'd only be a few boxes."

"You look like you could use a cold drink."

"There might be some canned sodas in the refrigerator." Sarah roused herself and opened the refrigerator door. The refrigerator was empty.

"I'll run over to the Pizza Palazzo and buy some Cokes," Cliff said.

"All right," Sarah said. "I'll open the windows in case there's a bit of a breeze. I can unpack a box or two while you're gone."

When Cliff had driven away, Sarah went around the house throwing all the windows open. Someone had just cut his grass, and the fresh scent dispelled the stuffiness. The green shadows of trees flickered on the wall. The sounds of town seemed overly loud, probably because Sarah wasn't used to them. Traffic noises seemed magnified, and children's shouts were startling.

I hope Mama and Pop like it here, she thought wistfully.

She went back to the kitchen and unpacked one of the cartons she and Cliff had carried in. Inside were towels and sheets, still bearing the clean, fresh smell of country air. Charlotte refused to dry sheets and towels in the dryer. She hung them outside in all but the worst weather. "They smell so much fresher that way," she'd say whenever Sarah ventured the opinion that Charlotte might find it easier to use the dryer instead.

Sarah put the dish towels in a kitchen drawer and stacked the bathroom towels in the bathroom cupboard, but when Cliff returned carrying two paper cups filled with ice and Coke, he found her standing in the middle of the kitchen, holding a sheet to her face.

"Hey," he said, setting her cup down carefully on the counter. "Is anything wrong?"

Sarah shook her head. "It's just that seeing these familiar towels and sheets here, in Aunt Millie's house, makes it seem so certain that Mama and Pop are really going to live here. Before, it didn't seem real to me."

Cliff took a sip of his Coke, watching her. "And their moving upsets you?"

Sarah folded the sheet and sighed. "Not exactly. I've known for a long time that they'd be moving here. I've even longed for it at times. But when I unpacked that box—" and she waved her hand at the empty carton "—it was like unpacking little details of our lives together. Displacing them."

She opened the kitchen drawer and pulled out a striped cotton towel. "This is a towel I embroidered for Mama as a 4-H project. See how crooked the stiches are? Later, when I was older and knew a little more about embroidery, this towel embarrassed me. I wanted to pull the stitches out and embroider the design again, but Mama wouldn't let me. She kept on using the towel." Sarah replaced the towel in the drawer, smoothed it thoughtfully, and closed the drawer. She felt as if she were closing it on part of the life she had spent with her parents.

She and Cliff sat down at the small painted kitchen table.

"Didn't you ever leave home? Didn't you ever live away from Charlotte and Elm?" he asked.

"Oh, sure," Sarah said. "I went to Kansas State after I graduated from high school. James was already there. I was gone for four years, but after James and I got married, we moved into the farmhouse with Mama and Pop. James was the youngest of five sons. There wasn't much opportunity for him on his family's farm, and Pop needed help. I got a job teaching at Curtisville High, and James farmed with Pop. It seemed natural to come home. We never even thought that we wouldn't live on the farm." She shrugged and smiled.

"But then you never totally separated from your parents," observed Cliff.

"No. I suppose not," said Sarah, but she didn't feel apologetic about it. She didn't feel as though she *should* have left them.

"Who is going to look after Lucy and Ben when your parents move to town?"

"I'll drive them to town in the mornings for day camp at the park, and if I'm working late, they'll walk here to visit with Mama and Pop afterward. During the school year, they can walk over here and stay with my parents until I'm free to pick them up. It'll work out fine."

"Fine for them. But what about you? How do you feel about living alone?" He spoke softly, but his eyes bored into her.

"You sound like Mama," she said with a little laugh.

"It's only natural that your mother worries about you," said Cliff.

"I think I worry about her even more than she worries about me."

"I didn't realize that."

"Well, it's not something I've ever talked about. Especially not with her or with Pop. They like to feel that they're still in charge of things, and it's hard when I have to take over. And I can see..." She let her voice trail off.

"See what?" Cliff prompted gently.

"How it will be in the future. Mama doesn't drive much, and Pop isn't supposed to. Someday I'll have to drive them everywhere, and they're both so independent that they'll hate that. And if either of them becomes a chronic invalid, I'll have to make arrangements for someone to take care of them.'' She bit her lip.

He was unprepared for how deeply her concern for her parents touched him. He'd known how naturally Sarah mothered her children: it was part of her personality. Now he saw the depth of her love and sensed the pain accompanying her thoughts of her parents' aging. Her empathy for others was one of her major strengths. It struck him that Sarah's nurturing wouldn't only be restricted to her family but would include the man in her life—that is, if a man were lucky enough to be included in it.

They had lapsed into a comfortable silence. Sarah watched Cliff, trying to figure out what he was thinking. Failing at that, she tried to figure out what *she* was thinking. That wasn't any easier.

She liked Cliff. She was romantically attracted to him. But she wasn't the type who gave her affections easily, and she didn't want to give them easily now. She didn't trust her intense attraction to him.

Sarah was still learning to let go of James, and soon her parents would no longer be living with her. Cliff had popped up in her life at a time when she, without quite realizing it at first, had been casting about for someone to lean on. Maybe she had subconsciously taken Charlotte's broad hints about needing a man more seriously than she'd thought. If Charlotte was right—if Sarah indeed needed someone—then Sarah didn't want to automatically transfer her all-too-natural feelings of dependence to Cliff. It wouldn't be fair to him. Or to herself.

The pale lemony light of dusk diffused through the room. They finished their Cokes, and as they rose to leave, Sarah said suddenly, ''I never showed you the rest of the house, did I? Would you like to see it?''

Cliff nodded and followed her into the living-dining area. There was a brocade couch and a few tables. It also had a small fireplace.

''It's just a tiny house,'' said Sarah. ''My Aunt Millie lived here alone for years. She never married. She left this house to my father when she died, and living here seemed like the perfect solution when he and Mama decided to move to town. Here's the bathroom," she said, flicking the light on. "And over here's the bedroom."

"Nice," said Cliff. The room had a homey feeling to it, with its bird's-eye maple bureau and the bed covered with a crocheted spread.

"Mama's going to bring a few things from the farm to make the house seem more like home," said Sarah. "I think she'll take the clock with the swans painted on it, and maybe the kitchen table to replace Aunt Millie's little painted one."

Sarah had turned out the bedroom light, and he was close behind her in the narrow hallway. It seemed to Cliff like the most natural thing in the world to reach out and cup Sarah's shoulder with one hand. She turned to him, her eyes glowing in the half-light. And at last they did what they had both been wanting to do all evening: they melted into each other's arms.

Cliff kissed her tenderly, caressing the back of her neck. She let herself ease against him, aware of his breathing, the scent of his skin, the slow massaging of his fingers beneath her braid. The encroaching darkness brought with it a sense of intimacy.

His hands came around to cup her face, and after a moment of searching her eyes, he moved his hands so that his fingers threaded into the hair behind her ears and lay against her scalp. Heat from their bodies in this narrow space enveloped them. The air seemed to hold its breath.

He kissed her lightly on the lips. And then he took his hands away, smiled and said, "If we get a move on, we can get back to the farm in time to say good-night to Lucy and Ben."

He helped her close all the windows, and they met at the back door.

"Ready?" he said.

She nodded, wondering if he knew how happy she felt, and arm in arm they walked into the shadowed dusk.

LATER THAT NIGHT at Windrush Valley Farm, Sarah found herself unaccountably restless. The other members of the household were asleep, but after she had tucked the sheet firmly around Ben and picked Lucy's beloved panda bear off the floor, checked the doors to make sure they were locked and put away the dishes from supper, she still didn't feel like going to bed.

She kept picturing Cliff in her mind, the warm acceptance in his eyes, the way he smiled. She remembered details much better than the overall picture. His nose was pointed at the end, and it was a nice nose. Not too long, not too short, but exactly right. His eyelashes were curly and tipped blond from the sun. His teeth weren't exactly straight, but they weren't crooked, either. Just a slight misalignment of one or two in the top row, which kept him from looking movie-star perfect.

He managed to turn even something so mundane as moving the boxes to her parents' new home into a recreational experience. Not that he did so much to make it one, but he was very good at letting her be herself. To someone who was beginning to realize that she'd lost sight of who she really was inside, that meant a lot.

What was it he had said to her one time? Oh, yes. He'd said, "I like you to be just Sarah."

No one else had ever said that. She was supposed to be mother and daughter and farmer, but never "just Sarah."

With him she could let go, tell him what she really thought about things. She could even pretend and not feel embarrassed. She'd been that way with James, but since his death she'd more or less clamped down on all the original aspects of her personality. She'd never realized, before Cliff came, how much she missed the way she used to have fun.

Before he'd gone home tonight, Cliff had asked her to keep Sunday afternoon free for an outing. His eyes had crinkled merrily as he extended the invitation, but that was the only clue that something out of the ordinary could be expected.

When she had inquired what he had in mind, he had only laughed. And when she asked if her parents or the children were invited, he said no. Then he told her he would call her after church and let her know what time he would pick her up.

When she asked him if there was anything she could bring, he had smiled and said, "Just Sarah."

AFTER HE LEFT SARAH that night, Cliff drove straight back to the inn, where he flopped across his bed and lay on his back staring at the ceiling. He was thinking.

Every time he looked at Sarah, he wanted to light up from inside. The feeling was nothing he could recognize from past experiences with women. There had been many flirtations over the years, but nothing serious until he met his former wife.

When he'd fallen in love with Devon, it had been a swept-away kind of thing. He'd met her at a party where everyone was trying to outshout everyone else. He'd managed to outshout her date, who peevishly went off to refill his glass at the bar. Her date's temporary absence had given Cliff time to ask for and receive one of Devon's business cards. He'd given her one of his. They'd made eyes at each other all night. Devon had phoned Cliff first.

Their sexual attraction was the definitive emotion of their early courtship. Together they were passionate and uncommitted; then, very shortly, passionate and committed; and soon, passionate and living together. They got married because they thought they couldn't live without each other and discovered thereafter that they couldn't live *with* each other, either.

Most of the time he was married to Devon, Cliff felt an aching loneliness. Their marriage might have looked ideal to outsiders. He supposed that it was the perfect marriage as touted in popular literature. He and Devon were upscale contemporaries, a two-career couple, caught up in a hectic whirl of business luncheons and dinners and obligatory parties, of trading both German-made cars for newer, more elaborate models every year. Their apartment was professionally decorated. They employed a maid who came in three times a week. They had everything except what Cliff wanted most—love.

Now he didn't miss the life-style, and he didn't miss Devon. And when he first came to Curtisville, he'd still harbored that hollow pain inside his chest, a pain some might call heartache. He'd made up his mind that he was going to be happy, yet he'd had no idea how to go about it.

Fate had provided Sarah and her wonderful family, and he had grown to care for them in a way that seemed natural and right. His own family had lived much the way Sarah's family did: close to the land, depending on each other for emotional sustenance. In the past few years, Cliff had grown away from those expectations. He'd forgotten how satisfying family life could be until he was reminded of it by the Norquists and the Morrows.

What a special gift they had. What a joyous way of life. He marveled at it.

To Cliff, it seemed that the times demanded thrills and pleasure. What commanded the spotlight—in other words, television time—was the flashy, the arrogant, the defiant and irresponsible. All these faults, and Cliff had been brought up to regard them as faults, were now transformed by the ubiquitous media into virtues. Movie stars flaunting their unwed pregnancies and either bragging about or decrying their own drug use; people going public about their private medical problems; scandals in government and world politics. Sometimes it seemed that this craziness was what modern life was all about.

Yet in the heartland of America, away from the television cameras and news wire services, were places like Curtisville, Kansas, where Sarah and her family and other families just like them believed that the old virtues would prevail. Where people brought up their children to know right from wrong, where families took care of their parents when they got old, where leisure time was spent at prayer meetings or in committees planning celebrations of a community's spirit, like Elm and his Pioneer Day.

Cliff lay awake in his room that night for a long time, comparing Curtisville to the places he'd lived in the past several years. Comparing Sarah to Devon. Comparing the person he was today with the person he had been a month ago.

When he finally fell asleep, it was with a burgeoning excitement. He couldn't help believing that here in Curtisville he would find the happiness that had eluded him for so long.

Chapter Nine

Cliff asked Sarah to meet him at the Country Inn on Sunday afternoon in a last-minute phone call that made her think there might be some difficulty with the afternoon's plans. Thoroughly mystified, she drove the station wagon into town and parked it in front of the inn door. On Sunday afternoon, most people were home with their families, and so the streets of Curtisville were nearly deserted.

She hurried inside the inn, saw no sign of Marlene, and ran up the stairs. She knocked on the door of room six.

After a long pause during which Sarah alternately wondered if he'd heard her and considered knocking once more, the door swung open.

Cliff's eyes lit up with unmistakable pleasure.

"I'm sorry about not being able to pick you up," he said, ushering her into his room. "I'm having unforeseen difficulties."

He waved his hand toward the bed, and her eyes widened at the pile of gray plastic arranged on top of the bedspread. It seemed to flow to the floor, where it somehow connected with a peculiar apparatus which Sarah, in one cursory glance, couldn't identify.

Sarah stepped closer. "What *is* it?"

"It's a raft. A *polyvinyl chloride* raft. Yes, I've been practicing that word since yesterday in case somebody asked me what it is."

"Why do you need a raft?" asked Sarah, frankly puzzled. She identified such things with Navy frogmen, Jacques Cousteau or maybe the Boy Scouts.

"I don't *need* it," Cliff replied impishly. "It's more that I wanted it. Or wanted a toy."

"A toy!"

"It's not like I have much to do in my spare time. And as you can see—" and he gestured at the small room "—this isn't much of a home. I get tired of these four walls and like to get out once in a while. I thought the raft would be fun. We're going to take it out on the pond in the park."

"Is that what we're doing this afternoon?" Sarah said in astonishment.

"Yes, unless you veto it," he replied.

The look of the raft tickled her sense of humor. She lifted one limp corner. "In its present condition, I don't believe it'll float, Cliff."

Cliff laughed. "It may never float if I don't figure it out. It has this foot pump, but I can't get it to work." He nudged at the machine on the floor with one big toe. His feet were bare. Sarah belatedly realized that most of the rest of him was bare, too. He wore only a pair of tan corduroy shorts.

"Maybe you've hooked it up wrong," said Sarah, diverting her attention from Cliff's bare chest to a large sheet of instructions on the dresser.

"If you'd read me the instructions out loud, then I could concentrate on pumping it up," suggested Cliff.

"I can't read them. They're in French." Sarah looked up at him with a perplexed expression.

"Turn it over. It's English on the other side."

"'Congratulations. You have just bought the finest in poly—'"

"Polyvinyl chloride."

"'Poly. Vinyl. Chloride. Rafts,'" said Sarah, completely deadpan.

Cliff's laughter made her raise her eyes from the paper. "Go on," he said, watching her appreciatively.

She sat down on the bed, frowning at the fine print. "It says a lot of stuff we don't need to know. Like never set a hot curling iron on the poly-you-know-what because if you do, it will melt."

"I never use a curling iron, so skip that," Cliff said, straddling the foot pump. A tiny corner of tissue paper stuck out of the end of the hose that he'd once connected to the raft. He tugged at the paper and it fell out.

"Stop reading. I think I've found the problem. The raft wasn't getting any air because the hose was clogged. Now I think we'll get somewhere."

He stepped on the foot pump tentatively, it made a whooshing sound, and the raft on the bed twitched.

"It's getting air now," said Sarah, leaning forward to feel the air moving inside. Cliff kept pumping.

"Open up the raft, will you, Sarah?" he said before changing feet on the pump.

Sarah pulled at the raft until it was fully opened. It was as long as the double bed and almost as wide.

"How many people will this raft hold?" she asked, standing up and eyeing the thing as it grew sides.

"Two. You and me," he said. The pump hissed rhythmically beneath his foot.

"Where did you get it?" she asked.

"I went to Wichita and bought it yesterday. I've been thinking about getting one for a while," he said.

"But Cliff, if you wanted a toy, why a raft? Why not a bike? Or a kite? Or a cocker spaniel?"

"Because, my dear Sarah, I wanted to have fun. I wanted to do something I've never done before. And I wanted to do it with you."

During this exchange, the raft had transformed itself into a raft instead of an amorphous piece of plastic. Cliff disengaged the pump and pulled the raft off the bed onto the floor. He stepped into it and sat down.

"Come on," he said, grinning up at her. "Hop in. We might as well take it for a dry run," and he laughed a little at his joke. So did Sarah.

Gingerly she stepped into the raft.

"Careful, you'll tip it over!" he cried. He grabbed a paddle off the floor and pretended to paddle furiously. "Sit down, quick! There are rapids ahead!"

She pretended to glance fearfully over her shoulder. "I'm not nearly as worried about the rapids as I am the crocodiles," she said, playing along with him.

"Yah! Take that! And that!" said Cliff, spearing the mattress with his paddle.

He fell back as though exhausted. He opened one eye and winked at her. "Who says nothing ever happens in Kansas?" he said weakly. He jumped up. "Now we have to go try it out on the pond," he said, holding his hand out. She accepted it, and he pulled her to a standing position.

"You don't mind, do you?" he said, his eyes searching her face.

"No," she said, thinking that if she hadn't agreed to spend this time with Cliff this afternoon, she could be poring over booklets about sorghum production or irrigation systems. Suddenly she didn't care. It felt good to have something else to do besides worry about the farm.

Cliff poked his bare feet into a pair of old tennis shoes beside the door and picked up the front end of the raft. Sarah picked up the back end, and they bumped their way downstairs.

Their muffled laughter summoned Marlene from the nether regions of the linen closet down the hall. Her eyes grew round at the sight of the raft.

"Now you know what I've been building in my room," Cliff said. "This was in the cardboard box I brought home yesterday."

"Do you know something I don't?" Marlene asked. "Has the weather changed again? Are animals lining up, two by two, in front of the hotel? What is that thing made of, anyway?"

"This raft is made of polyvinyl chloride," Cliff enunciated clearly.

"Fine," Marlene said, retreating to her closet. "Let me know if it recovers."

They maneuvered the raft out the front door, and Cliff said, "Here, I can manage the raft alone. You carry both paddles."

Cliff balanced the raft on top of his head. Two boys on bicycles glided by, their mouths wide open at such an unusual sight proceeding down Main Street.

It was a short walk to the park, and twice Sarah had to stifle laughter as people passed in their cars, gawking out the windows. Both times, Sarah managed to hide herself behind him. She wasn't yet ready to practice what, in Curtisville, might be called public madness.

The park was quiet, and the small pond created by the damming of a little creek which merged with the Bluestem River at the edge of the park was deserted except for a few ducks, which retreated to the other side of the pond in alarm.

Cliff dropped the raft in the water and steadied it among the cattails in the shallows at the edge of the pond. Sarah pulled off her sandals and set them a careful distance from the water.

"The way this works is that you get in first, and I'll push off. At least I think that's the way it works." He had a sudden thought and turned to look at Sarah, who was looking patient but amused. "I hope you don't mind getting a little wet."

"Why? Has that thing sprung a leak already?"

"I'm not sure water won't come over the sides."

"I didn't come dressed for swimming," she informed him. She had worn a loose shirt and a pair of Indian cotton pedal pushers.

Cliff remembered, from that time at the swimming hole, how she would look if she had. He only had a moment or two to regret that she wasn't wearing a swimsuit.

Sarah got in the raft, leaned back against the plastic and watched while Cliff waded into the water before getting inside. He brought a few streamers of slimy weeds into the raft with him, and the weeds landed on a portion of Sarah's bare leg, but she reached out and tossed them over the side. He respected her for that. Another woman might have made a fuss over being subjected to slimy weeds slithering on any part of her person.

Cliff paddled in silence out to the middle of the pond. He stopped, shipped his paddles and felt around the edges of the raft where the seam was.

"It seems like a pretty sturdy little tub," she said.

"It does, doesn't it? And fun, too, don't you think?"

Sarah laughed. Out here in the middle of the pond, she felt freed from the constraint of the farm. All her problems seemed far away.

She leaned back and relaxed, watching Cliff as he rowed. He paddled slowly around the pond's perimeter.

"Have you spotted any subs yet?" asked Sarah.

"Not a one."

"I don't think you will, either," said Sarah. "The enemy doesn't seem particularly restless this afternoon."

He smiled and kept paddling. How quiet it was, and how far removed they seemed from the rest of the town. Out here on the water, sounds of people and what little traffic existed echoed hollowly around them. Sarah was hypnotized by the dipping of Cliff's paddle. The air smelled of algae.

"I go out for a walk in the evening sometimes. This is a nice place to stop. It's so quiet and peaceful. Now I'll be able to paddle out here, pull in my paddle and lie back to gaze at the stars," Cliff said.

Sarah let her head fall back. Cliff did the same. The vaulted blue sky arched over them, and on the other side of the pond, trees shimmered with green brilliance as their leaves caught the sunlight.

Too bad this two-person boat isn't made so that the two people can sit side by side, thought Cliff, but then he changed his mind. It was such a pleasure to sit opposite Sarah, watching as an expression of quiet contemplation slid over her even features. She sat with her legs extended, her head thrown back to expose the long, clean line of her throat. Her hair was brushed smoothly off her forehead as always, but there was a softness around her face where several wisps had fallen forward. He wondered why she seemed totally unconscious of her beauty.

He liked the effect of her soft cotton shirt as it hugged her body. The fabric draped her breasts and nipped in at her waist, where it was loosely bloused. The pants she wore tucked tightly into the v between her legs, and her thighs were clearly outlined by the thin fabric.

Just when his imagination was about to supply a whole assortment of clothes Sarah might wear and positions she might assume, she lifted her head and smiled at him.

"Ben and Lucy would enjoy this," she said.

"I'll take them out sometime. I suppose two kids would be equal to one adult in a two-person raft."

"You've been so good to them, and I appreciate it. They miss their father," she said.

"I'm sure they do. I know it's hard for you, bringing up two children on your own."

"I've had lots of help from my parents," she reminded him.

"It's not the same," he said.

"No, it's not," she said with a sigh.

"Sarah, if I can do anything for you or your children, let me know. I like them, and I have extra time. I could take Ben fishing or toss a baseball around with him sometimes, things like that."

"You've already helped Lucy by decorating her bike for the Fourth," Sarah reminded him.

"That was fun. It's the kind of thing I enjoy more and more as I get older."

"You're very good with children," Sarah observed. A tiny breath of wind sprang up from nowhere, and she turned her head to catch it full in her face.

Cliff studied her profile and said, "I wish I'd had some children of my own."

Sarah's head snapped around. "You do?"

"Sure," he said. "I've found out that there's more to life than buying a new car every year. The sense of continuity one gets from having children must be very rewarding."

"We have three generations of our family living in our old farmhouse," Sarah said. "They represent three stages of growth. I have the best of it, I think. I'm in the middle, the bridge between my children and parents. And my children will have children, and then I'll be at the stage where Mama and Pop are now. I'll have learned from living with my parents during this trying time of their life. I'll have that advantage when I'm their age.''

Cliff imagined Sarah thirty years from now. Somehow it was easy to do. She would be tall and stately, with a corona of silvery-gilt hair. She would be dignified and wise and as beautiful as ever.

But Sarah was still talking.

"As much as I disagree with Pop sometimes, he's been a wealth of information for me. He still is.''

"I like your father. I wish I felt that he accepted me.''

"He will in time, Cliff. I think he's already beginning to respect your judgment.''

"He asked me the other day what I thought about a couple of new wheat herbicides that just came on the market,'' Cliff said.

"You see? He wouldn't have done that if he didn't respect you.''

Cliff reached for the paddle, his hand brushing her bare leg. His fingers paused for a moment with the shock of touching warm skin, then he gripped the paddle firmly.

"It's time to go in,'' he said regretfully. "If we stay out here any longer, we'll get sunburned. Next time, let's bring some sunscreen lotion.''

It was the first time Sarah had thought about a next time. She had to admit to herself that she hoped there would be. It was wonderful to spend time alone with Cliff, away from her family.

He rowed them to shore, and the raft slid easily into the shallows until the bow touched the bank.

"Careful,'' he cautioned, gripping her hand tightly as he helped her out of the boat. The water felt cool on Sarah's feet as she splashed the few yards to the bank. They hadn't thought to bring a towel, so Sarah wiped her feet as thoroughly as she could on the long grass and slipped her feet into her sandals.

Again Cliff carried the raft and she carried the paddles. The only sound was the slap of Sarah's sandals on the sidewalk.

Outside the inn, Cliff lowered the raft and dug in the pocket of his shorts for his keys. "When I was in Wichita I bought the neat's-foot oil I promised to buy Ben for his baseball glove," he said. "It's in my car." He unlocked his car and took a small bag containing the oil off the front seat. He handed it to her.

"Thanks a lot, Cliff," Sarah said. "I've had a wonderful time."

"You're welcome," he replied. "Tell Ben that if he wants to wait, I'll help him oil his glove tonight."

"I didn't know you were coming over!"

"Charlotte invited me to sample her rhubarb pie," said Cliff. "So I guess it's official."

"I guess it is," Sarah said, and she couldn't help returning his ready smile.

She climbed into her station wagon and rolled down the window. "What time will you be there? Ben will want to know."

He hoisted the raft onto his head again. "I'll see you about six," he said.

Rounding the corner and watching Cliff in her rearview mirror as he manipulated the raft through the narrow door of the inn, Sarah felt somehow renewed. She couldn't remember the last time she had had anything remotely resembling fun. She'd done things that were meant to be recreational, but she'd certainly never felt recreated by them.

For instance, she'd participated in a school fair last spring with Lucy and Ben, and not too long ago she'd gone flying with Tim Vogel. Afterward, however, she'd experienced no sense of peace or freedom as she did now.

Probably it was because she was never the object of anyone's full and undivided attention. To her children, she was Mom. To Tim, she was like a big sister, and during the flight in his plane he'd been more interested in the plane than in her response to it. With her parents, she never felt like an equal.

But when she was with Cliff, she felt different. She felt validated. She felt real.

She had felt, when they were floating serenely on the pond's surface, as though she had stepped out of the ordinariness of her life as easily as a snake shedding its skin.

When she was a child, Sarah had often come across the discarded papery husks of snakes in the blackberry patch, and she'd gingerly knelt down and poked at them with a wary fingertip until they crumbled into dust. Her brother Duane, twelve years older and wise about such matters, had explained that snakes were a farmer's friend. They ate rodents that could destroy the crop. And so Sarah had never been afraid of them.

But snakes, once they left their skins, did not have to resume occupancy of them. Sarah could not shed her life so easily. She'd have to go back home today and pick up where she'd left off, cajoling Lucy out of her current bad mood, answering Ben's questions about whatever project had captured his attention this afternoon, and trying to read up on irrigation systems to boot. And Cliff was coming over tonight, so her time would be limited.

Sarah grinned to herself. That Charlotte! Charlotte hadn't breathed a word about Cliff's being invited for rhubarb pie tonight. You'd think she'd say something about it, wouldn't you?

Charlotte's unabashed matchmaking was so transparent that it was almost funny. Her mother was determined that Sarah would not be left alone on the farm when she and Elm moved to town. Charlotte had never bought Sarah's protests that she wouldn't be alone when they left the farm, that she'd have Lucy and Ben.

"It's not children I'm talking about," Charlotte would always say when the subject came up, making it clear that she worried about Sarah's living on the farm without a man.

"But there are Tim and the rest of the Vogels right over on the next farm, within walking distance," Sarah would point out. "And Henry is here every day, not to mention the other guys who work for me."

"Your cousin Henry and a bunch of hired men aren't what I'm talking about, either," Charlotte said, compressing her lips into an uncompromising line.

From the looks of things, and judging from the way her mother threw the two of them together whenever she could, Sarah surmised that what Charlotte was talking about was Cliff Oenbrink himself.

Chapter Ten

"Sarah, I would have started your spaghetti sauce for you if you'd mentioned it," Charlotte said as she pecked Sarah on the cheek. It was five o'clock on Friday afternoon, and she and Elmer were planning to spend the weekend at the house in town. They were going to ride into Curtisville with Henry.

"I can handle it, Mama," Sarah told Charlotte, but she was beginning to regret not asking her mother for help, especially since she and the children had invited Cliff to eat supper with them.

After Henry's car disappeared over the hill, Sarah hurried back inside to supervise her work crew. She had planned to come home at noon to make the spaghetti sauce, but Henry had unexpectedly summoned her to the Inman place to take a look at termite damage in the house he occupied there, and problems with termites weren't conducive to thinking about cooking supper.

"Lucy, *please* stir the sauce. No, not so fast," Sarah said in exasperation. She grabbed the spoon and demonstrated, wondering if she and Ben and Lucy were capable of producing an edible meal. It was a real challenge. Cooking, as everyone knew, wasn't Sarah's strong point. She could only hope that Cliff had a cast-iron stomach in case something went wrong.

Sarah was trying to prove to herself and to her parents that Lucy and Ben were indeed in a position to be a great help to her when Mama and Pop moved to town for good. She wanted to train them now, before the fact. Farm children often learned responsibility early. Both Sarah and her brother Duane had.

"Careful, Ben, with that knife," cautioned Sarah.

"I *am* being careful," said Ben, who was slowly and deliberately slicing lettuce into a salad bowl.

Quilter, Charlotte's calico cat, jumped on the kitchen counter. Sarah used the back of her hand to wipe the perspiration from her brow. "Ben, please get that cat out of here," she said.

"I just washed my hands. You *told* me not to pick up an animal after I wash my hands or while I'm touching food," said Ben patiently.

Muttering to herself, Sarah scooped Quilter up in her arms and petted her for a moment before putting her on the back porch. Quilter's sides were beginning to bulge. She was expecting her first litter of kittens soon.

"Lucy, I'll stir the sauce, honey," Sarah said. "You go set the table."

"I hate to set the table. Anyway, it's *hot* in here," said Lucy, stepping down from the stool where she'd stood to reach the spaghetti sauce.

"Yes, I know," Sarah agreed.

"Is it okay if I let Spanky in?" Lucy asked, pausing with her hands full of silverware as she passed the screen door where Spanky stood patiently with his tongue lolling out.

"Absolutely not," replied Sarah. Had she remembered to put the basil in the spaghetti sauce? She couldn't recall.

Lucy passed Spanky by and sang softly to herself as she walked around the table doling out knives and forks and spoons. Ben sliced carrots into the salad. Sarah swatted a fly buzzing against the window screen and let a spoonful of spaghetti sauce cool in the spoon before tasting it. She *had* put the basil in after all. The sauce tasted pretty good. Cliff would like it, she thought. She removed the sauce from the stove and turned off the burner.

The ensuing series of events started with Lucy, who meant to go outside and pet Spanky in consolation for his not being allowed to come in the house. But Quilter, hovering in wait for just such an opportunity, slipped inside the screen door as Lucy was about to go out.

A startled Lucy slammed the door on her finger and yelled. The shout scared Quilter, who jumped on the kitchen counter and skidded onto the stove. The burner was still hot enough to let Quilter know that she was someplace she shouldn't be, and she let out a pained yowl. This startled Ben so that the knife slipped and he cut his finger. Quilter set off at a run, knocking the pot of spaghetti sauce over. It spattered all over Sarah as it fell.

Lucy began to cry. Ben bit his lip and watched a thin red line of blood appear on his cut finger. Sarah's eyes widened in horror as spaghetti sauce oozed onto the floor. Quilter was nowhere to be seen. Spanky, roused from his sleep on the porch, jumped against the screen door and barked.

At that point, Cliff arrived for supper, pulling his car to a stop beside Sarah's pickup after a spirited whoosh down Lornbacher Hill. He was surprised and yet pleased to see Spanky showing so much vigor by jumping around on the porch. But when Cliff stood at the screen door, it became clear that things were amiss in the Norquist-Morrow household.

From where he stood in front of the door, Cliff took in the crying Lucy, the spattered Sarah, the stoic Ben. He calmed Spanky by stroking his head until Spanky subsided with a wag of his tail and a resigned retreat to the corner of the porch. Then Cliff cautiously opened the door and stepped inside.

"Holy cow!" exclaimed Cliff in astonishment when he saw the mess. "What happened here?"

"Everything," Sarah said hopelessly. Her supper was in ruins. So were her plans to unite her small family into a team of cooks.

Cliff sat down on a chair and lifted the sobbing Lucy into his arms. She hiccuped softly against his chest.

"Should I go on making the salad, Mom?" asked Ben, wiggling his finger experimentally. "This cut is only a little scratch, nothing to cry about."

"Yes, please. I mean, no. Oh, I don't know." Spaghetti sauce had spattered all over her clean shirt and pants. As for the spaghetti sauce, they could hardly eat it now. What should she do? Invite Cliff to sit down to a meal of grilled-cheese sandwiches? Break out a can of Spam?

"I have a good idea," said Cliff, easing Lucy off his lap. "First we clean up this mess. Then we go to the Pizza Palazzo and order the biggest pizza they have. Okay?"

"O-*kay!*" said Ben, dropping the knife into the stainless-steel sink with a clatter.

"I have a good idea, too," quavered Lucy.

"What's that, sweetheart?" asked Cliff.

"We can let Spanky in the house. He'll eat up all the spaghetti sauce."

Cliff looked at Sarah. "Is spaghetti sauce on Spanky's diet?" he asked.

"It is now," she said. She went to open the door for Spanky, herself.

While Lucy was crowing at the sight of Spanky gobbling up the spaghetti sauce, Sarah said to Cliff, "I'd better go change my clothes."

He grinned at her. "That might be a good idea," he agreed.

Sarah ran upstairs with one ear cocked toward the noise in the kitchen. What fun the three of them were having over this spilled sauce!

"He won't eat the tomatoes," said Ben with a note of authority. "Spanky just *hates* tomatoes." Sarah smiled at this. She wasn't sure about Spanky's tastes, but she knew for sure that Ben hated tomatoes.

She descended the stairs just as Cliff and the children were wiping the last of the spaghetti sauce off the counter and cabinets. An orange-muzzled Spanky sprawled under the table, a sated expression on his face.

"Eating up all that sauce was the best trick Spanky's done yet," Ben said.

Lucy said disdainfully, "It's just about the last one he knows how to do," whereupon Ben offered to brain her with a frying pan.

"The important thing," interrupted Cliff when Ben and Lucy's exchange looked as though it might get out of hand, "is to decide what kind of pizza to order when we get to the Pizza Palazzo.''

The ensuing discussion lasted almost until they reached town. Sarah rode in the front seat of Cliff's car with Cliff. The kids rode in the back seat. *Like a family,* was Sarah's inadvertent thought, but she pushed it out of her mind.

At the Pizza Palazzo they ordered a Sicilian Sockeroo, a huge pizza with everything on it.

"I can eat the most slices of pizza," claimed Ben.

"I bet you can't," challenged Cliff, and they bet each other a dime, but Ben won.

"I can eat the most spaghetti, too," said Ben when they were on the way home. In his fist he clutched the shiny new dime he had won from Cliff on their bet.

"I'm not sure I want to bet you again," joked Cliff. "I've already lost one dime."

"You probably couldn't eat the most of Mom's spaghetti," said Lucy, who was beginning to get sleepy. "It's not so good."

"Yeah, Grandma's is better."

"Well, fortunately Cliff isn't ever going to find out who makes the better spaghetti sauce," Sarah said, hoping to put an end to this discussion.

"Ever?" asked Cliff, and his glance danced in her direction.

Sarah didn't know what to say, but she need not have worried. Silences between the two of them could be counted on to be filled by one or the other of her children.

"Mom's not such a good cook," Ben said. "We all kind of know that."

Sarah wanted to shrivel up and disappear. Why must her children take it upon themselves to inform Cliff of her shortcomings? Anyway, they were talking about her as if she weren't even there.

"Hey, I'm sure your mother knows how to cook lots of things," Cliff said loyally.

"Not very good things. She doesn't even make Kool-Aid right."

"Ben," said Sarah warningly.

"Well, you don't, Mom. You don't put enough sugar in."

"The dentist said—"

"I don't like the dentist," said Lucy, and yawned.

I'm really going to have to do something about Lucy, Sarah thought despairingly. *It seems as though that child never likes anything anymore.*

Cliff pulled his car up beside the barn. "Here we are," he said cheerfully as Spanky wandered toward them, then sat down in the dust. Sarah noticed how tired the dog looked. Usually Spanky would have bounded toward them, poking his damp nose into the kids' hands as they walked toward the house and clowning around in hopes of being invited inside. The heat must be affecting him, she thought. Or maybe it was the spaghetti sauce he'd eaten, although Spanky had always been happy to function as a canine garbage disposal.

"All right," said Sarah as she opened the back door. "I want everybody in pajamas and into bed. Right now!"

"Everybody?" said Cliff under his breath, but Sarah was shooing the children upstairs, and he didn't think she heard him.

Sarah whisked several stray dog hairs from the living-room couch. She sat down and patted the cushion beside her.

"Kids," she said weakly as Cliff joined her. "Kids. I might have known they'd tell you that I'm not a very good cook."

"I thought you were a home ec major."

"I was, but I always hated cooking. I was better at sewing. I don't even do that anymore, because Lucy doesn't like the things I make. She's so negative about everything lately. And Ben's so demanding."

"They're great kids. They're both cute and lots of fun. I enjoyed taking them to eat pizza."

"Would you like to watch television?" she asked him. The way he looked at her sent shivers up her spine.

"No. I'd rather talk with you." He picked up her hand and began tracing the lines in her palm. It tickled, but she didn't pull her hand away.

"Mo-om, Lucy won't give me the toothpaste. Give me the toothpaste, Lucy!"

"I will not!"

"She's spraying me with the WaterPik, Mom!"

Sarah refused to mediate. "I expect both of you to get your teeth brushed without killing each other," she called, and after a giggle and a scuffle, all was quiet upstairs.

"That was a smart thing to do," said Cliff.

Sarah shrugged. "I've never let myself get caught in the middle of their arguments. If I did, they'd be fussing with each other all the time just to get my attention."

"Shucks, then it won't work," said Cliff with a twinkle.

"What won't work?"

"Picking on Lucy or Ben to get your attention."

"You have my attention, Cliff," she said serenely.

"But there's always something else going on," he pointed out, and as though to punctuate this statement, Ben and Lucy presented themselves for good-night kisses. At the first sound of their bare feet on the hardwood floor, Sarah removed her hand from his. She kissed both children good-night, and Lucy insisted on kissing Cliff on the cheek.

"Sleep tight," Sarah called after them as they disappeared upstairs.

"Now about getting your attention," said Cliff when the door-slamming and giggles had subsided.

"Yes?"

"I've been seeing you almost every night since I arrived in Curtisville."

"I've noticed," Sarah replied pleasantly. She gazed steadily at his face, a face so familiar to her. It was a nice face, a gentle face. A face filled with what might be called loving kindness. Behind the face, she knew, was a person of solid worth.

"The trouble is, I seldom see you alone."

"How much of a problem is that?"

"It's getting to be more and more of a problem," admitted Cliff. He took her hand again, then reached for the other one. He didn't want to take any chances that she might bob up from the couch and flit away.

"We're alone now," she pointed out.

"Yes, but usually there are your parents, and your children, or even your cousin Henry. And sometimes, like on the Fourth of July, the whole town of Curtisville. Sarah, I like your family. Your kids are wonderful. But I'd like it to be just us sometimes."

"I'm so caught up in other things right now, Cliff. There's the sorghum, and working the acreage I don't have planted right now, and the business of running the farm."

"There's you and me. Doesn't that count for anything?"

"Not on a financial balance sheet, it doesn't."

"Sarah," he said, and he pulled her into his arms and kissed her. Then he said, his arms still wrapped around her, "How does that affect a financial balance sheet?"

"Cliff, you're not being fair," she said.

"Sometimes I don't like to play fair," he admitted before kissing her again.

"The children may still be awake," she protested halfheartedly when his lips reluctantly pulled away from hers.

"Want to go check?" he murmured into her ear.

Sarah listened. She heard no noises from the children's rooms, which were located directly over the living room. She relaxed a bit.

"Sarah, we're not inexperienced kids, and I don't think we should act like we are. I want to be with you. I want you." She didn't pull away, but the color drained from her cheeks and she stilled within the circle of his arms.

"I was an inexperienced kid when I married James," she said, resting her temple on his collarbone.

"But you're not now," he pointed out.

"I still feel inexperienced. Because he was the only man in my life, ever."

He kept his arm around her and stroked her arm slowly. "Well, I'd like to be the second," he assured her.

"I don't know what to say," she said after a long silence. Her eyes were troubled, but she wouldn't look at him.

"Say you feel the same way," he urged softly.

"And then?"

"And then we let nature take its course."

"I don't know how I feel," she said helplessly. "I don't know *what* I should feel."

"Dear Sarah, it's not that confusing. It's simple, really. We care about each other. We can be more to each other than we are right now."

"You're my friend," she told him. "I'm attracted to you."

"You see? It's not that difficult," and he smiled at her.

She thought about it. While she was thinking, he tightened his arm around her and brought his left hand up to cup her chin. Slowly he turned her face so that they gazed deeply into each other's eyes. "Sarah," he said, and then with her name still on his lips, he lowered his lips to kiss her.

She closed her eyes and gave in to the emotion that flooded over her. As a child of the prairie, she didn't know much about the ocean. But it seemed to her that the sound of a faraway sea sang in her ears and pulsed in her veins, washing her free of her cares so that she could immerse herself in Cliff's lovemaking. She was surprised at how natural it felt to lift her quivering arms and slide them around his shoulders.

He murmured something against her lips and trailed cool fingers momentarily across her cheek, winding them in the base of her long braid. She sighed and cast herself adrift upon this new experience, not caring where she was going, knowing only that she was going with Cliff, and that was enough.

His kisses deepened, and she met them with a longing that she had thought lost to her for all time. A great trembling surged within her, an aching to be closer to Cliff, and it seemed that inside her heart was a hollow yearning to be filled. She was immersed in the new reality of textures she had forgotten. The stubble of Cliff's beard bit into her soft cheek, and his chin abraded hers. Beneath her hands his muscles rippled and hardened. His was not the sweet-soft skin she was accustomed to caressing on her children, but taut and unmistakably male.

His fingers tightened at the base of her scalp, and his fingernails pressed hard against her skin. She was faintly aware of the minty taste of him, and of the faint scent of his after-shave. She wished there was some way that two people could kiss all over at once, instead of just one place or another, and that seemed like a very silly thought, and then not so silly.

Yet he seemed reluctant to do more than kiss her on the mouth, and restlessly she shifted beneath him. When he didn't understand what she wanted, she gently removed his hand from around her waist and placed his hand on her breast.

"Oh, Sarah," he said, because he hadn't known that this was what she wanted and because she had surprised him. He had learned that she was a particularly moral woman; now he was learning that she was a very sexual woman. In Sarah, how did these two sides of her personality converge?

He gazed down at her, and her lips were parted in longing. She looked at him across a distance of wonder and unbelief, and her heartbeat fluttered wildly beneath her breast. He couldn't take advantage of her, not in the state she was in now. She was a woman, he must remember, who had denied herself male companionship since her husband died. He was well aware that many men would be willing to provide her with a quick fix of whatever they thought she needed. He wasn't most men, though. And what he had to give Sarah was more than temporary satisfaction.

At that moment he felt torn between his own eagerness to explore this new facet of their relationship and the sense that the timing was all wrong. He wanted her, but not until they were both sure that their psychological fit was right. At the moment, it wasn't.

She caressed his head briefly, then began to unbutton her blouse.

His hand stayed hers. Her eyes flared with the unspoken question, *Why?*

"Because it wouldn't be right," he said gently. "Not yet."

She was clearly dismayed. "I thought you wanted—"

He caught her lips up in a kiss of almost unbearable tenderness.

"I do. And it will happen soon, I hope. But I don't want you on an impulse. I've just realized what I'm asking of you. I want you when you've had time to think it over. I love you, Sarah Morrow. I have fallen in love with you over and above the attraction we both felt from the beginning, and I want you to know that. But I don't think you are capable of undertaking a physical relationship unless you love me."

"Love?" she whispered. The word felt unfamiliar on her lips. Love was something she felt for her children, for her parents and for her land. Love was something she had shared wholeheartedly with James. But did she love Cliff Oenbrink?

"Think about it, my wonderful Sarah." Cliff straightened his clothes and kissed her gently on her forehead. He stood up.

"You're not leaving?" Sarah, stunned by the swiftness with which Cliff had ended such a romantic interlude, had not entirely returned to reality yet. It didn't seem real that Cliff, who had so recently been physically close to her should be standing a few feet away now. He should be beside her, touching her, kissing her, not striding across the living room toward the door.

"I'll call you," he said, and then he was gone.

The only thing that kept Sarah from feeling rejected was that he had said he loved her. He loved her! What, exactly, did that mean to Cliff? Dear God, what did it mean to her?

She smoothed her hair and pressed a forefinger against each eyelid. An inane ditty ran through her thoughts, something about love and marriage and how they went together like a horse and carriage. Cliff had spoken of love only a few minutes ago, and now she was already linking the word in her mind with *marriage*. In this day and age, that must be the utmost stupidity.

Like a robot, Sarah went about the living room, straightening cushions, picking up empty envelopes from the morning's mail, and fishing Lucy's Barbie doll clothes out of the crevices in Elm's armchair. As she automatically straightened the room the way she did every night, she reflected that she could very well be falling in love with Cliff Oenbrink. She couldn't help contrasting the warm feelings she felt for Cliff with the only other occasion on which she'd fallen in love.

For Sarah, the last time she'd been in love was also the first time. James had been her only serious boyfriend. They had seemed right for each other from the first.

Sarah Norquist and James Morrow became aware of each other in seventh grade. He'd won a little lapel pin for raising a prize heifer in 4-H, and he'd shyly presented it to her on the school bus one day as he passed by her seat. Before the end of the year, Sarah and James had been sitting together on the school bus every day.

Later she had worn James's high-school ring, sized with adhesive tape, on her ring finger. On the night she'd graduated from high school, he'd given her a diamond engagement ring he'd bought with the previous summer's earnings from whacking wheat with a custom-cutting crew. They were so much in love that their friends didn't think they'd make it all the way through college before getting married, but they had.

Their long engagement hadn't been easy, especially the physical side of their relationship. They'd slept together before they got married when they were away together at college, but James had graduated first and then they'd been apart during Sarah's senior year.

Sarah had missed James terribly after he graduated. She came home to Curtisville most weekends during her senior year, staying with her parents, so that she could see James. They didn't have any privacy in Curtisville. James refused to make love to her in her father's house when they were still unmarried, and his parents' house had been a hive of activity.

They stole frantic, highly charged moments in his car out on Old Mill Road, or in the Norquist orchard with crickets chirring in the timothy grass where they lay, or in the big gray abandoned barn at the Morrow farm where pigeons wheeled above the roof. In the coldest months, when it was impossible to find a warm, private place outdoors, James would travel to see Sarah at school, and they'd rent a cheap room in a motel somewhere, and the room, with its leaky faucets and dim light bulbs, would be transformed by their love. And they'd felt guilty about what they were doing, even though they certainly had enjoyed themselves.

But with James, Sarah had always known it was right to be making love with him because everyone knew they would be married as soon as they both earned their college degrees. Sarah had worn his engagement ring on her finger ever since she was seventeen years old. They knew that nothing would ever come between them. They were an established couple, and in those days when they had to make do with stolen moments, they could see their future spreading before them just as rippling and golden as the wheat fields spreading to the sky. It was a given that Sarah and James would marry and have children and grow old together right here on Windrush Valley Farm, just like Charlotte and Elm and all the generations before them.

And they did get married in their home church on a clear and hot June day, and they did have children. And then James died, ending their bright dreams forever.

Now, heaven help her, she was beginning to feel close to a man who wasn't James. She had thought that this wasn't possible for her. She had never envisioned herself letting another man into her life. That the man was Cliff Oenbrink, someone new to her and to her family, was somehow startling. She hadn't been prepared for it.

Yet Cliff, with his warm, friendly smile, was exactly the person she would choose if she was going to open herself to another human being. He had said that he loved her. She believed him, and she regarded his statement with the utmost wonder and delight. To be in love with Cliff would expand her world, open new vistas of sharing and intimacy. She hadn't dared to dream that it could ever happen to her.

She had realized tonight that she wanted to make love with Cliff Oenbrink. When he had held her in his arms and kissed her so convincingly, when he had told her that he loved her, there was nothing she wanted to do as much as to lie beside him, sharing his life as well as his bed, listening to his dreams and telling him hers, and daring to plan a future together. And she wanted even more than that.

She longed to feel his hands caressing her breasts and his leg parting her thighs and nudging into the cleft between, and she wanted to murmur coaxing endearments into the hair on his chest and to cry out as his body assuaged her emptiness. How she had missed that side of herself, how she had longed for the peace sexual fulfillment always brought her.

At last she had the chance to experience it all again with Cliff, and her impulse had been to take that chance, never minding how she'd feel about it later. But Cliff knew her even better than she knew herself, and he had kept a clearer head. He had realized even before she had that, without the certainty of an ongoing relationship, Sarah would feel uncomfortable giving herself to any man.

She wasn't sure if her feelings for him were strong enough to be labeled love. She had serious doubts about the wisdom of loving a man who was not of her world and who was free to leave it whenever he wished.

Sarah glanced once more around the living room and sighed. She let the cat out for the night. And then she climbed the stairs slowly to her bed, where she said her customary bedtime prayer and, for the first time, included Cliff's name.

Chapter Eleven

"That dog looks fairly beat," Elm said about Spanky one night that week after supper.

"Do you think I should take him to the vet?" Sarah asked. She was lazing in a hammock that Elm had strung up from corner to corner of the porch. She was thinking that this was the way life should be. Life should hold you up. It should cradle you and rock you gently. Life should be like a hammock.

"The vet? I don't know," Elm replied thoughtfully.

Charlotte lowered her head so that she had two chins and watched Spanky over the top of her glasses. "Janice was just out here looking in on Ben's lambs," Charlotte said. "I wish I'd thought to ask her to look at Spanky, too."

"It's just too hot for Spanky," Ben said, repeating what Sarah had said so many times this summer. Ben ran over to where Spanky lay soaking up the shade of the sycamore tree and ruffled Spanky's coat. The dog flapped his tail a few times, but then everyone's attention was commanded by a car speeding over the top of Lornbacher Hill.

"That car's going way too fast," observed Elm in alarm.

"I'm just glad Lucy Anne isn't riding her bike out there. Why, isn't that Tim's new car?" Charlotte said, half-rising to her feet.

The sporty white Laser screeched to a stop in front of the back porch, kicking up a spurt of dust. Tim jumped out. Sarah knew right away that he was upset.

"It's happened," said Tim, looking red-eyed and distraught. "We've lost the farm." He sank down on a porch rocker and buried his face in his hands.

"No," said Elm, shaking his big head in denial. "No."

"I must go to Mina," Charlotte said immediately. She began to untie her apron.

"Mama, wait and see what Tim has to say," said Sarah, reaching over to rest a comforting hand on Tim's arm.

Tim heaved a shuddering sigh and raised his head. His eyes registered shock and unbelief.

"I—I came home from the airport today," said Tim. "Ken Shumaker from the bank was there. He told Dad—" and Tim's voice shook.

"Take it easy, Tim," Elm said. "It's okay."

"He told Dad that there wasn't any more they could do. He told Dad we'd have to file for bankruptcy."

A heavy silence settled over them. Even Lucy stood solemnly, her hands clasped behind her, staring at Tim.

"I can't tell you how sorry I am," Sarah said at last. She looked helplessly from Elm to Charlotte. There had been other local bankruptcies, but none had struck as close to home as this one.

Tim recovered enough to level a long, serious look at Charlotte. "If you want to go over and talk to Ma, Mrs. Norquist, I'll drive you," he offered. "I know she'd be glad to see you."

"Of course," Charlotte said. She bit down on her lip, trying to keep it from quivering. Charlotte was practical enough to know that tears wouldn't help anyone.

"I'll go, too," decided Elm.

"Dad's in shock," warned Tim. "He may not want to talk."

"That's all right," Elm said. "If we were the ones, I'd like it if Frank came over to see me. Wouldn't matter much what he actually said." He cleared his throat and stared hard at the corrugated metal side of the barn as though he couldn't bear to look at Tim.

"Tim, if you want me to come," Sarah began.

"No, not now," he said quickly. "After I take your parents to our place, I'd like to come back."

Sarah nodded slowly, understanding that Tim wanted to talk. "Okay," she said.

Charlotte and Elm settled themselves in Tim's car, and they took off over the crest of the hill.

"Mom, what's happened to Mr. and Mrs. Vogel?" asked Lucy, who looked troubled. "Why was Tim almost crying?"

"Does bankruptcy mean they have to move away?" asked Ben. Bewilderment flickered in his eyes.

Sarah sighed. "The Vogels' farm hasn't been making enough money," she said, trying to keep her explanation simple. "Sometimes when that happens, a farmer can't pay the money he owes the bank. Then the bank takes over the farm and the farmer has to move. That's what has happened to the Vogels."

"Will Tim move, too?"

"He'll have to, Lucy. He won't be able to live in the farmhouse anymore because the bank will sell the farm to someone else." A hard lump grew and burned her throat, and she found it difficult to speak. She couldn't imagine strangers living in the Vogel house, working on Vogel land. She turned and stumbled blindly into the house, hoping the children wouldn't notice her tears.

Ben and Lucy clung to her, wanting to comfort her and needing her reassurance. Sarah knew that this was a time when she needed to be strong for them, but she didn't feel strong. She felt sad.

The sound of Tim's car broke the silence. She stood up and tried to smile at the children, who looked troubled and frightened.

"Well," she said with as much confidence as she was able to muster, "I guess I'd better wash my face before I see Tim. He's very unhappy right now, and since I'm his friend, he'll want to talk about what has happened. Go tell Tim I'll be out right away, will you? And can I count on both of you to get your pajamas on, your teeth brushed and into bed by yourselves?"

"Of course," said Ben with unaccustomed dignity.

"How about you, Lucy?"

"I don't want to go to bed," Lucy said automatically.

"*Lucy!*" hissed Ben.

"All right," Lucy said with reluctance.

"Good. Go out and talk to Tim for a few minutes. No questions, though. I'll tell you more about this in the morning. In the meantime, don't worry. There's nothing we can do about this now but help the Vogels any way we can."

"Okay, Mom," said Ben. He tugged a subdued Lucy toward the door.

Sarah watched them go out to greet Tim on the porch, and then she splashed cool water on her face. When she reached the porch, Ben and Lucy had already gone back into the house, and Tim, looking drained, was sitting on the top step. Quilter wound through the porch railing, as she so often did, and then she came over and jumped into Tim's lap. Tim scratched her gently behind the ear.

"This cat's so pregnant that she's going to get stuck between those railing posts one of these days," observed Tim, and Sarah was glad to see that Tim could notice a thing like that at a time like this.

She sat down beside him and linked her arm through his, resting her head on his shoulder. They sat like that for a long time, drawing comfort from each other. Sarah was glad that she could provide solace for Tim. He had been wonderful to her when James died.

At last Quilter jumped up and slinked into the shrubbery to investigate a rustling noise. A low-flying june bug flopped heavily against the porch light above them. Stars began to appear in the sky.

"I feel like somebody died," said Tim suddenly.

"So do I," agreed Sarah.

"I mean, losing our farm is so final that it's really like a death in the family."

"I know."

"Ma's holding up real well. Maybe too well. But it's Pa who worries me."

"Your father keeps everything inside."

"He always has."

"How have your brothers taken it?"

"Okay, I guess. They expected it. I did, too. But that doesn't make it any easier. Damn! I wanted to liquidate and pay off our creditors long ago. Pa refused to do it. Instead, he mortgaged our house and the land around it. Now everything's gone."

"Oh, Tim. How awful."

"Pa said he didn't know any other way of life. He said he wouldn't know what to do if he didn't farm. Well, he'll find out now, won't he?" Tim's grin was twisted and bitter.

"How about you, Tim? What will you do?"

Tim shrugged. "I'll keep crop dusting, I guess. They call us crop dusters 'gypsies' because we travel wherever there are crops to be sprayed. I can do that the rest of my life."

Sarah sensed a certain false bravado. "Don't stray too far from home, Tim. Your mother and father need you now."

"They didn't pay any attention when I gave them good advice. 'Get out now!' I said over and over. Pa was too stubborn. Ma, too. Now we're going to lose everything."

Sarah couldn't speak. Hot tears stung the back of her throat. She knew how she would feel if she was losing Windrush Valley Farm. Still, she would have her family and her friends. Not everything would be lost.

"Tim, you and your folks have something very precious. No one can ever take it away from you. You still have each other, Tim."

"Do we? My brothers are busy congratulating themselves because they've lined up steady jobs. My father won't talk to any of us. And my mother runs around chirping like a bright little chicken who doesn't know the sky has fallen."

"Your mother is only trying to reassure everyone," said Sarah. She knew Mina Vogel. Mina would put the best face on anything, no matter what.

Tim shook his head. "You can't understand unless you've been through it, Sarah. But right now it's as though we Vogels are all a million miles apart. It's like we've all created our own little worlds where we've retreated so we can get through this. Alone."

"Maybe you can be the one to bring everyone together," said Sarah a little desperately, although from what Tim was telling her, she doubted it.

"I just want to get out of here," Tim said vehemently. "Out of Curtisville. I can't stand people staring at us on the street and saying, 'They couldn't even hang onto their land.'"

"No one will say that," said Sarah.

"Won't they?" Tim shot back, fixing her with a challenging look. "Then why is that every time I walk into the Chatterbox everyone stops talking and Ida Rae runs into the kitchen? It's been like that ever since word got out a while back that we were close to losing our land."

"They probably just don't know what to say," Sarah said. She paused. "You're not seriously thinking of leaving Curtisville, are you, Tim?"

"Yeah. I'd give anything to be out of here. To forget about everything."

"Your family needs you, Tim. Don't go. Stay and help them get through this bankruptcy proceeding."

Tim stood up. He looked torn, indecisive.

"Let me put on a pot of fresh coffee," she said. "Let's go inside and talk things over."

"Not right now, Sarah. I can't talk about it anymore."

Sarah realized that he was serious about leaving Curtisville. She clutched at his arm.

"Tim, please don't do anything rash," she said in sudden fear. She had a haunting sense of déjà vu. Years ago when Tim's older sister Norrie had run away, Mina and Frank had been nearly inconsolable. No one knew why Norrie had left, and she had never been found. Now Sarah felt a stabbing certainty that Tim would leave, too. And she was afraid that if he did, his parents might never recover from the additional emotional stress.

"Tim?" she said, holding her breath.

Tim did nothing to reassure her. He only squeezed her hand momentarily and said, "Sarah, thanks for listening," and then he loped down the stairs and folded himself into his car.

"Tim," she repeated urgently, running down the steps after him, but he had already gunned the engine and was accelerating up Lornbacher Hill into the darkness.

The air, heavy with humidity, seemed hot and oppressive after he left. Sarah's forehead was damp with perspiration. She turned back toward the house, feeling as though it was too much of an effort to move her arms and legs. The upstairs lights were off, indicating that the children were asleep. She longed to be over at the Vogels', but she couldn't leave the children here alone.

She stood indecisively on the porch for a few minutes, letting the cool breeze play on her face and trying to shake off her anxiety. Quilter leaped out of the shrubbery and rubbed against her legs. Sarah absentmindedly bent over and stroked the cat. The porch hammock swayed gently in the wind.

"Life is some crazy hammock, isn't it, Quilter?" she murmured. "Sometimes it dumps you right out of your safe place." The cat gave a little chirrup and went to stand expectantly at the screen door. After a moment Sarah opened it, and they both went into the too-quiet house.

When she had dumped Cat Chow into the waiting Quilter's dish, Sarah dialed the Country Inn from the kitchen phone. She seldom called Cliff there, but this was an emergency.

A hurried conversation with an inquisitive Marlene produced Cliff at the lobby phone.

"Cliff, the Vogels have lost their farm," she said when he answered.

"Oh, no." Cliff was silent. "Do you think I should go to see them?"

"Mama and Pop are over there now. Tim just left here. Oh, Cliff, I can't believe it. And Tim—I'm worried about Tim."

"I can't talk here," said Cliff in a low voice while Marlene's attention was diverted by another guest. He knew that whatever he said in front of Marlene would soon be relayed to Ida Rae and various other townspeople.

"I just thought you'd want to know," said Sarah. She drew a deep breath, forcing the air into her lungs. She felt so depressed that it was almost too difficult to breathe.

"May I come over? Should I stop at the Vogels' first, or would they only be embarrassed if I did?"

"I'd be happy to see you, Cliff. As for the Vogels, I don't know. Mina would feel as though she had to put on a front for your benefit, and according to Tim, she's doing enough of that already. And Frank's taking it awfully hard. Maybe you should wait until tomorrow to see them."

"All right, I'll keep the Vogels for later, but I'll see you soon," said Cliff, and then he hung up. He didn't like the way Sarah sounded. He didn't think she should have to be alone.

When Cliff arrived, Sarah was pacing the back porch. Her braid fell over one shoulder, and her eyes were as bleak and cold as a prairie winter. He gathered her into his arms and held her, listening to her breathe softly against his ear.

"Oh, Cliff," she said brokenly. "I wish you could have seen Tim. The anguish in his face," and she let her words taper off, remembering.

"What is Tim planning to do?" he said as Sarah pulled away.

Sarah shook her head. "Tim's been involved with the farm only part-time for a couple of years. Leonard and Bernie have jobs, and Tim can continue crop dusting. Frank will have to find some kind of work. They've lost everything. Cliff, I simply can't believe what's happening to them."

He folded her hand inside his. He'd seen it happen too many times to too many farmers, and he was sad that this had happened to Sarah's good friends.

"I always walk when I feel unhappy," said Sarah. "Do you want to walk to the top of the hill with me?" She knew she had to do something. If she sat down in her present mood, she was afraid she'd never want to get up again.

"Sure," Cliff said. He strode along behind her as she preceded him down the porch stairs. She seemed lost in thought as they walked slowly up the hill. Sarah kept her arms folded in front of her, hugging herself.

Cliff inhaled deeply of the scent of weed and leaf and grass. The land smelled earthy and fertile. This was a goodly land. But it was blighted.

Thousands of American farmers had been forced to quit farming last year. Most of them had been farming all their lives. While government bureaucrats argued over what to do about the farm surplus and how to boost foreign sales of farm products, people like Frank Vogel were quietly going under. To Cliff, these people had always been more than statistics. But the case of the Vogels brought the plight of the American farmer home to him one more time, and painfully.

"How will the Vogels manage?" Cliff asked.

"They'll find a little place to live somewhere. They'll survive, with God's help."

Cliff might have guessed that Sarah, with her strong faith, would answer in these terms. Her voice sounded forlorn. He saw that she was shivering, even though it was a hot night. He stopped, and he pulled her into his arms. Her fingers coiled against his chest like a child's. It was then that he realized that she was crying softly against his shirt.

Around them the fields stretched, whispering in the night. He didn't know how to comfort her. He couldn't right the wrongs of the world for her, even though he would have liked to.

Sarah sniffed, and then she straightened, pushing him away. "I'm sorry, Cliff." She seemed determined to pull herself together, to give him the picture of strength she always gave everyone else.

"You don't have to apologize to me for an honest emotion," he said. He reached out and stroked her hair. She wiped her eyes on the back of one hand. He noticed the fine, downy hair on her cheek.

"We should go back to the house in case Ben or Lucy wakes up," she said, turning around. He kept his arm around her as they climbed down the hill.

"It's fear that keeps us going, you know," she said in a low voice. She slipped her arm around his waist and hitched her thumb through one of his belt loops. It was a companionable thing to do, he thought. It was the kind of thing she would do only with someone with whom she felt very comfortable.

"What are you afraid of, Sarah?" he asked, because he had never thought she was afraid of anything.

"I'm afraid of the future. Afraid of losing what we have. Farmers live with fear."

They had reached the back porch.

"Will you come in?" she said. Her face was pale and strained. He wondered how much she needed him, and if she needed him for the same reasons that he needed her.

"I don't think I'll come in, Sarah. Unless—" The question in his eyes was unmistakable.

She kissed him on the lips and let her cheek rest against his. "Not tonight," she said gently. "I can't think about anything but the Vogels and their trouble."

"I love you, Sarah. If I can help—"

"Thanks, but you already have helped. I don't know what I would have done without you tonight, Cliff." She opened the screen door and went inside.

"I think I'll stop by and see the Vogels tomorrow afternoon. Would it be okay if I come over here afterward? I have some new fishing flies I'd like to show Ben."

"He'd love that. If you're here in time for supper, you'll get to taste Mama's eggplant parmigiana."

"I wouldn't miss it. Good night, Sarah." He started to walk away.

"Cliff," she said, startling him.

He turned. Her features were blurred by the mesh of the screen door.

"Cliff, come to church with me sometime."

"Well," he said awkwardly, because he hated to refuse her anything.

"Please," she said. "It would mean a lot to me."

"All right. That will be nice." He couldn't recall the last time he'd gone to church. It must have been before he married Devon.

"This Sunday then. We'll pick you up at the inn at ten-thirty. We'd be pleased if you'd come home with us to Sunday dinner afterward."

He smiled at her. "That's a deal," he said with a wave.

Cliff took his time driving back to the inn, and when he was there he tried to do some paperwork. He found that he couldn't concentrate, and finally he put the papers back in his briefcase and stared out the window.

A streetlight across from the Chatterbox illuminated the town's unfinished mural of Curtisville's history. The mural didn't show the aftereffects of the tornado, the individual hardships of the people, the grieving of parents for children who had been swept away by the wind. How could it? Things like that were what people wanted to forget.

Forget they did, and what helped them to forget was their faith. It buoyed them up in times of trouble; it was reaffirmed in times of triumph. These were times of trouble, there was no doubt about that. He admired Sarah's faith. He envied it, too.

He stared at the mural for a long time, thinking about what Sarah and her family had given him. They had accepted him, a stranger, into their midst. They had made him see that there were still people of intrinsic value and worth in this country, people who lived by the traditional values that he had lost somewhere along the line. He was happier here in Curtisville than he had been in a long time, and Sarah and her family were mostly responsible.

The long Sunday afternoons after a dinner like the dinners his mother had served; the gentle camaraderie of three generations living together in one house. They had made him part of that. He would always be grateful.

"Sarah, I love you," he whispered, wishing he was telling her in person. Did she know how much? Did she know what she meant to him, really?

He longed to hear her say the words "I love you" to him, but she never had. He didn't want her to say them if the feelings weren't there. He didn't, after all, expect love to strike Sarah all at once. He considered both of them beyond that kind of love.

His love for Sarah had been a steadily growing happiness that sprang from the part of himself he had once thought outgrown. It had an element of physical attraction, certainly. But the physical element wasn't paramount. It added spice to their relationship, but it hadn't added substance, at least not yet. His love for Sarah was based on trust, openness and honesty.

Cliff knew from experience that a too-early sexual relationship could obscure true feelings. It usually made for a pseudo-intimacy brought about by the emotional impact of going to bed together. People who slept together too soon actually felt more intimate than they usually were. As much as he wanted to know the pleasure and peace of Sarah's body, he longed even more to have a mature and loving relationship with her. He didn't want any part of false intimacy. He'd had enough trouble with that already.

Cliff wanted to prove to Sarah how much he loved her in so many ways that she couldn't doubt it. He wanted her to feel the same emotion he felt, and surely she would eventually.

He would help her friends if he could. He would make things easier for her at the farm now that Elm and Charlotte were moving to town. He would accompany her to church. He would befriend her children.

In short, he would love her. It was what he had to offer—and it was such a simple gift to give.

Chapter Twelve

"There!" Charlotte exclaimed in satisfaction, standing back and admiring the neat rows of newly sealed jelly jars on the kitchen counter. Their jewellike contents glowed in the streak of sunlight beaming through the window.

Lucy batted at a bevy of fruit flies swarming in search of their lost meal and said impatiently, "Is it all right if I go outside now, Grandma?"

"After you sweep the floor, Lucy Anne," reminded Charlotte.

Lucy tugged the broom out of the closet. "This broom doesn't sweep the way it does when you sweep," she complained. "It only sweeps short sweeps."

Charlotte smiled. "When you're taller, you'll be able to sweep long sweeps, too," she promised her granddaughter.

"I get to wash the big pot," Ben said. He stood on a kitchen stool and ran plenty of hot water into the huge pot Charlotte used for making jelly, squeezing in lots of liquid detergent so that the bubbles flew up and tickled his nose.

"Sure is a mess in here," commented Elm helpfully from the door to the dining room.

"Oh, go away," Charlotte said in exasperation, but she smiled at him as she said it.

"It's impossible to measure out thirty-three cups of sugar without spilling some," Ben said over his shoulder.

"Sounds as though you had a busy day," Sarah said as she strode in the back door and threw herself onto a kitchen chair.

The house was a cool oasis after the heat of the fields on this July day.

"We had pretty much fun," Ben said.

"No, we didn't," Lucy said as she shoved the broom and dustpan back in the broom closet. "I would have rather been out climbing trees." She regarded Charlotte and Ben with an aggrieved expression.

"But doesn't the jelly look nice, Lucy Anne? Stop and look at it just a minute. And won't it taste good with your morning toast!" Charlotte grasped Lucy by the shoulders and made her stop to admire the product of their labors.

"I guess it's okay," Lucy conceded grudgingly. "Can't I please go outside now?"

Charlotte released Lucy, and Lucy ran out the door and down the back stairs.

That child is getting to be a problem, thought Charlotte. She'd tried to help, but these days Lucy took everything the wrong way. Charlotte had been focusing more attention on the children and less on Sarah, since Sarah seemed to need less and less attention from her these days.

It was hard to let go of Sarah. Charlotte had had someone to worry about as long as she could remember. First she had taken care of her small siblings. Then she had her own children to raise. Now there were grandchildren. She was more than ready to leave the worrying to Sarah. But that Lucy!

Ben finished washing the pot and went in search of Spanky, who had been banished to the barn all day so that he wouldn't be underfoot.

"I haven't done much to get supper started," Charlotte said. She sat on the chair beside Sarah. Her shoulders and elbows and fingers ached. It might be her last year for jelly-making. She had already missed making jelly last year.

"No need to cook," said Sarah. "Cliff is going to bring us fried chicken. He's driving all the way to McPherson to get a take-out dinner."

"Cliff reminds me so much of Duane," Charlotte said fondly. "Remember the time Duane drove to McPherson just to get a certain flavor of ice cream?"

"Butter crunch," Sarah said. "Norrie Vogel went with him, and they brought back enough ice cream for everybody." Her brother had been eighteen then, so she, Sarah, must have been six. She remembered begging to be allowed to drive to Mc-Pherson with Duane and her beloved Norrie, but Duane, who had been about to enter basic training in the Air Force, had vetoed the idea. He'd wanted to be alone with Norrie.

"The Vogels all came over, and we ate those two huge boxes of butter crunch ice cream on our back porch in one sitting," Charlotte said. They lapsed into silence, remembering a beloved brother and son.

"Hey, Henry told me that Frank Vogel found a job!" Sarah said suddenly. She'd almost forgotten this important news item.

"Doing what?"

"Repairing farm machinery. Frank's always been handy at that."

Charlotte sighed. "Well, I'm glad. The fact that Frank's employed will make Mina feel better, I know."

"Have you talked with Mrs. Vogel lately?"

"We chat on the phone every day. She tries not to talk about losing the farm, but I know it's hard for her to talk about anything else. Do you realize that the Vogels haven't been to church in weeks? I think they're too embarrassed to show their faces." Charlotte's forehead wrinkled in concern.

"Maybe we should invite them for Sunday dinner to celebrate Frank's new job," Sarah said. "We haven't all eaten Sunday dinner together in a long time."

"Oh, Sarah, that's a good idea. We can use the best china with the silver rims and the cut-crystal pickle dish and—"

"Mama, we don't have to make such a big deal out of it. I was thinking of a simple family meal."

"We can decide later what china to use, I suppose. I'll ask Mina tomorrow." Charlotte stood. "I guess I'll go get cleaned up," she said. She held out her hands so Sarah could see them. "Just look at this. I've got sugar burns from boiling up all that fruit and letting the syrup get so hot that it popped and spit at me. I'd better put some ointment on them." Fatigue suddenly settled down on Charlotte like a hot, heavy quilt. She hadn't realized how very tired her work had made her. Yes, this would *definitely* be her last year for making jelly.

Lucy danced in the door and opened up the refrigerator to get some cold water. She poured herself a glass. "Do you want some, Mom? Grandma?"

"Just a little before I go rest," said Charlotte.

Lucy carefully poured the water. Charlotte drank deeply, then set her glass in the kitchen sink and ruffled Lucy's bangs before going off to find the burn ointment.

"I'm going to hop in the shower," Sarah told Lucy. "If Cliff shows up with that fried chicken, let him in and keep him company until I come down."

Lucy grinned happily. "You mean I get Cliff all to myself without Ben?"

"Sure," Sarah said. She hadn't really thought about it before, but Ben always tried to command Cliff's attention.

"Okay, Mom," said Lucy. "I'll wait for him by the bend in the creek. I'll be able to see his car from there." Lucy headed for the door.

Sarah left to take her shower, pleased that Lucy was acting positive about something for once.

When Cliff arrived at the farm, he noticed Lucy pounding up Lornbacher Hill behind his car. He slowed down, smiling at the way her hair ribbon bounced and then came untied. She called, "Cliff! Cliff! Wait for me!"

With her leaf-brown eyes and golden hair, Lucy was such a pretty child. She looked a lot like he imagined Sarah must have looked at her age. She climbed into the front seat beside him and inhaled deeply.

"I smell something good," she said.

"I hope you like fried chicken as much as I do," Cliff replied.

"Especially when I'm hungry like I am today. I helped make the jelly and then I went down to the creek. There were minnows swimming in the shallows and I threw in small stones, then big ones."

"I bet the minnows didn't stick around to see what you would throw in next," Cliff said.

Lucy giggled. "You're right," she said.

"Say, there's a question I've been meaning to ask you," Cliff said.

"Okay," Lucy replied.

"I've noticed that everyone calls you Lucy except your grandmother. She always calls you Lucy Anne. Is that what you prefer to be called?"

"Not really. Grandma just calls me Lucy Anne because Anne is her middle name, too. And it's my mother's middle name. So we have three Annes living in the same house. Charlotte Anne, Sarah Anne and Lucy Anne. Grandma says she hopes there'll always be an Anne at Windrush Valley Farm. I'm going to name my first child Anne."

"Oh," said Cliff, "but what if it's a boy?"

Lucy wrinkled her nose. "I'm never going to have any boys. Never, never."

Cliff hoped he didn't look amused as he pulled to a stop beside Sarah's pickup truck.

"Do you think you'll live on the farm when you grow up?"

"Sure. Can I carry the box of chicken inside?"

Lucy took it for granted that the farm would always be here, much as Sarah had, once upon a time. Well, if Cliff had anything to do with it, the farm would always belong to Lucy's family. He wasn't about to let their fortunes go the way of the Vogels'.

Earlier in the afternoon a sudden rain had subdued the dust and washed the air to a new freshness. As he and Lucy walked toward the house, Cliff asked, "How did the jelly-making go?"

Lucy, clutching the box of chicken tightly against her chest, said, "Oh, Ben got to pour the sugar. Ben gets to do everything. I only got to sweep."

"And so you're feeling a little left out, is that it?"

"Uh-huh," said Lucy.

They stepped inside the house, and Lucy set the chicken carefully on the kitchen table.

"Well, I've got a job for you," said Cliff.

"What?"

"It's a secret. Can you keep a secret, Lucy?"

"Sure. I promise."

"A promise is a promise," Cliff said solemnly.

"I know. I won't tell."

"Okay, then. I want you to help me measure the kitchen."
Lucy cocked her head at him. "Why?"

"Because I want to give your mother a present."

"A present? What is it?"

"Your grandmother isn't around anywhere, is she?" asked
Cliff. "I don't want her to know the secret."

"Grandma is resting and Mom is taking a shower. Grandpa
is asleep on the living-room couch."

Cliff closed the door between the kitchen and dining room
and unreeled a tape measure that he took from his pocket.
"You hold this end," he told Lucy, "and I'll hold the other."
They stretched the tape measure the length of the cabinet next
to the sink and Cliff measured the height of the counter. Then
he measured the depth and width of the cabinet.

"When are you going to tell me what the present is?" whispered Lucy.

"It's a dishwasher," Cliff whispered back.

Lucy's eyes lit up. "That means I won't have to wash dishes
with Mom or Grandma anymore!" she said.

"Shh! They'll hear you. Now don't tell anyone. Remember,
you promised!"

"I know," said Lucy. "Oh, boy! A dishwasher!" She giggled and then clapped her hands over her mouth.

"When will it get here?" she asked softly.

"As soon as Sears delivers it," said Cliff, pocketing the tape
measure. "Maybe in a week or two."

"Oh, *boy!*" repeated Lucy.

"Oh, boy, what?" asked Sarah, breezing into the kitchen.
She propped the door between kitchen and dining room open
again.

Lucy and Cliff exchanged conspiratorial glances.

"Oh, boy, I can hardly wait to eat the fried chicken Cliff
brought," said Lucy with another giggle.

"I could smell it clear upstairs," said Sarah. "Lucy, will you
help me set the table?"

"Let's use paper plates, Mom," Lucy said. "Then there won't be any dishes to wash."

Sarah couldn't figure out for the life of her why this statement ended in a torrent of giggles, nor why, out of the corner of her eye, she caught Cliff pressing his forefinger to his lips as he gave Lucy a warning look.

CLIFF ATTENDED CHURCH with Sarah and her family that Sunday. Sarah sat erect beside him, hands neatly folded over her Bible, frowning a bit in concentration at several points during the sermon. She sang the hymns by memory in a clear, low voice.

Cliff found himself caught up in the age-old ritual, and it reminded him of his boyhood when he'd attended church every Sunday. He'd even served as an acolyte. Those days seemed regrettably long ago.

When he stepped outside into the shadowless noon, he felt a jolt. The cool interior of the church contrasted so sharply with the hot bright outdoors. Cliff felt an absurd longing to retreat to the cool comfort of the church and all that it represented—peace, hope, fellowship, continuity. He hadn't realized until now that he'd missed going to church so much.

Sarah slipped her arm through his. "Are you ready to leave?" she asked.

"I'm ready for some of Charlotte's wonderful home cooking," he answered.

Dinner was a pleasant time. The Vogels were there, and, in contrast to the last time Cliff had seen them shortly after they'd found out they were going to lose their farm, they seemed to be resigned to their fate. Frank talked at length about his new job. Tim was grave but polite, thoughtfully inquiring about Cliff's success in setting up new accounts for Agritex.

Afterward when the Vogels had left and he was bidding Sarah goodbye, Cliff said, "Thank you for inviting me to church."

She slanted a hopeful look up at him. "Does that mean you'll go again?" she asked.

"Probably," he said.

"Next week?"

"Probably."

"I'm not trying to push you, Cliff. I don't want to make you feel uncomfortable about going."

"You're not. I wouldn't want to go back if I hadn't found something I was looking for there."

She smiled up at him and touched her forefinger lightly to his lips. Nothing he could have said could have meant more to her than that.

A FEW NIGHTS LATER, Sarah and Cliff sat side by side in the hammock, swaying back and forth. The curvature of the hammock dumped them toward the center so that their sides touched. They held hands.

Charlotte and Elm had gone to a movie in McPherson with their longtime friends, the Wilsons. Ben had spent the day with a friend in town, and Lucy had retired, yawning and unprotesting, about an hour ago. It had rained earlier, and the air smelled fresh and sweet.

"I saw Tim Vogel again today," said Cliff.

"How was he? He hasn't been over here since Sunday."

"He asked me if I knew anyone who might want to buy his car."

"His car? Why, Tim just bought that car a few months ago!"

"Well, he wants to sell it for the highest offer now."

Sarah sat in shocked silence. Clearly Tim must need the money that the sale of the car would bring. She couldn't imagine him parting with his new car otherwise. But Tim was working regularly, and as a crop duster, he made good money.

"What did you tell him?" she asked finally.

"I suggested that he ask the oldest McClellan boy if he wants to buy it. I heard that Carl's looking for a sporty car to drive back and forth to Salina to work."

"Did Tim mention where he's going to live after he leaves the farmhouse? Is he planning to live with his parents?"

"He didn't talk about his plans. We only talked about selling his car." He paused. "Your hair sparkles in the moonlight. It looks like spun gold."

She smiled up at him. "My, what a rapid change of subject," she said lightly.

"Well, I don't want to talk about Tim Vogel and his problems. I'd rather talk about you and me."

"I thought you cared about the Vogels."

"I do, but I care about you more. I wish—" He stopped, wondering if he was being selfish. No, he wasn't being selfish. He honestly thought that Sarah tried too hard to be all things to all people.

"You wish what?"

"That we had more time together. More privacy. I've mentioned it before, you recall."

"I know," she said more seriously. "You've been very patient, Cliff." Taking the risk that she would overturn the hammock, she leaned forward and bent over him, kissing him sweetly on the lips.

He wanted her to understand exactly why he wanted to spend more time with her. He didn't want her to think that his feelings for her were merely physical.

"You must know that I've grown to love you. I didn't merely fall in love. My love for you took root, sprouted and blossomed. It means more to me than anything," Cliff said.

"Roots, sprouts, blossoms. You're certainly putting your feelings into words that I can understand," Sarah said. She was touched by Cliff's sincerity, but she also felt slightly wary. He seemed to find it so easy to put his feelings for her into words, and yet she knew she wouldn't feel comfortable telling him how much she cared for him, even though she was considerably fond of him. No, more than fond . . . but was it love?

He wrapped his arms around her, liking the way she smelled of Ivory soap, and he kissed her more deeply. Her breasts flattened against his chest, and he drifted his hand downward to the roundness of her hip.

Sarah settled herself across him, letting her fingers roam upward until they tangled in his dark wavy hair. Desire rose in her, warm and insistent, refusing to go away. She didn't want it to go away. She slid her hand down to his jaw to hold his lips to hers, and he sighed and shifted in the hammock so that their bodies were more perfectly aligned.

The hammock swayed, lending an air of unreality. Sarah felt suspended in space, in time, floating somewhere with Cliff. His gently caressing hands were all she cared about. Those and his mouth. And his breath, flowing into hers, and his heart, beating next to hers.

"I want—" murmured Cliff.

"I know," she whispered back.

"No, I mean—your hair," he said, touching her braid.

She eased backward and stared at him, not understanding what he meant.

"I want to take your hair down," he whispered.

"I will," she said, struggling to right herself.

"No, don't move. Let me," he said, and reverently he reached around her and fumbled with the band until it fell away, and then he slid his fingers through the soft silky strands until the braid came undone and the hair fell around Sarah's shoulders almost to her waist.

"It's so pretty," he said, lifting it off her shoulders with both hands. "It's like corn silk." The heft and weight of it were more than he had expected. He had thought it would be as lightweight as it was pale. He lifted strands of it to his lips. Her hair smelled fragrant, like wildflowers.

He kissed her again, pulling her over him in the hammock so that her hair fell around his face and curtained them off from the night. Her breath was hot against his cheek, her pulse pounded against his hands, and all his senses seemed magically heightened. Her body, pressing against his, seemed pliant and emanated heat. With her heavy hair trailing across his face and her body pressed the length of his, he felt enveloped in her heat and light.

By contrast, Cliff felt dark, like the side of the moon unilluminated by the sun. As they kissed, he felt himself opening up to her stimulus, drawing into himself the burning light that was Sarah. His breathing speeded up until it merged into the same deep and steady rhythm as hers.

He opened his eyes to the sight of her eyelids threaded with tiny blue veins. The curve of her cheek was exquisite. As though moving in slow motion, he pushed her hair to one side and drifted his lips across one pink cheek, tasting salt, and then he found the glossy hollow of her throat.

"I do love you, Sarah," he said, and he slid his hand beneath her blouse and released the constricting band so that her breasts hung free, and she twisted so that the full weight of one lay in his hand. She was still positioned above him, the sun to his moon, and despite his sense of her as something celestial, there was an earthy quality about her too.

Cliff curved his fingers to correspond with the contour of her breast. She sighed in acquiescence and shifted slightly away from him to make herself more comfortable.

"Sarah, sweet, sweet, don't move away," he murmured, and then an incandescent glow on the far side of Lornbacher Hill sent sharp fingers of light up into the nighttime sky, warning of an approaching car. Sarah's eyes, starting slowly, opened wide. Wordlessly they broke apart, and Sarah rearranged her clothes and began to fumble with her hair.

"You're going to put it back in the braid?" said Cliff. His voice sounded husky, deep.

"Yes, if I can find the rubber band."

"Here it is. Who's coming? It isn't time for your parents to be back, is it?" He glanced at his watch. Time had flown. Indeed, it was time for Charlotte and Elm to return.

The sedan belonging to the Wilsons rolled down the hill, pulled to a stop, and discharged Charlotte, Elm and Ben, who had been picked up at his friend's house in town. They found Sarah rocking sedately in a rocking chair. Cliff was reclining in the hammock.

Sarah waved to her parents' friends and got up to greet her son.

"Ben, it's very late. You'd better go right up to bed." Her heart still pounded from the excitement of Cliff's lovemaking. Her breasts felt heavy, swollen. She wondered if her hot cheeks looked as red as they felt. She put a cool hand up to touch one, then yanked it away, hoping that Charlotte and Elm hadn't noticed.

"I want to check on Spanky and see if he is asleep in the barn, Mom. I can, can't I?" said Ben.

"Yes, go ahead," Sarah said. "Take the flashlight." She reached inside the back door and handed the flashlight to Ben. He ran off across the yard, shooting a wavering beam of light at the barn. Sarah glanced quickly at Cliff. Her gaze was warm. His eyes rested upon her only briefly, betraying nothing of his passion a few moments ago. Sarah's heartbeat fluttered and then settled into its normal reassuring rhythm. She took a deep breath and tried to relax.

"How was the movie?" Cliff asked Elm. Cliff slapped at a mosquito while Elm considered before answering.

"It was pretty good, I guess. Except I didn't like the way it portrayed parents and teachers as dolts. That's the trouble with too many movies these days. They give kids bad ideas about authority figures." Elm moved stiffly into the house, letting the screen door slam behind him with its characteristic *thwump*.

"Did you like the movie, Mama?" Sarah asked. Charlotte stood beside her, fanning herself with one hand as they both peered toward the dark barn waiting for Ben to return.

"I agree with your father," Charlotte said. "My idea of a good movie is *Cocoon*. I'm going to stop going to the movies if they don't start making my kind of movie again."

They heard a sharp clatter in the barn as though Ben had knocked something over. Then the flashlight bobbed frantically toward them, and behind it loomed Ben's white face.

"Mom! Mom!" he cried, running headlong up the steps and into Sarah's arms. The flashlight hit the wooden floor of the porch with a metallic clang. Ben's face was streaked with tears.

"Ben! What's wrong?" Sarah's heart clenched in her chest. Instinctively she knew what was wrong before Ben got the words out.

"It's Spanky! Oh, Mom, Spanky's dead!"

Chapter Thirteen

They buried their beloved Spanky, dead of old age at the respectable age of fifteen, in a grove of trees on the edge of Oley's Creek. Cliff attended the funeral, because Charlotte insisted that there be a funeral, and Ben haltingly read a heartwrenching poem entitled "Good Dog," which he had written himself. Lucy stood sullen and tearful at the edge of their little group, refusing Sarah's comfort.

Spanky's death was hard for Ben, but he seemed to weather the crisis of losing the family pet better than Lucy. The little girl was angry and defiant. She didn't understand why Spanky had to die. After a short service, she disappeared into her room and refused to come out despite Sarah's pleading.

"Let me take care of her," whispered Charlotte as she and Sarah stood outside Lucy's bedroom door listening to her sobbing into her pillow.

Worried, Sarah left Lucy to her mother's gentle persuasion. In the lull afterward, Cliff used the opportunity to offer to drive Sarah to town to pick up a part Henry needed in order to repair one of the tractors.

Sarah seemed so tense that Cliff suggested stopping for a walk along the river in the park on their way home from picking up the requisite tractor part. He parked the car on Main Street, and they walked down the flight of stairs on the bridge. On the riverbank they paused, drew in deep breaths of cool air, and began to walk along the path.

"Lucy's been hard enough to get along with lately," Sarah said. "I don't know how to help her snap back from this setback."

She sat down on a large flat rock next to the path. They weren't far from where they had been when Cliff first kissed her on the Fourth of July. Remembering, he sat down beside her and laid an arm around her shoulders. It was another sultry July day. Molten sunshine shimmered on the surface of the placid river, and the sun shone brassy and hot beyond the bank of trees.

"How long has Lucy had this negative streak? Or has she always been that way?"

"I never noticed it until six months ago. No, maybe it's been a year. I guess it's just a stage she's going through. Kids are always going through stages. If it's not one stage, it's another."

"She seems jealous of Ben," Cliff observed.

"I think that's normal," Sarah replied. "At least, it must be normal when siblings are close to the same age, as Ben and Lucy are. My brother Duane and I were twelve years apart. That's like two different generations."

"Do you remember Duane, Sarah? You were very young when he was killed."

"I was seven, but I think about Duane often. Why, just the other day Mama and I were recalling a day when Duane and Norrie went all the way over to McPherson and bought us two huge containers of butter crunch ice cream."

"Norrie?" Cliff asked, because he couldn't place the name.

"Norrie Vogel. Tim's older sister."

"Oh, now I know. The one who disappeared and never came back. What do you think happened to her?"

Sarah shook her head sadly. "I don't know. Maybe we'll never know. We couldn't figure out why she went away. It was just the strangest thing."

"Tell me about it," Cliff said, nudging Sarah's head with his chin so that it rested on his shoulder.

Sarah swallowed. Even now it was hard for her to think about Norrie.

"It was on my birthday. Norrie was my idol, and so pretty with her twinkling blue eyes and long blond hair. I wanted to look just like her when I grew up, only I knew I never would."

"But you *are* beautiful," interjected Cliff. "Go on."

"Norrie had made me a little crocheted collar to wear with my sweaters. She left it on the sideboard at the Vogels' house with a note asking her mother to give it to me for my birthday. I was thrilled that she'd made me the collar, but I couldn't believe she'd left without giving it to me herself. Norrie loved me. I was crushed because she didn't stay for my party."

"And then what happened?"

Sarah shrugged. "We were all terribly distraught. Remember, my brother's helicopter had crashed in Vietnam only one month before. We hadn't even recovered from that tragedy before Norrie disappeared as if into thin air. None of us ever saw her again."

"No one had any clues about what happened to her?"

"There was nothing." She shuddered. "Spanky's death certainly has made me gloomy. I seem to be thinking of nothing but sad things today."

Cliff stood up and pulled her to her feet. Today she wore a peach-colored dress with a full skirt; she looked like a girl. Her hair was piled loosely on top of her head, and little strands of it fluttered around her hairline.

"How about this to cheer you up? The Philip Pharr Dancers are coming to Wichita next Sunday. I read it in the paper. Would you like to go with me?"

"Why Cliff, I'd love to. Who are they? I don't believe I've ever heard of them." They fell into step beside one another and walked slowly toward the stairs up to the bridge and Main Street.

"They're one of the better modern dance troupes around. I saw them in Minneapolis a long time ago and vowed that I'd catch any performance of theirs that happened to be nearby. I hope it's not too late to get tickets."

It was hard to imagine what Cliff's life must have been like when he lived in Minneapolis and Kansas City and Oklahoma City. He had told Sarah once that he'd put his family farm behind him to seek life in the fast lane and that with his ex-wife, he'd found it. Curtisville must seem altogether too placid to him if he was used to the likes of the Philip Pharr Dancers, of whom Sarah had never even heard before today. Her ignorance made her feel downright provincial. Did Cliff see her that way, too?

"We could take the children," Cliff continued.

"No, let's make it just us," Sarah said quickly.

"It should be easier to get seats for two than for four," agreed Cliff. They reached the steps to the bridge, and Sarah preceded him up. Her legs were long and graceful, and his gaze lingered on them until they reached the top. Once there, Sarah said suddenly and unexpectedly, "Cliff, Mama and Pop are going to stay in town this weekend. They've invited Ben and Lucy to spend Friday and Saturday nights with them."

It took a moment for the import of this statement to sink in. He stared at her in dawning awareness.

"I was thinking," continued Sarah in a low tone, "that you might like to come over Friday night after they've gone."

"Are you planning to make spaghetti sauce again?" asked Cliff in a jocular tone. He knew right away that he'd been mistaken to make a joke.

Sarah's eyes, dark and serious, shot up, and she began to walk toward his car.

"I'm only kidding," he assured her quickly, seeing that for Sarah this was a serious matter and that he had managed, in his nervousness, to offend her. This was a serious matter to him, too. He didn't know why he had joked about it. Maybe it was because he felt an indefinable tension when he thought about being alone and uninterrupted with Sarah for any appreciable length of time. His gaffe made him unnaturally silent.

They reached his car and he opened the door for her. Frustration beat frantic wings in his stomach, and he tried to think about getting their conversation back on track. He wanted her to know that he didn't really take the matter of their becoming lovers lightly.

When he was inside the car sitting beside her, he took her hand in his and lifted it gently to his lips.

"Sarah," he said. "I wasn't consciously trying to be facetious. It's just that we've been waiting for such a long time to be alone together, and I can't quite believe that it's true that we will be. I didn't know how to respond.''

In her apprehension at making clear their opportunity to be alone during the coming weekend, Sarah had never stopped to think that Cliff might be anxious about it, too. It was hard, somehow, to imagine a man being nervous about the first time he made love with a woman. She smiled tentatively, seeing Cliff in a new light.

When Sarah smiled, Cliff knew in a rush of relief that everything was all right again. He leaned over to kiss her on the lips. He would somehow atone for his own ineptitude, for trivializing the prospect of their becoming lovers for the first time. A knot rose in his throat. It seemed to him that he owed her a great debt for accepting him into her life and into her family circle and for just being Sarah.

He looked away as she straightened her clothes and hair. When he looked at her again, he was overcome with tenderness for her. He was undone by the stillness of her features. Shade from the overhead trees rippled across the shiny surface of the car's hood, but it was hot in the car anyway. He reached over and turned on the ignition. The engine stuttered into life, and cool air began to whistle out of the air-conditioning vents. It blew the wisps away from Sarah's face. She seemed to be made of cool marble.

"I love you, Sarah," he said. He wanted to kiss her mouth, and he wanted to kiss the inside of her forearm, and he wanted to kiss the secret whiteness of her belly.

She turned to him. "I wouldn't make love with you if you didn't love me," she said in a whisper. "I wouldn't make love with you if I didn't love you."

It was the closest she had come to saying the three words that he longed to hear.

"You have time to think it over if you want to change your mind," he said.

"I won't change my mind," Sarah told him.

He shifted the car into gear and headed out of town. He held her hand, but they didn't talk all the way back to the farm.

ON FRIDAY AFTER she came in from the fields, Sarah drove her parents and the children to the little house in town and broke several speed limits rushing back to the farm.

She wanted everything to be right. Was this a seduction? If it was, she was ill prepared. Not a single black nightgown did she own, nor did she possess a filmy peignoir. She owned a perfectly serviceable shift of cotton that no one could see through, which was why she'd bought it. But as for seductive lingerie, forget it. And there was no place in Curtisville to buy such items. She wouldn't feel comfortable buying them here, even if there had been. She knew what Ida Rae, who might very well hear of it, would make of such interesting information as the widow Morrow buying black nighties.

The telephone rang, but Sarah ignored it. She didn't want to buy aluminum siding for her house, and she didn't care to donate money to send unknown children to the circus. She didn't want to talk to any of her friends. She wanted to get ready for Cliff, and that was what she would do.

She arranged a bouquet of wildflowers on her dresser, spilling water on the cherry wood in her nervousness. She wiped up the water. She poked at the flowers in their vase, studying the effect, and then gave up and turned her attention to other things. She tugged at the bedspread until it hung straight. She turned down the top of the spread and plumped up the pillows before covering them again.

When she realized the import of what she was doing, she sank down on the edge of the bed. She was preparing her bed— her marriage bed—for another man. A sweep of regret made her suddenly tearful. How could she be thinking of sleeping with Cliff in the bed she had shared with James?

Their two children had been conceived here, maybe on these very sheets. She blinked away her tears and peeked under the bedspread at the sheets, which were newly washed and dried outside in the sun as per Charlotte's requirements. No, she was safe there. The sheets were ones that Sarah had bought last January at a white sale. Their design was misty-colored field flowers spread on an ivory background.

Her eyes flew involuntarily to the gold-framed picture of James hanging on the wall. Well, actually it was of James and the two children. He had surprised her with the picture on Mother's Day not long before he died. She stood up and stared at it. James was smiling. He held a child in the curve of each arm. They'd visited a professional photographer to have it taken, and James looked very happy. But then James had always looked happy. It was one of the things she'd loved about him.

She knew she couldn't make love with Cliff under the watchful eyes of her husband. Quickly, without allowing herself to think about it, Sarah lifted the picture off its hook and shoved it into a drawer in her dresser. She glanced around, trying to find something else to hang on the empty hook.

Her eyes fell on a plaster cast that Lucy had made of her palm print in first grade. It was lying on the table next to the bed, and Sarah picked it up. She turned it over. The teacher had thoughtfully provided a little silk hanging loop on the back for parents who might want to hang the cast. Sarah hung the cast of Lucy's small hand on the wall, and then she stood back to assess the way it looked. It seemed a little bit lost, that small round bit of plaster on the large expanse of the wall, but other than that, it was fine. If she decided to leave it there, maybe she could dress it up with a calico ribbon later.

What about music? Maybe Cliff liked to listen to music when he made love. As well as she knew him, she still didn't know some things about him. She stood indecisively for a moment. The family stereo was a small one, and it reposed in a cabinet in the dining room so that they could listen to music when they ate meals. Not that they did this often, because Elm liked twangy country songs, Charlotte preferred classical, and the kids were developing a distressing taste for rock music.

And that was another thing: what kind of music would Cliff want to listen to? There was something to be said, certainly, for the high-minded rapture of classical music, but on the other hand, she couldn't discount the primitive allure of a thumping rock beat with a smoky voice wailing in and around it.

She decided to leave the music to Cliff. Maybe they should have discussed all this sooner, but all they had discussed about preparing for this evening was birth control. He had inquired if she was protected: she had nodded mutely, glad that her gynecologist had allowed her to continue taking birth-control pills because of a minor hormone imbalance. She made a mental note to make sure her prescription wasn't due to run out.

Somewhere, Sarah supposed, there were people who caught a certain glint in each other's eyes and fell into the nearest thicket and had intercourse. She and Cliff were not like these people. For a moment, she wished that they were. It would be easier. But not as responsible. And there wouldn't be this heightening sense of anticipation, this eager, disquieting longing to be consumed by the other person. If the consummation came too quickly, the pleasure waned quickly also. At least that was how Sarah felt about it. She suspected that Cliff did as well.

She peeled off her clothes, imagining that Cliff was undressing her. He would disrobe her slowly, thoughtfully, until she stood before him, white and trembling. Goose bumps shivered up her arms, down her sides, down the backs of her legs. Sarah regarded herself frankly in the mirror over her dresser. She was tall and full figured, with breasts that drooped instead of tipping upward like a young girl's. The triangle of hair at the juncture of her legs looked like pale curly feathers. She needed to shave her legs.

Sarah was ready to step into the shower when she heard a car heading down Lornbacher Hill. She almost got in the shower anyway, but she thought better of it and ran to the window in her bare feet to see who it was.

It was Cliff, wearing shorts and a shirt unbuttoned above them.

But he wasn't due here for another hour. That was the time they'd agreed upon.

She pulled the drapery around her so that he wouldn't see that she had no clothes on. Which was pretty silly, considering.

He glanced up at her and lifted his hand in greeting. "Sarah? Want to go for a swim in the swimming hole?"

"I wasn't expecting you for another hour," she called back.

"I know, but it's such a hot day that I quit work early. I thought the creek would be nice and cool." He grinned up at her, and she wondered if he knew she was standing there naked.

He looked so expectant, so happy to see her, that she didn't want to disappoint him.

"Sure, that'll be nice," she said lamely, letting the curtain fall back across the window. She went to put on her swimsuit, a new two-piece, and she ran the water noisily in the sink and tried to scrub some of the perspiration off her face and neck. The washcloth came away gray. It had been dusty in the fields today.

The dirt she hadn't washed off would come off when they swam, she figured. With one last look around her bedroom, she kicked her clothes under the bed because there was no time to pick them up. She thought the room looked nice, but she wondered now how the seduction scene would go. She'd had it all figured out in her head—who would lead whom, who would stand where, how they'd get to the bed. But that was before Cliff had shown up unannounced and ready to swim.

Downstairs, he greeted her with a kiss. "Shall we walk or ride?" he asked.

"Oh, let's walk," said Sarah, and they headed out of the house into the gritty heat.

"First the bad news," Cliff said when they were walking along the farm road.

"Bad news?"

"We can't go see the Philip Pharr Dancers because the tickets to the Wichita performance are all sold out. I'm sorry."

"Oh, so am I!"

"I wish—" he said and stopped in mid-sentence.

"You wish what?"

"I wish that there were more cultural things to do here."

"In Curtisville?"

"Yes. Or in Salina or McPherson."

"You miss the big cities where you've lived."

"I miss the entertainment. Oh, a Dixieland band is great for the Fourth of July, but it's nice to see a world-class ballet now and then."

"I wouldn't know," Sarah said.

"That's why I wanted to take you to see the Philip Pharr Dancers," Cliff said.

Sarah thought it was time to change the subject. She didn't like to think about how unsophisticated she must seem to Cliff.

"I wonder if it will rain," she said, looking up at a wide blue sky.

"I doubt it."

"I'm thinking about putting in an irrigation system on the home farm, did I tell you that?" She felt much more at ease with topics she understood.

"I think it's a great idea."

"Pop doesn't think so. Between Pop and Lucy, my greatest ideas get shot down."

"Your father will come to his senses, especially if he realizes that you're going to plant a lot of your acreage in row crops from now on."

"It would be so nice to have a big pivot irrigation system," said Sarah, picturing it in her mind. The pivot would sit in the center of the field, timed so its arms on their rubber, motor-powered wheels made a complete circle of the land in four days. In those four days, the crop would receive the equivalent of three inches of rain. She would no longer have to cast a practiced eye at the sky every morning and spend the rest of the day worrying about whether it would or wouldn't rain. She would be able to water her crops herself. The pivot could run twenty-four hours a day during dry weather.

"How much would a pivot cost?" asked Sarah.

"They run about twenty-five thousand dollars," said Cliff. "That's just a shorty pivot. It would cover about a quarter of a forty-acre field."

"That's too much money," said Sarah. "I shouldn't even be thinking about it until I find out how much I can get for this sorghum I'm growing."

"I rode out to one of your far fields the other day," Cliff told her. "Your sorghum looks fat and sassy."

"And will stay that way if the rain keeps up," said Sarah.

"You're not worried, are you?" Cliff asked. He took her hand in his.

Sarah shook her head. "I know I'm doing all I can to recoup the loss of my wheat crop. It's just that being so close to the Vogels makes me stop and think."

"If you're going to stop and think, think positive," suggested Cliff.

"Is that what you do?" she said, shooting him a curious look.

"Most of the time. Abraham Lincoln is one of my heroes, and he said something like, 'We're all just as happy as we want to be.' I decided to be happy after a long period of unhappiness, and I found out I couldn't be happy if I was always thinking about negative things."

"It's hard not to think about them sometimes," said Sarah. They had almost reached the creek and were cutting through a tangled thicket of blackjack oak. They heard the sound of water running over rocks ahead.

"You have to train yourself. You have to surround yourself with upbeat people." They stopped beside the creek.

"Upbeat people like you?" Sarah smiled over at him and tested the water with her big toe. "Ooh, that's cold!" she exclaimed.

Cliff pulled his shirt and shorts off. "I'm in a positive frame of mind at this point in my life. It's because of you. And your family."

Sarah stopped midway in pulling the oversize T-shirt she wore over her head.

"You give us too much credit," she said.

"No, that's not true." Cliff stepped into the water, hesitated for a moment and plunged beneath the surface. He came up tossing the hair out of his eyes.

"I came to Curtisville not knowing what happiness is," he said. "I found it when you and kids and Charlotte and Elm more or less adopted me." Sarah stood before him, covered only by the new two-piece swimsuit. He had never seen her with so few clothes.

She waded knee-deep in the water, leaving little curling wavelets in her wake. The water obscured her from the knees down, but the rest of her was plainly in sight.

One of the first things he noticed, of which he had only dimly been aware before, was that there was no roll of flab around her waist. Her figure tapered smoothly from midriff to hip, taut and slightly muscular. He knew why. Sarah worked hard on the farm. She was always pushing or lifting something. In terms of exercise, Sarah's work on the farm was the equivalent of visiting a health spa every day.

Sarah felt a curious pride when Cliff looked at her, knowing that he liked the way she looked. She had felt self-conscious the last time she had been here with him, but she had hardly known him then.

She submerged her body. He was tantalized by the sight of her skin, made unnaturally white by the water. He looked down at himself. The hairs on his chest seemed magnified by the effect of the water. He looked at her. Her breasts seemed bigger and were so buoyant that they displaced the top of her swimsuit. He glimpsed, briefly, one rosy areola. He turned his eyes away, sure that she wouldn't want him ogling her.

"Aren't you going to take your hair out of that braid?" he asked her.

She grinned. "What is it, Oenbrink? You seem to have it in for this poor innocent braid."

"That's exactly what I don't like about it," he said, reaching to pull of the band at the bottom of it. "It looks entirely too innocent. Here in the water, you should look like a sea nymph."

Sarah snickered at that, but she obediently turned her back to him so he could unfurl her braid. He fanned the wet hair out across her back, but she laughed and swam away, kicking water in his face. He swam after her, finally catching her near the opposite bank. She turned gracefully and, borne up by the water, let herself lie in his arms, her hands looped loosely behind his neck.

He kissed her, and she tasted green and mossy. No, the green and mossiness was only a fragrance of the swimming hole. Sarah herself tasted like Sarah.

"Mmm," he said, burying his face in her wet hair. She laughed and struggled, slipping away from him as easily as an eel.

"You *are* a sea nymph," he said, plunging after her.

"And what are you?" she asked in a new spirit of playfulness.

"You tell me," he said, continuing his pursuit.

She dived underwater. "You could be Captain Hook," she said when she burst to the surface again. "You could be the yellow submarine."

"I could be Moby Dick," he told her.

"No, I was Moby Dick the day you surprised me here. I remember I was glad I was wearing my swimsuit."

"You mean sometimes you don't?"

"Not always."

"Sarah!"

"Well, I don't," she said, lunging into his arms and resting there, out of breath from her exertions.

"Then," Cliff said softly, "let's go skinny-dipping."

"Oh, but Cliff," she objected.

"Why not?"

"Because," she said faintly as he unhooked the top of her swimsuit. He let it remain where it was. It wobbled in place, held against her by the current.

"Well?" he said, his lips close to hers.

She smiled tremulously up at him, and then the top of her swimsuit floated away.

She touched the elastic of his swim trunks. "And you?" she said softly.

"Yes," he said, and she rolled the elastic down, and he stepped out of his suit.

Standing only a foot away from him, Sarah slipped out of the bottom of her swimsuit and stood facing him.

"Oh, Sarah," he said in a choked voice.

He pulled her into his arms. Her body, cool and white as though it was carved out of alabaster, slid against him. It felt so natural and right. He touched her beneath the water, tentatively at first, then more boldly.

"I thought we were going to swim," she said, clinging to him. Her hair floated behind her like drifting seaweed.

"Later," he said as he buried his face in her neck. "Later."

IF THERE WAS A PRIZE for innovative foreplay, thought Cliff, surely they would have won it. He had not known that the old swimming hole in Oley's Creek was fraught with such possibilities.

It was not, he and Sarah mutually decided, the place to consummate their union, especially when the sky had gone dark and a lonely bullfrog decided to serenade them.

"I wondered what kind of music you'd like as accompaniment tonight. I never thought of a bullfrog," Sarah told him as they slipped on their clothes and left the creek, swimsuits in hand.

Cliff only hugged her close and adjusted his steps to hers as they walked slowly back to the farmhouse.

"What if someone comes and finds us walking along, wearing very little and carrying our damp swimsuits?" asked Sarah apprehensively.

"It won't happen," Cliff assured her.

Sarah giggled. "I can't imagine explaining this to Tim Vogel," she said.

"I'll do the explaining," said Cliff.

"How?"

"I'll tell him you're a sea nymph and I'm Captain Hook."

Tim, being more literal-minded and not into acting out his fantasies, as far as Sarah knew, would never understand. For the sake of her reputation, she could only hope that he was occupied elsewhere tonight.

They slipped inside the house, which was dark because Sarah had neglected to turn any lights on.

The house seemed so familiar. Its smells were the smells the house had absorbed from years of the cooking of Norquists, of the dust from their bedclothes and the odors of their bodies. She could almost hear the house breathing around them. She wanted to tell the house, "Yes, I'm bringing Cliff here. He is mine and I love him."

"Sarah?"

"Yes," she answered.

"Sarah, don't turn on any lights."

She agreed with him, and linking her little finger with his little finger, she drew him inside the house much as she would draw him inside herself, gently, caringly, lovingly. They mounted the stairs to her room.

They were both still damp from their swim, and silently they stood in the pool of moonlight shining through the window and took off the few clothes they wore. They saw each other only in outline. She was aware of the sharpness of his nose as he bent his head toward hers, and he saw the pendulousness of her lower lip as though for the first time.

She lifted her lips to his, surprised that she felt such calm and certainty. She drank of his kiss as she would drink from a tall glass of cool water at the end of a long, hot day.

Only their lips touched until he clasped each of her hands in each of his, drawing her closer until her breasts tipped the wet hair on his chest. Then her breasts were crushed gently against him, and the hair tickled her chest. He released her hands and ran his down her hourglass shape, reaching around behind her to pull her closer. He slid one leg between hers.

She felt her legs go slack, and she steadied herself against him. Slowly he pushed her backward until the backs of her knees felt the edge of the bed, and she sank gracefully beneath him, going under like a sinking ship.

He loomed above her, bathed in moonlight, and she felt as though this were her first time, ever. He made it new and different for her. She could not think of anyone else.

"Cliff," she demanded, altering the slant of her body so that it would be easier. "Cliff. I love you, Cliff."

"Oh, Sarah. Oh, my love," he cried, and raw with hunger, he flung himself into her and cried out again.

AFTERWARD, WHEN HER HEAD rested on his thigh, and he half sat propped against the headboard, he combed his fingers through her long lovely hair.

"Did you really mean it?" he asked, because the memory of her saying the three words he had longed to hear was blurred with passion.

Her eyes became round, bottomless. She lifted herself on one elbow and, reaching out, put her hand around his neck and pulled him down to her. She kissed him, and he tasted himself on her lips.

"I meant it," she said. "I love you, Cliff. I love you."

He surrendered to her softness, thinking that he had never cared so much for anyone. Especially after tonight, he couldn't imagine being without her. Ever.

Chapter Fourteen

Anyone could see that Lucy still wasn't her old self. Even the delivery of the dishwasher on the following Tuesday didn't make Lucy feel better about Spanky's death. One thing Lucy did manage to enjoy, however, was her own importance when Sarah came in from the fields and saw the dishwasher installed in its place beside the kitchen sink.

"*I* helped measure for it, Mom," Lucy said.

"I can't imagine how you managed to keep it a secret for almost two whole weeks," Sarah told her.

Sarah was stunned that Lucy and Cliff had conspired with the rest of the family to keep her at the Inman place all day so that the new dishwasher could be installed without her knowing it.

"You mean you went out and bought us a *dishwasher*?" she said over and over to Cliff. "I can't believe it. I just can't believe it!"

"I had to do something to repay all of you for the many meals I've eaten at your house," Cliff said.

"But a dishwasher! Oh, Cliff, you shouldn't have!" Sarah couldn't stop smiling at him.

Charlotte had noticed that Sarah had been smiling almost nonstop since last weekend. Sarah was full of bright, beaming smiles when Cliff was near. Sarah indulged in shy secret smiles when she thought no one was looking. Charlotte wasn't quite sure what had happened between Cliff and Sarah that last weekend she and Elm spent in town, but she had a pretty good idea. Only one thing could have brought that particular glow to a woman's skin, that sparkle to her eye.

It wouldn't have happened in her day, thought Charlotte. A man and a woman had to wait until they were married in those days. But things were different now, and Charlotte tended to think that it was a good thing. When she recalled the courage that she, Charlotte, must have possessed in order to move to Curtisville at the age of twenty to marry Elm Norquist and spend the rest of her life with him. Why, she and Elm had never even seen each other without their clothes on before they got married!

Charlotte was tickled about the new dishwasher. Instead of giving Sarah a useless bit of folderol like a bracelet or a necklace, Cliff had chosen to give her something she could use and would value even more. He was a smart man to do this. He knew that Sarah was the practical sort.

The dishwasher was equipped with all sorts of knobs and dials, and it had a shiny black front. It looked nice in their kitchen. It would be good for Sarah not to have to wash dishes anymore, although Charlotte herself would miss standing at the sink with her hands in warm water and iridescent soap bubbles climbing halfway up her arms. The warm water always eased her stiff joints.

Probably if she were to add up the hours and minutes she had spent standing in front of the window over the kitchen sink, they would add up to a large number. The scene had been a never-ending source of inspiration to her. Charlotte derived a good deal of comfort from gazing at the hazy hills in the distance. She often thought of the Bible verse,

I will lift up mine eyes unto the hills from whence cometh my help.
My help cometh from the Lord which made heaven and earth.

Comfort or no, Charlotte knew that she wouldn't be looking unto the hills from this kitchen window much longer. The weekends they had spent in town had convinced Elm that he was ready to move into town permanently. He liked hobnobbing with his cronies, and he was beginning to resent the lone-liness of the farm. If he lived in town, his chairmanship of the town's annual Pioneer Day would be so much easier.

"We'll move into Aunt Millie's house next week," he told Charlotte on the day that the new dishwasher came.

"Don't you think we'd better discuss the move with Sarah beforehand?" Charlotte asked anxiously.

"I have a hard time discussing anything with Sarah these days," Elm complained. "She has her own ideas about things. She'll probably be glad to have me off the place."

"Oh, Elm, you know that's not true," soothed Charlotte, but secretly she wondered if it was. Sarah's confidence had been growing by leaps and bounds lately. Charlotte wondered if Cliff had anything to do with that. She hoped so.

Charlotte had done her best to nurture a romance between Cliff and Sarah, and it had apparently worked. The thing was, did Cliff also see Sarah as the kind of person he'd want to marry?

Charlotte leaned against the kitchen cabinets, which vi-brated with the hum of the new dishwasher. Ben laughed about something with Elm in the living room, and Sarah and Cliff murmured to each other out on the porch. Charlotte stored these sounds in her memory bank, to take out and treasure in time of need. Leaving all the familiar smells and sounds of this place behind was a heartache. How she would miss the farm, and Sarah, and the children. And the calm, gentle evenings when they all sat on the porch after supper. And her garden. How she would miss everything!

But heartache or no, she must face up to the fact that it was definitely time to move.

CLIFF WAS PLEASED that Sarah liked the new dishwasher. He felt a stab of sadness that never again would he see Sarah standing at the sink washing dishes with her double-jointed knees thrown backward in graceful arcs. He did, however, fully enjoy the neat convexity of the curves of her backside when she leaned over to load the dishwasher.

He was gently caressing those very curves one night when he asked Sarah a question he'd been wanting to ask all week.

"Do you think your parents suspect we're lovers?" Cliff asked.

"I think Mama does. Pop's so busy planning Pioneer Day that I don't think he gives us a thought."

"Is that why they're moving to town? To give us more privacy?"

"They'd already planned to move before you ever showed up, Cliff."

"But still," said Cliff. He didn't like the idea of Charlotte and Elm leaving the farm on his account.

"Hush," said Sarah, bending over and kissing him. So enticing was she that she captured his total attention, and no more was mentioned of Charlotte and Elm that night.

CLIFF EASILY BECAME Sarah's obsession.

Everything reminded her of him. Everything was a signal that honed her body in readiness.

It might be that she had suffered too long a drought, and that anyone who came along might have been absorbed into her like a rainfall on parched land. But Sarah didn't think so. For her, there was no such thing as a simple sexual act. The act had to grow out of a deeper emotion. That was the way it had happened with James; it was the way it had happened with Cliff. It was Sarah's pattern. She had never learned to love in any other way.

She had never been so aware of her body before. It was suffused with sensation. Her lips wanted to smile all the time. Her eyes found beauty in the most mundane things. Her skin was overwhelmingly sensitive to touch. Once Lucy absentmindedly stroked her arm as they sat on the couch watching television together, and she almost jumped out of her skin. This startled Lucy, and it embarrassed Sarah. How could Lucy know that at that moment, Sarah had been reliving the magic moments of the night before when Cliff had stroked her all over before he would even so much as kiss her on the lips?

A freeze-frame of how Cliff looked at the moment of climax was frozen behind her eyelids, and every time she thought about such moments, Sarah got dizzy. First Cliff's eyes would squeeze shut, then suddenly his muscles would tense before relaxing completely, and his face would become a mask only barely resembling the Cliff that the rest of the world saw. Finally he would melt into her arms, and she would experience the bright, blinding sensation that their two spirits had merged into one. He was never more hers than he was at that moment.

Afterward he would be sweetly tender. He loved to look at her, admiring at leisure the pink and white and tan of her, the blue veins of her breasts and inner thighs, the roundness of her belly. Even the pierced holes in her ears were deemed worthy of inspection. He would touch her with gentle fingertips, exploring minutely the tiny wrinkles at the corners of her eyes, the crease under her breasts, the way her little toes turned over on their sides, and he would pronounce her beautiful. If anyone who had examined her so attentively thought she was beautiful, Sarah reasoned, it must be true. She accepted his pronouncement. She felt beautiful when she was with Cliff.

Their bodies together, her mind told her, were only two adult bodies, one male and one female, doing what they were created to do. But in her heart, their bodies were much more than ordinary. They were magnificent.

And so the summer segued into August. Sarah spent her days daydreaming as she guided the tractor through her fields, and she spent her nights, when they could be sure of privacy, locked in Cliff's arms. When they slept together, they had a rule that part of them must always be touching, even if it was only their two little fingers or the sides of their legs. When she got up to get a drink of water, he would awaken too, and when she came back to bed, he would draw her close as if to tell her that he couldn't bear to be parted from her for even so short a time.

All this made Sarah feel a heady exaltation, but it also made her feel ever more dependent on Cliff's presence.

In a moment of doubt, she allowed herself to think about how she'd feel if Cliff fell out of love with her. For her, making love with Cliff had ineffably strengthened their bond. Their physical intimacy had transformed her, had made her into a person she hadn't been before. If Cliff were to go, so would the new Sarah disappear. And she didn't want to be the person she was before, ever again.

If Cliff dropped her, she'd have to deal with the embarrassment, in this small community, of being the one who was left rather than the one who did the leaving. People might stare at her in church. They would whisper behind her back. And Cliff, no doubt far away by that time, after leading her down a path liberally strewn with primroses, would be on his merry way in the company of a more worldly, more sophisticated Devon-equivalent.

But maybe that wouldn't happen. Cliff seemed steady and rock solid. He liked her family. He went to church with her on Sundays. He loved her.

"He loves me," she would whisper to herself when she was sure no one could hear. "He loves me."

Which was reassuring. Sarah couldn't help thinking that she was too happy, that her happiness couldn't possibly continue, and that she was tempting fate to think that it could.

THE HOOT OF THE pickup's horn was borne to her on the wind. Sarah shaded her eyes with one hand and recognized the blue pickup truck belonging to Frank and Mina Vogel. Mina climbed down from the cab, calling, "Sarah!"

Sarah shut down the tractor engine and jumped down between two rows of sorghum. Mina Vogel's pickup truck was parked at the perimeter of the field, and Mina was standing in an ankle-high tangle of bindweed squinting into the sun.

"Mina, is everything all right?"

Mina's plump face was overshadowed by worry.

"Have you seen Tim, Sarah?"

"Not for a couple of days." Sarah felt a twinge of guilt. She had been so busy seeing Cliff every night that she'd given only perfunctory thoughts to Tim.

"Tim didn't come home last night," said Mina. "I'm worried."

"Have you checked with anyone else?"

"I just came back from the airport. They said that he was hanging around there late last night, but no one seems to know why."

"Maybe he was going to a job somewhere." Tim often worked as a crop duster in neighboring states, and he liked to hitch rides in airplanes with pilots who stopped at the local airport to refuel.

"He always lets me know if he's going to be gone, even for one night."

They stood silently while Sarah thought this over. A few feet away, a baby pheasant skittered across the road.

"I don't know what to tell you," said Sarah, feeling helpless. She wanted to do something, anything, to help Mina Vogel, but she didn't know Tim's whereabouts.

"Thanks, Sarah. I'll let you get back to work." Mina turned back toward her truck. The wind whipped her skirt around her knees.

"Please phone me tonight," Sarah called after her. "I'd like to know if you've heard anything."

Mina waved and nodded, and in a few minutes, her pickup was spinning toward the highway in a wind-whipped cloud of yellow dust.

Sarah went back to her work, but she couldn't stop worrying about Tim. It sounded to her as though Tim had left town, and in light of his remarks about wanting to put Curtisville and everything it represented out of his life, she feared that he had done just that.

Scoured by the wind and drained by the ninety-five-degree heat, Sarah quit work early and went to the house to make some phone calls of her own. Discreet inquiries of Tim's friends produced no leads. A call to the airport elicited the information that Mina already knew—that Tim had been seen at the airport last night but not since then.

Sarah knew the name of the man for whom Tim had worked in Wisconsin, and she called him.

"No, I haven't heard from Tim since he left," said the man. Sarah hung up, more concerned than ever.

When she still hadn't heard from Mina after supper, Sarah telephoned the Vogel home.

"Mina? Is there any news from Tim?"

She could tell that Mina had been crying.

"No, Sarah. There's no news. But I found out that Tim sold his car to Carl McClellan."

"Oh, no," said Sarah. Her heart sank.

"Yes, I'm afraid so. I—I hope that Tim doesn't do anything rash."

"So do I," said Sarah, feeling heartsick.

"I'll call you if I hear anything new," said Mina before ringing off.

"What do you think Tim's gone and done?" Elm asked after Sarah told her parents that Tim couldn't be found.

"I don't know," said Sarah grimly, and went for a solitary walk up the hill.

The wind had died, and she wished she'd meet Tim walking over the top of the hill to meet her as he sometimes did. Tim didn't show up, but she recognized the headlights of Cliff's car when it was still far away. He stopped and swung open the car door on the passenger's side. Sarah climbed in, and Cliff pulled over to the side of the road beside the hedge of Osage orange.

"I heard a rumor that Tim Vogel air-hitchhiked out of town last night with another pilot who was happy to have a copilot," he told her.

"Where were they going?"

"The other pilot had filed a flight plan to Springfield, Missouri," Cliff said.

"That doesn't mean much," Sarah replied hopelessly. "Tim could be almost anywhere in the United States by this time."

Still, when they got back to the house, Sarah called the airport in Springfield and asked about any late-night private flights from Curtisville. The woman who answered the phone knew that a single-engine plane had refueled there late last night, but whether the pilot had a passenger named Tim Vogel, she couldn't say. Sarah thanked her and hung up.

There was no news from Tim that day, nor was there news on the next day or the next. The Norquists, the Morrows and the Vogels lived for the ring of the telephone. They never answered it without a certain apprehension.

Everyone in Curtisville was talking about Tim's disappearance. Sarah was unable to defend Tim's actions. Public opinion was certainly against Tim. And that was something else he'd have to face when—and if—he ever came back to Curtisville.

On the fourth day after Tim's disappearance, Sarah stopped by the Vogel place to take Mina a few jars of Charlotte's plum jelly. While she was there, the postman's car crunched to a stop at the rural mailbox at the end of the driveway.

"I'd better see if there's a letter from Tim," said Mina, hurrying outside.

Sarah walked with Mina to the mailbox. As they turned back toward the house, Mina shuffled through the letters and magazines.

"This is Tim's handwriting!" Mina exclaimed. Her fingers trembled as she tore the envelope open.

"Is he all right? What does he say?" asked Sarah. She picked up the envelope from the ground where it had fallen and tried to read the postmark. It was hopelessly smudged.

A check fluttered to the ground, but Mina hardly noticed. Her eyes were rapidly scanning the letter. Sarah said in surprise, "Why, look at the amount of this check, Mina!"

Mina took the check. "Tim says he's sent us five hundred dollars less than the amount Carl McCellan paid him for his Laser." She thrust the letter into Sarah's hand and began to walk swiftly back toward the house.

The terse note from Tim said little more than not to worry, that he was safe.

"He didn't give me a reason why he left," sobbed Mina when they were inside the house.

Sarah held Tim's wrinkled note in her hand. She was so angry that her vision blurred. How could Tim be so heartless? His mother and father were going through one of the worst times of their lives, and Tim Vogel had left them here to face it without his help. Tim was her friend, and Sarah loved him like a brother. But if he were standing here in front of her, she'd give him a piece of her mind.

"I don't understand why Tim had to do this, Mina," Sarah said slowly.

Mina dried her tears. "He sent us the money he got from selling his car, and it will be a big help," Mina said in resignation.

"That's true," Sarah said. "I'm glad Tim gave you the money. I don't like the way he went about it, that's all."

"I'm aware Tim doesn't mean to hurt us," Mina said, twisting a handkerchief in her plump hands. "Maybe he thinks he's helping by running away like this. But it hurts a lot. It reminds me so of Norrie!'' Mina began to sob again, and Sarah thought that the soft muffled weeping would break her heart.

These people, so proud and hardworking, had lost their daughter, they had lost their land, and now they had lost their son, too. After receiving Mina's assurance that she could cope, that she would be all right, Sarah walked slowly back to Windrush Valley Farm, and she dreaded telling her children and parents that Tim Vogel was apparently gone for good.

Certainly Tim was acting irresponsible. Sarah felt strongly that he should live up to his obligations to his parents. He was the only son still living at home, and he could have chosen to make things easier for them. Frank and Mina were bogged down in a maze of bankruptcy proceedings and hoped that they could salvage a bit of decency and self-respect. Sarah hated him for putting them through this extra hardship.

But she knew that she loved Tim too much to be angry with him for long. And she hoped, for his parents' sake, that Tim Vogel would come home to Curtisville soon.

To Sarah, it seemed as though her days swung between incredible highs and lows. The highs were when she was with Cliff and when she was on her land, watching her flourishing crop of sorghum as it spread a dense green canopy of leaves over the soil. The lows were when Mina Vogel called to report no more word from Tim and when Lucy woke her in the night with nightmares.

Once Sarah tiptoed into Lucy's room after one of Lucy's bad dreams and found Lucy wide-awake, her heart hammering in her little chest. Sarah gathered her daughter in her arms and soothed her, finally venturing to ask what was wrong.

But Lucy couldn't—or wouldn't—tell her.

Probably Lucy was still reacting to Spanky's death. Or maybe she was anticipating Charlotte and Elm's impending move away from the farm. Whatever it was, Sarah felt powerless to help Lucy.

It was Cliff who took Ben under his wing and found things for the two of them to do, such as riding the farm's two Honda ATVs together. He also began to find things to do with Lucy.

He and Lucy built a tree house down by the creek, enlisting Ben's help. Cliff included her in fishing trips with Ben. Lucy responded well to Cliff, but she still seemed out of sorts most of the time.

"I think I've taken Spanky's place," said Cliff one day in characteristic good humor. "I think I've become the family pet."

"You're more than just a family pet," said Sarah quickly.

And this left Cliff to ponder what he really was to this family. And what they were to him.

Certainly Sarah was his love. He cared about Ben and Lucy. He was fond of Charlotte and Elm.

They were family to him, which was comfortable to think about. In his mind he was forming another comfortable thought: it would be pleasant to be a permanent part of their family circle. They had become indispensable to his life in Curtisville.

But had they become indispensable to his life, period?

That was what he'd have to work out.

Sarah, in the meantime, had other things to work out. One of them was balancing her duties to the farm, her parents and her children. Sarah confided to Cliff that she often felt torn in three directions.

"If only I weren't so busy," fretted Sarah.

"You're doing the best you can," Cliff reminded her. He often helped by bringing them take-out dinners so that Sarah wouldn't have to cook in the evening. Sometimes he ferried Charlotte and Elm out to the farm with him, and Charlotte would carry in pots of food that she had cooked in the afternoon, and they would all sit around the dining-room table and eat supper the way they used to before Charlotte and Elm moved.

Such help was much appreciated by Sarah. She usually heaved a sigh of relief when Cliff drove Elm, Charlotte, and occasionally, Ben and Lucy back to town after such suppers. Then she would relax on the porch all by herself, thinking that solitude was not such a bad thing after all.

It was at such times that she reflected how different her life was from the life she had expected to lead. She'd certainly never planned to farm Windrush Valley Farm alone, but more than that was different about her life.

For instance, she remembered her mother and her grandmother sitting together on this very same porch after dinner. They would catch up on their mending at such times.

Did anyone ever mend anything anymore? Sarah had learned to darn socks in Girl Scouts. As far as she could see, it had done absolutely no good for her to hunch over a sock stuffed with a light bulb, weaving navy-blue thread back and forth in a futile attempt to accomplish a smooth darn that wouldn't blister the wearer's heel.

Now there were iron-on patches for holes. Or, as happened in her house, they threw socks with holes in them away.

Sarah had known back then, even as she learned to do it, that she'd never have to darn socks. She'd thought it was because she would be rich when she grew up. Well, she didn't darn socks, but it wasn't because she was rich. Another of life's little jokes.

Actually all that time she'd spent learning to darn socks in Girl Scouts might have been better spent in learning how to make love to a man. Such knowledge would certainly contribute more to maintaining a happy home life than darning a guy's socks. However, she could imagine the uproar if such a skill were listed in the Scout handbook. Lucy would be joining the Scouts soon. Sarah wondered if Girl Scouts still learned to darn socks.

Usually by the time Cliff came back alone, Sarah was ready for her solitude to end. He would sweep her into his arms and whisper loving comments in her ear until she led him upstairs to her bedroom.

Ben and Lucy spent many nights with their grandparents, because then Sarah wouldn't have to drive them into town to the recreation department's day camp the next day. They thought it was a great adventure. Ben said, "We can walk to the park right after breakfast!" They loved their summertime activities at the park. As farm children, they had often felt deprived because they had no playmates but each other.

"How are your parents adjusting to life in town?" Cliff asked idly one night. Ben and Lucy were upstairs asleep. He and Sarah were talking in the kitchen.

"I think they're doing great," said Sarah, pouring them each a glass of iced tea. "Mama plays cards once a week with some other women who live on her street. Pop seems happy too."

"I see Elm holding a meeting of his Pioneer Day committee in the Chatterbox almost every morning when I go in there for breakfast," Cliff said.

"Pop's worked on the Pioneer Day committee as long as I can remember," Sarah said. "They used to meet at our house until Mama complained so much about Charlie Olsen's cigars."

"When is Pioneer Day, anyway?" Cliff asked.

"In September, the weekend after Labor Day."

"What happens on Pioneer Day?"

"It's a celebration of the pioneers who settled here. There's an art festival in the park and a play put on by the kids in the recreation department. There's even a Chautauqua, which travels from community to community with actors and actresses who play the parts of people who are historically significant to the plains."

"All that sophisticated stuff," Cliff said with a little laugh.

She might have guessed that Curtisville's annual celebration would seem altogether too homespun and ordinary to Cliff. After all, it was the kind of thing he had left home in order to avoid, wasn't it? She stood up abruptly and busied herself with petting an unusually nervous Quilter so that Cliff wouldn't know that she felt inadequate to compete with the kind of life—and the kind of people—to which he was accustomed.

Quilter shifted from foot to foot and wound through Sarah's legs like a vine.

"Tell me, Cliff, do you know anything about cats giving birth? Quilter looks mighty on edge tonight." The cat paced restlessly from corner to corner of the room.

Cliff centered his attention on the cat instead of Sarah's slim ankles. "We used to have lots of cats on our farm," he said.

"There were always kittens around, but I don't remember anything about the cats actually having them."

"Well, Cliff, I'm sure they did. Cats only come from cats, not pigs or chickens."

"I know, smarty. What I mean is that the cats just went off into the barn and emerged with a litter of kittens a few weeks later. That's all there was to it."

"All there was to it!" exclaimed Sarah. "What a typically male response!"

Quilter meowed piteously, but she refused to go outside when Sarah held the door open. Sarah offered cat food, but Quilter wouldn't eat.

"I guess I'd better leave her alone," Sarah said. "She'll know what to do."

"Good idea," Cliff agreed, pulling her into his arms, and in a few minutes, Quilter was forgotten.

When Cliff was ready to leave, Sarah suddenly remembered Quilter.

"Help me look for her, Cliff," she said, and so Cliff delayed his departure long enough to participate in an all-out search for the cat.

After looking everywhere else, they found Quilter in the basement, huddled inside the top-loading washing machine. Her sides were heaving in labor.

"We can't leave Quilter in there," Sarah said distractedly. "She's lying right on the ribs of the agitator."

"She seems comfortable enough," Cliff said with a yawn.

"I'm afraid to move her," Sarah fretted. "It looks as though those kittens are about to be born." Indeed, Quilter was panting heavily, her eyes half-closed.

"Would you like me to boil water?" Cliff offered.

"What good would that do?"

"It's what they always do in the movies when someone is having a baby," he reminded her.

She shot him an exasperated look. "I could call Janice, I suppose. Cliff, what time is it?"

"It's almost midnight. I don't think Dr. Janice would appreciate a late-night phone call about a cat who seems to be giving birth to kittens in a perfectly normal manner."

"Quilter does look as though she knows what she's doing, doesn't she? Oh, I forgot. I promised Lucy that she could watch when Quilter had her kittens."

"Are you sure—"

"Of course. It will be a good education for Lucy. Anyway, she needs something to cheer her up."

"What about Ben?"

"Ben watched our last cat have kittens when he was Lucy's age. He's not interested at this point."

"Want me to get Lucy?"

"No, I want to. You keep an eye on Quilter."

While Sarah was gone, Cliff eyed the cat warily. He wouldn't want to admit it, but this process scared him. That's why he had tried to joke about it. If he could have, he'd have gone home. But he knew that Sarah expected him to stay and join in the fun. Some fun.

As if she knew what he was thinking, Quilter implored him with her unblinking green eyes and a spirited but muted, "Mrow."

"You're not crazy about this, either," he whispered, and then looked around to make sure no one had heard him. He felt a little silly talking to a cat.

Quilter meowed again, and after that, Cliff knew that even if he managed to talk his way out of this, he didn't have the heart to go home until all her kittens were safely born.

Lucy and Sarah appeared, Lucy picking her way carefully down the basement stairs in her long bathrobe. She peered into the washing-machine tub with wide eyes.

"Why did she decide to have her kittens in there, Mom?" Lucy asked.

"It must have seemed like a safe place," Sarah said.

"It's dark and cool," Cliff added.

"Gee," Lucy said. "I hope she's not going to live in the washing machine with her babies!"

"No," Sarah said with a smile. "We'll move Quilter and her kittens to a clean box in the barn as soon as we can."

"She sure seems tired," Lucy said.

Sarah explained why Quilter was panting so hard and why her sides were heaving. "It's a perfectly natural process," Sarah said. "Quilter knows exactly what to do."

Cliff brought kitchen stools down to the basement, and once in a while Quilter allowed one of them to stroke her soothingly between the ears. Then, with quick efficiency, one, two and then three kittens were born.

"Wow!" Lucy said, her eyes as round as saucers. "Oh, gee. Wow."

The kittens were tiny and wet, but Quilter licked them all dry with a vigorous tongue. One was calico, just like Quilter, and one was black-and-white, and one was a gray tabby.

"They're so tiny," Lucy marveled. "And look how little their tails are!"

"And see what good care Quilter takes of them," Sarah said.

They watched the new mother as she positioned herself so that the kittens could nurse, and Sarah felt a lump in her throat at the sight of the mother and her three new babies.

"It's a miracle," said Lucy before she yawned. "It's a beautiful miracle."

"And it's almost dawn," Sarah replied. "I haven't had any sleep." She felt exhausted, but elated.

Lucy trailed up the stairs to bed. She turned to speak to Cliff at the top.

"It's so late to go home, Cliff, that you might as well sleep over," Lucy said. She yawned again and stumbled toward her room.

"Interesting idea," Cliff said, preparing to kiss Sarah good-bye at the back door.

"Yes, but not a very good one," said Sarah, who had definite ideas about what should and should not go on under her roof when her children were present.

"Maybe we should get married," said Cliff, and then he couldn't believe he had actually said such a thing out loud.

Sarah stared at him long and hard. Her eyes were rimmed with fatigue. She couldn't figure out if he actually meant it. Maybe it was just one of those comments he tossed off from time to time to distract her.

"Another interesting idea," she agreed, and she smiled a weary smile before pushing him out the door into the curling mist of a gray dawn.

Chapter Fifteen

No more was mentioned of marriage after the night when Quilter's kittens were born. Sarah wondered if Cliff had been thinking about it, but she was loath to be the first to bring up the subject. Cliff had been tired that night; she had been tired.

Besides, she couldn't shake the idea that Cliff was not long for Curtisville. He subscribed to a Minneapolis newspaper, which was delivered every day by mail. He spoke often of his friends in Kansas City. These were signs to Sarah that Cliff had never really given up his concept of himself as a big-city type. He didn't fit into the Curtisville mold. As much as Sarah loved him, she doubted that he ever would.

Sarah felt woefully inadequate around Cliff at times. He dressed so nattily most of the time, and when he met her as she came in from the fields, she thought he must look down on her sweaty clothes and the dirt clinging to her work boots. He never gave any sign of this, but she was sure that somewhere in his subconscious, he thought of her as a hick.

Sarah tried to look as sophisticated as possible. She took to piling her hair on top of her head in elaborate styles. Cliff never failed to ask her to take it down.

"I like to see your hair hanging free," was all he ever said.

She fell more deeply in love with him every day, and at odd moments she found herself hoping that he would mention marriage again. She was hoping, but she was afraid, too. She knew that if he decided that it was time to explore the possibilities of marriage, she'd have to lay it on the line with him. She'd have to tell him that her main worry was that he would tire of Curtisville—and of her.

That he loved her now was unmistakable. Sarah, however, had schooled herself, much as it hurt, to think of herself as nothing more than a passing fancy for Cliff. He was in Curtisville, and she happened to be handy. His falling in love with her was the choicest luck and owed much to their circumstances of propinquity. She couldn't believe that he would stay in love with her for any length of time.

"I have a few days of vacation coming," Cliff told Sarah casually one night as they were driving back from a movie in McPherson. "I've been thinking about going home to Medallion."

"I'm sure your mother and father will be happy to see you," Sarah said.

"That's not the only reason I want to go," he said, and she had the feeling that he was building up to something. She turned inquiring eyes toward him.

"I'd like you to go with me," he said, and then cleared his throat.

Stunned, Sarah could only stare at him.

"But why?" she managed to say.

"Because I love you. I want them to love you too."

She thought this over. She couldn't help but be touched by the invitation, although she couldn't be sure what Cliff's motives were. Motives aside, however, she could hardly pick up and leave home without a care in the world.

"Cliff, I have so many responsibilities. The farm, for one thing. And Mama and Pop. And the kids. I can't just go."

Cliff had apparently figured all that out ahead of time. "Henry could look after the farm for a few days," he said. "Your mother and father seem to be doing beautifully on their own. Ben and Lucy could come with us. In fact, I'd planned on it."

Sarah considered this. A vacation was certainly appealing. Besides, she was curious about Cliff's parents. He'd spoken of them only briefly, although affectionately. She wasn't sure she could know Cliff—or judge her chances of having a lasting relationship with him—without first meeting them.

"When would we go?" she asked.

"Whenever it would be best for you. The end of next week?"

Henry had mentioned that his bowling league would end its season in a few days. This meant that next weekend Henry would have more time available to do Sarah's work. "I could be gone for four or five days," Sarah said slowly. "Wednesday through Sunday, maybe."

"Does that mean you'll go to Medallion with me?" Cliff's voice held a note of excitement.

She smiled at him. She loved to do things to make him happy. "Yes," she said. "I'm glad you asked me."

Cliff grinned at her. He'd been prepared to be even more persuasive. "That's wonderful, Sarah," he told her. "I can hardly wait for you to meet my parents. And I'm looking forward to showing you all the splendors of Medallion, Illinois." He laughed and reached for her hand.

"What will we do there, Cliff? Will there be enough to keep the kids occupied?" This was the one thing that worried her.

"We can certainly keep busy for a mere three days, which is how long we'll stay in Medallion. It takes a day's traveling time to drive each way. When things get a little dull, we'll go to downtown Medallion and watch one of the town's two traffic lights changing colors. When that gets boring, we'll sit on the sidewalk and watch the cars rust." He laughed again.

"It doesn't sound as though you like the town much." Not liking one's hometown was incomprehensible to Sarah.

"I certainly wouldn't care to live there," Cliff said, as though living in Medallion would be a great inconvenience to him.

The way he spoke told Sarah a great deal.

If Medallion was a lot like Curtisville, and Cliff had assured her that it was, she'd feel right at home there.

But she didn't think that Cliff would. She had detected a note of disparagement in his tone whenever he talked about his hometown and his roots. It seemed even more evident to her than ever that Cliff preferred bright lights and big cities.

"ARE WE THERE YET?" asked Ben, who had grown tired of counting cars.

"Not yet," Sarah said patiently.

"Is this what it's like to have kids?" asked Cliff. "They've asked if we're there yet at least ten times."

"They'll ask it ten more times before we get there," Sarah said. "You'd better get used to it."

"Yeah," Cliff said, but he was smiling as he said it.

They had started out early Wednesday morning, and they expected to arrive in Medallion around four in the afternoon. Cliff's parents were eagerly awaiting their visit.

"Cliff's told us so much about you," Emily Oenbrink had told Sarah on the phone when she was officially inviting her and the children.

I didn't know that, Sarah had thought as she handed the phone back to Cliff. If Cliff was taking her up to his parents, did that mean that he had serious intentions toward her?

Sarah was nervous about the meeting.

"Don't tell Mrs. Oenbrink that I'm a bad cook," Sarah had said to Lucy as she tied her hair in twin ponytails before they left on the morning of the trip.

"I wouldn't lie, Mom," Lucy said. "She might ask me."

"She probably won't ask," Sarah had said doggedly. "And you don't need to tell her."

"I can't talk about you at all?"

"Just don't say anything negative," instructed Sarah, giving the right ponytail a final pat.

"I won't tell her you leave your clothes all over the bathroom floor after you've taken a shower," Lucy had said kindly before bouncing away.

"Thanks a lot," Sarah had muttered under her breath.

Ben was looking forward to the trip because he would be able to see the place where Cliff had grown up. Besides, the Oenbrinks had a dog.

"We'll go see the farm where I lived when I was a boy," Cliff promised. "We'll see the water tower where I sprayed 'Class of 1967' in orange paint the night I graduated from high school. We'll eat hamburgers at the old Daisy Grill, and you can try one of their soft-ice-cream sundaes, Sarah. You'll love it."

Cliff continued to speak in favorable terms about Medallion now that they were on their way there. Sarah couldn't figure out the discrepancy in his glowing anticipation now versus the disparaging things he had said about it in the past. Or maybe the disparaging things he said were only part of his lively sense of humor. In any case, this paradox in Cliff's thinking intrigued her. It made her all the more curious about the town where Cliff had grown up.

Medallion, Illinois, was a little over five hundred miles from Curtisville. They stopped for a leisurely lunch at a roadside rest stop in Missouri. After they ate the sandwiches Charlotte had packed, Sarah and Cliff discreetly held hands while Ben and Lucy played tightrope walker on a low rock wall. Yellow grasshoppers catapulted up out of the knee-high grass, and Lucy shrieked with laughter when one slid down the front of Ben's shirt, effectively ending the game.

"Are we there yet?" asked Ben again as they crossed the state line into Illinois.

They drove for miles without seeing another car. When they did, the heat transformed the approaching vehicle into a dancing dot on the flat black ribbon of the road ahead. Fat green fields on either side of the road told them they were still in farming country. The fields spread out in front of Medallion like a commodious lap.

Sarah recognized the town by its rusting water tower high above the railroad tracks. Like Curtisville, the town had its own grain elevator.

"Our prairie cathedral," Cliff called it when he pointed it out.

Main Street led right through the middle of town and was shaded by big oaks. It had rained recently, and the leaves dripped raindrops on the windshield of the car. Their tires hissed on the pavement, and the air smelled of wet asphalt.

Cliff turned down a quiet side street paved in brick. "My parents bought their present house after they sold the farm," he said. "It's not as big as our farmhouse was, but it's just right for them."

"Why, this street looks a lot like streets in Curtisville," said Lucy in surprise when she saw the neat front yards planted with zinnias and marigolds.

"Medallion *is* a lot like Curtisville," Cliff said.

Sarah held her breath as they drove into the driveway of the Oenbrinks' brick house. She was still nervous about meeting Cliff's parents. What had he told them about her? What did they expect?

Emily Oenbrink peered out between two slats of the venetian blinds before running out the door to meet them. Although she was seventy-two, she was as spry as one of Ben's lambs.

Without hesitating, Emily embraced Sarah in welcome. Her husband, Harold, who was right behind her, was stooped and balding, but his brown eyes were lively, and he welcomed Sarah with a warm handshake.

The children hung back shyly until a fox terrier erupted from the house, yipped a few times, circled them once and then jumped on Ben's legs. Ben immediately sank to the ground and let the dog, whose name was Dibs, lick his face.

They ate dinner early because that's what Cliff's parents always did. Afterward, when Sarah was helping Emily clean up the kitchen, Emily asked many interested questions about Sarah's running of her family farm.

"I don't know how you manage," Emily marveled. "I don't think I could have run our farm all by myself."

"Sarah makes it all seem easy," said Cliff, ambling into the kitchen in search of a second piece of his mother's prize chocolate-almond cake, which she had served for dessert. He rested a proprietary hand on Sarah's shoulder while his mother cut another piece of cake, and his hand was still there when his mother turned around. Emily's surprise at this affectionate gesture was obvious, and so was the knowing look that leaped into her eyes.

I wonder if she approves of me, thought Sarah. Somehow Emily's approval had become very important.

Tired from their long car trip, the children went to bed soon after they ate, and since the Oenbrinks customarily retired early, Sarah and Cliff found themselves alone in the living room.

"Well?" said Cliff, smiling at her. "What do you think?"

"Of what?"

"Of my parents."

"It's what they think of me that I wonder about," she said.

Cliff crossed the room and pulled her to her feet. He curved his arms around her and rested his cheek against hers.

"They love you, naturally," he said.

"Is that what you want?"

He tilted away from her in surprise. "Of course," he said.

"Mmm," she said. She waited a moment. "I feel as though I'm on display."

She felt Cliff's lips curve against her cheek. "You are. I want them to know what a wonderful woman I've found."

"Your mother makes me feel comfortable here. I was afraid she might not."

"Mother is the soul of hospitality. Also, I'm sure that she was even more curious about you than you were about her. She's glad to know that at last I've found someone she considers my type. She couldn't stand Devon."

Sarah sat down on a chair. Cliff pulled up the ottoman from in front of his father's easy chair and sat down in front of her.

"Why didn't she like Devon, Cliff? Devon has always sounded—well, interesting."

Cliff grinned. "You're much more interesting to me," he said. "For instance, I'm interested in your mouth, and your neck—" and here he bent over to plant a kiss in the hollow of it "—and your breasts."

Casting a frantic glance toward the hallway, Sarah said, "Cliff!"

"And I'm interested in the rest of you. What do you say we go for a ride out to the local lovers' lane? Hmm?"

By this time he was tugging the hairpins from her hair, and it tumbled in a yellow froth around her shoulders.

"Cliff, I don't know," she said with a wary glance down the hall where the bedrooms were. She pushed her hair back out of her face.

"Come on," Cliff whispered, pulling her by the hand and tiptoeing across the floor. When she started to object, he planted a hand across her mouth. Her eyes gestured wildly in the direction of the bedrooms, but in answer he only removed his hand from her mouth and replaced it with his lips until Sarah thought that their heavy breathing must be audible all over the silent house. He whispered close by her ear, "It's our only hope for privacy."

Her knees were weak, and her heart seemed ready to leap out of her chest. Caught up in the giddy excitement of an adventure and barely restraining the urge to giggle, she followed Cliff outside and into his car. She sat beside him as he coasted the car expertly out of the driveway before he started the engine well out of hearing range of the house. By the time they reached the corner, Sarah was convulsed with laughter.

"You must be experienced at such quiet getaways," she said at last, snuggling close to him on the seat. His marvelous spontaneity was one of the things she loved about Cliff.

He threw her a long mischievous glance. "When I was growing up on the farm, I learned how to park my car on a hill after I'd been out on a date. When I was going with Brenda Pearson, our curfews were too early to suit either of us. After my parents were asleep, I'd roll my car down the hill after sneaking out of my house around midnight, and Brenda would slip out her window and meet me on the corner of her street. We spent many a long night out on the Overlook Road learning what every teenager ought to know."

"Cliff! I didn't realize that you were such a naughty kid!"

"Oh, I wasn't. I was a model kid in the daytime. I'm not sure you'd call what Brenda and I were doing *naughty*. I've always viewed it as educational."

"Is the Overlook Road where we're going tonight?"

"You bet," he said as they passed the sign that read Medallion, Pop. 3,506.

Overlook Road was situated on a wide bluff overlooking the Medallion River, and the lights of the town were visible through the trees. Several other cars, widely spaced, occupied secluded thickets. Cliff drove to the end of the road and cut the engine.

It was a deep-breathing summer night. They sat quietly listening to the crickets resuming their song. The tall grass on the bluff looked as dark as water. The white light of the moon rimmed every leaf and bough, and a wind sighed restlessly in the trees.

Cliff flicked on the car radio. The sound of a soulful jazz trio blended with the rhythm of the chirping crickets. Cliff slid the car seat backward, and Sarah twisted around so that she was leaning against the door on the driver's side. Cliff rolled down the window, and the night air wafted in the scent of new-mown hay.

Sarah leaned her head on Cliff's shoulder. "Is this what Brenda would do when you brought her here?" she said after a while.

"Mmm-hmm," said Cliff. "And this is what I would do." He tipped her chin upward, and then he tasted her as he would taste a much-longed-for delicacy.

"What else would Brenda do?" asked Sarah when he had tasted his fill.

"Maybe you can figure it out," said Cliff, running a finger around the edge of her ear in time to the throbbing beat of the drum playing on the radio.

"This?" said Sarah softly as she experimented. "This?"

"Yes," he said, losing himself to the sensations. "And yes. And this is what I would do."

"And then she would—?"

"Mmm. Exactly. Mmm."

"This, too?"

"No, my love. That's entirely new with you," he said, and then the clarinet on the radio was featured in a solo, but Sarah and Cliff played an original duet.

"MY GRANDFATHER," said Harold Oenbrink, "came to live on the prairie when he was a bachelor. He built himself a little sod house. It wasn't much of a house. He built it into the side of a hill."

"How'd he keep warm?" Ben wanted to know.

"He had himself a stove. Why, instead of cutting firewood, he'd chop down one big tree. He didn't cut it up, he'd just put one end of it in the stove, leave one end hanging out the door, and keep pushing the rest of the log in as the fire burned it up. Oh, he was a character, my grandfather."

Harold leaned back in his chair.

"That's enough stories for tonight, children. We have to get up early in the morning to leave for home," Sarah said. She rose to her feet and held out her hand to Lucy. Surprisingly, Lucy took it. Ben followed along.

It was the last night of their visit, and it had gone well. Cliff seemed to enjoy pointing out local landmarks, although Sarah thought she detected a certain underlying eagerness to be gone. She had approached Cliff about this, but he had only laughed.

"Medallion and I parted company years ago," was his only comment, and that was all he would say. Why Cliff disliked the place remained a mystery to her.

Much to Sarah's relief, both Emily and Harold had taken a personal interest in the children from their very first day when they had all gone to lunch together at the Daisy Grill where everyone ordered one of the Grill's famous hamburgers.

"Cliff grew up on these hamburgers," Emily said before biting into hers.

"Ben, if you eat lots of these, you'll get muscles," Cliff said with a wink.

"Really?" said Ben. He was inclined to believe anything Cliff said.

Lucy howled with laughter. "He's pulling your leg, Ben," she said.

"That's where he'll get the muscles, Lucy. In his leg." Cliff munched on his hamburger, enjoying Lucy's skeptical look.

"I already have muscles anyway," sniffed Ben.

"So do I," Lucy said proudly. Just to show them, she flexed an arm.

"Are you a tomboy?" Emily asked Lucy with interest.

"No, but I like to climb trees."

Emily smiled fondly. "So did I when I was your age," and thus was established a special relationship between them. For the remainder of their visit, Lucy trailed Emily around the house like a small shadow. Emily's attraction seemed to be that she treated Lucy as an equal. As for Harold Oenbrink, his stories of the old days fascinated Ben.

"I like Mr. Oenbrink's stories," said Ben now as he climbed into the twin bed in the room he shared with Cliff.

"Me, too," said Lucy.

"His stories are almost as good as Grandpa's," said Ben.

"No, they're not," Lucy protested before padding into the bedroom she shared with Sarah and climbing unbidden into bed.

"I'm going to miss Mrs. Oenbrink," Lucy told Sarah as Sarah tucked a few stray items of Lucy's clothing into the open suitcase on the floor.

"So will I," Sarah said.

"Not like me," insisted Lucy. She sat up in bed and hugged her blanket-shrouded knees. Sarah closed the suitcase and sat down on the side of the bed. She felt an inordinate amount of tenderness for this small daughter of hers. Lucy had been trying to overcome her tendency toward the negative on this trip. She hadn't even told Emily that Sarah wasn't a good cook.

"Maybe Mrs. Oenbrink reminds you of Grandma," suggested Sarah.

Lucy's eyes were round and solemn in the soft light from the bedside lamp. "She reminds me of Grandma a little. It reminds me of Grandma a lot that I have to say goodbye to Mrs. Oenbrink tomorrow."

"That bothers you, does it?" Sarah said sympathetically.

"Uh-huh. Grandma moved to town so I don't see her as often, and now I have to say goodbye to Mrs. Oenbrink. Maybe I'll never see her again, Mom." Suddenly Lucy seemed perilously near tears.

Sarah hardly knew what to say. She remained silent.

"You know, Mom, it seems like I never see anybody again. Everybody goes away. Even Spanky." A big tear rolled out of the corner of Lucy's eye and slid down her cheek.

"Oh, Lucy," Sarah said, and she held out her arms. Lucy settled into them and began to sob quietly against her shoulder.

When Lucy could speak, she said, "I didn't even say goodbye to Spanky. When I woke up in the morning he was just dead."

"Sometimes we don't get to say goodbye," Sarah said. "That's why it's important to be nice to people—or dogs—while we can."

"I wasn't very nice to Spanky sometimes. I used to make fun of him because he couldn't do his old tricks."

"He did fumble around a bit in his old age, didn't he? I thought Spanky was even more lovable when he'd miss catching the biscuit once in a while."

"He always acted kind of—kind of—" Lucy couldn't find the right word.

"Surprised," supplied Sarah. "He always seemed surprised when he looked down and saw his dog biscuit lying on the ground."

Lucy managed a small grin. "Yeah, I guess he did. And then it was almost like he smiled. At himself and how funny he was."

"It's nice to remember the good things about Spanky, don't you think?"

"Yes," said Lucy.

"And as long as we remember him, he's never really gone, is he?"

Lucy shook her head. "I guess not," she conceded reluctantly. "I miss him a lot, though."

"Of course you do, honey. We all miss him. We'll go on missing him for a long time." She smoothed Lucy's hair away from her damp cheeks.

"Like we miss Daddy," said Lucy. "I didn't get to say goodbye to him, either."

Tears rose in Sarah's eyes now.

"But that's okay, Mom. I've figured it out. Someday Quilter will die, but I hope it won't be soon, but what I mean is that she will have to someday, because everything does. Part of her will still be alive in her kittens, and part of her will be alive in our minds."

"I suppose that's true, Lucy."

"And that must be true about people. As long as we remember Daddy, he's never really gone. And he's still alive in our hearts, isn't he, not just in heaven?"

"Yes," said Sarah faintly. "Oh, yes."

Lucy settled back on the pillows, her cheek resting on her panda bear. She yawned. "I'm really sleepy tonight. I love you, Mom."

"I love you too, Lucy," Sarah said. She bent over and kissed her wise daughter gently on the forehead, and then she left the room.

When she reached the living room, the phone rang. Cliff answered it. Harold glanced up curiously from his evening paper.

"Yes," said Cliff into the receiver. "Yes, Charlotte, we'll be back tomorrow."

Sarah hurried to Cliff's side. The gravity of his expression concerned her.

"Does my mother want to speak to me?" she whispered anxiously.

Cliff covered the mouthpiece with his hand. Sarah knew from the expression in his eyes that the call was serious in nature.

"Sarah, I'm afraid it's not good news. It's your father."

"Pop?" Sarah said. "What's wrong?" A panicky feeling rose in her throat.

"He's had a slight heart attack. They've put him in the hospital," Cliff said as he handed over the receiver.

"Mama?"

Charlotte's voice sounded surprisingly strong. "It's nothing to worry about, Sarah, although I admit he gave me quite a scare. Your father felt pain in his arm when we were out for our walk tonight, and we had to stop in at Mattie Sawyer's house and call the doctor. Mattie drove us to the hospital, and your father is resting now."

"And you?"

"I'm all right."

"Do you want us to start for home tonight?"

"No, no, it's entirely unnecessary. In fact, I'd only worry about all of you on the road so late. I'm going to stay with Mattie tonight. By tomorrow morning, your father will be itching to get over to the Chatterbox to have coffee with the boys. Take your time driving home, Sarah, and have a safe trip."

"We will, Mama," said Sarah before hanging up.

"I guess everything is under control," said Sarah. "I wish I'd been there."

"They seem to be getting along fine without you," Cliff pointed out.

"I suppose you're right," Sarah said.

Emily hovered sympathetically in the background. "What an awful thing to happen," she said. "Is there anything I can do?"

"Sarah, are you all right?" said Cliff.

"I don't know. It frightens me. Mama said not to worry. I wonder if I should believe her." She paced the floor.

"I would if I were you. If it were worse, she'd tell you." Cliff said.

Haltingly, Sarah related her conversation with Lucy about the ongoing cycle of life and death. "In spite of Lucy's little lecture about life and death, I'm not ready to face either of my parents' deaths," she said.

"Shh," Cliff said comfortingly, reaching for her hand.

With a meaningful look at her husband, Emily said, "Harold come help me put some coffee on. We'll have a piece of pie with Cliff and Sarah before we all say good-night."

After they had gone, Cliff wrapped his arms around Sarah as if to protect her from all unhappiness.

"Your parents are so kind," she whispered to him. "They knew we wanted to be alone."

Cliff held her loosely and looked at her face. "Are you *sure* you're all right?" he said anxiously.

Sarah nodded. "I'd be even more all right if you could hold me in your arms all night long," she murmured.

"If only I could," Cliff said. "If only I could."

At that moment Cliff knew that he didn't want to go on like this. He and Sarah were together in their hearts, but apart in too many other ways. He wanted to be with Sarah all the time, day and night.

Cliff knew that he wouldn't be satisfied with anything less than marriage.

Chapter Sixteen

Much to Sarah's relief, Elm's heart attack indeed proved to be a minor one, and he was released from the hospital in less than a week, but his doctor refused to let him continue as chairman of the Pioneer Day committee. Preparations for the annual celebration in September were put on hold for the time being.

Elm refused to recuperate at the farm, saying that he'd rather live in town where he was closer to the doctor and the hospital. Reluctantly Sarah agreed that this was best. Secretly Sarah suspected that Elm didn't want to renew the friction between the two of them. And, he said, he didn't want to be fussed over by two women. One woman's fussing was enough for him.

Charlotte fussed, but with moderation. She wasn't about to upset Elm in any way. Or Sarah, either.

Sarah fluttered and danced attendance on Elm for a day or two until she realized that she might be doing him more harm than good. After that, with her father on the way to recovery and Charlotte coping capably, Sarah was able to concentrate on the farm again.

The method of thick seeding that she had used when planting her sorghum had held weed growth to a minimum. The dense leaves shaded the soil and reduced evaporation. One bit of luck was that rainfall continued to be more than adequate. Sarah counted her blessings and answered with cautious optimism when other farmers asked her how her crop was doing. But secretly she was thrilled. She had tried something new. And so far it had worked.

Cliff rode out to meet her in the fields one day a few weeks after they had returned from Medallion. She recognized his car from a distance, wondering what he wanted. She hailed him heartily and walked rapidly to meet him.

"This is a good crop you've got here," said Cliff, pushing his brimmed cap back off his forehead. His eyes swept over the rich green of her plants. "It looks like its going to mature well before the first freeze."

"I hope so," Sarah said. "I'm proud of it."

"I didn't come out to admire your crop," he said with a grin. "I came out to admire you. And to ask you to come to Wichita with me this Saturday."

Sarah's happiness at seeing him dissolved into dismay.

"This Saturday, Cliff?"

"A friend of mine is the director at the community theater there. I knew her in Kansas City, and she sent me two tickets to their latest play and to the cast party afterward. Will you go with me, Sarah? It's really a treat. They're doing an original musical."

"Is it an overnight trip?"

"We could drive back the same night, although it's a long drive back from Wichita so late. If we want to spend the night, we could stay with my friend. She and her husband have a big house. They've invited us and several other people they used to know in Kansas City."

Sarah turned away and focused on the horizon. Her sorghum rustled in the breeze. Overhead a hawk circled.

"I can't leave the children with Mama and Pop this weekend, with Pop just out of the hospital. Lucy and Ben would be too much for Mama to handle."

"Then we can drive back that night. I'm sure you could find a baby-sitter for them."

Sarah shook her head. "I promised Mama I'd do her shopping for her on Saturday afternoon. I can't do it Saturday morning because a man from Sunshine Irrigation is coming out to talk to me about installing a pivot irrigation system. It's a busy day for me, Cliff."

"Sarah, you have to make time to have fun," Cliff said irritably. "You can't just leave it to chance. You have to plan your recreation."

Suddenly a dark cloud appeared on the horizon of their relationship.

"Some things are more important than running down to Wichita to see a play, Cliff," Sarah said quietly.

He slid an arm around her shoulders. "Hey, don't be angry. I was only trying to lighten up your life a little." He smiled at her, a smile that was usually infectious.

She wouldn't let him make light of her refusal. "Can't you see that helping my parents is important to me?" she said.

"Of course," he replied. "And getting out of Curtisville now and then is important to me."

Sarah kicked at a lump of dirt. It scattered. She glanced at Cliff. His lips were set in a firm line. She had always known that Curtisville wasn't enough to hold him; nor was she. Her spirits dropped like lead, and instead of the fresh green scent of summer, she smelled defeat.

"Then I suggest that you go ahead to Wichita without me," she said tonelessly.

"Sarah—"

"Never mind," she said, shaking his hand off her arm. "It's really fine with me if you want to go alone."

"Is it?" he said unbelievingly. "Is it?" Her resigned tone flabbergasted him. If the tables had been turned, and she wanted to go to a play in Wichita without him, it wouldn't have been all right with him at all. He'd thought she felt the same way about him, and he was floored to find that she did not.

"I have no desire to keep you from doing the things you enjoy most," Sarah said.

The things he enjoyed most? Didn't she know that he most enjoyed being with her, no matter what? But she was striding away from him, her shoulders hunched, her braid bobbing against her back. Something about the set of her head on her neck seemed brittle and nervous. She held her chin high, and her braid flapping against her back looked for all the world like a golden head of wheat. Cliff shook his head. Maybe the heat was affecting him. Maybe he wasn't hearing her correctly. This all seemed like a bad movie, speeded up until it was incomprehensible.

"Sarah," he said again.

"I have to ride over to the Inman place before quitting time," she tossed over her shoulder.

He didn't pursue her, though she thought he might. He only stood staring after her in a perplexed way, his cap in his hand.

She got in her pickup truck and barreled toward the highway. She put on her sunglasses when she was halfway there, not to guard against the glare of the sun, but because when she met Henry, she didn't want him to see that she'd been crying.

CLIFF, STILL NOT UNDERSTANDING what had gotten into Sarah, went to Wichita and had a miserable time. He stayed at his friends' house, drank too much at the cast party and met an actress who liked him more than he liked her. The actress followed him to his friends' house where they sat around, and she smoked brown cigarettes, reminding him of his past follies. Finally he managed to excuse himself and go to bed alone.

He dreamed of Sarah that night, a Sarah wearing blue jeans and tiny pearl earrings, standing with her legs thrown back in that peculiar double-jointed way of hers as she looked out over fields emerald green with sorghum.

He drove back to Curtisville on Sunday in time for church. He'd attended Sunday-morning church with Sarah regularly. But she wasn't there on this day, and he didn't run into Elm and Charlotte or the kids, either. He didn't stop on the front lawn to socialize with the parishioners but left as soon as possible.

He was concerned that something might have happened to Elm, so he stopped by the little house and, to his relief, found an apparently healthy Elm and Charlotte relaxing and eating tuna sandwiches.

"What, no Sunday dinner today?" Cliff asked.

Charlotte laughed. "I'm taking a break from Sunday dinner," she told him. "It's too hot to cook anyway."

"What are Sarah and the children doing for dinner?" he asked casually, and was sorry that he asked when Charlotte regarded him intently.

"Why, I suppose they're having Sunday dinner at the farm," she said. "Why don't you ride out there, Cliff? I know Sarah would be happy to see you."

I wonder, thought Cliff. It was the first time he had ever doubted that Sarah would welcome him if he showed up.

He wasn't sure whether Charlotte and Elm knew of his invitation to Sarah to attend the play or of the reason that she had refused to go. Her reason, after all, was tied up with helping her parents. After a few more minutes' conversation, Cliff decided that Charlotte and Elm did not know of the refused invitation and would be upset if they did, so he didn't inform them.

"How is the Pioneer Day committee getting along without you, Elm?" asked Cliff.

Elm, who had regained his color and was looking fit again after his heart attack, shook his head mournfully. "Not too well," he said. "They can't get anyone to take it over."

"They'll manage to have Pioneer Day, won't they?"

"Maybe not," said Elm.

"I don't see how we can cancel Pioneer Day," worried Charlotte. "Curtisville wouldn't be Curtisville without it. Besides, Elm is so well organized that he has everything written down to do. He just can't get anyone to do it."

"Look," Elm said. He opened a folder on the kitchen table. "Here is the lady to contact for the balloon concession. And here's the guy who arranges the booths for the craft show."

"You've certainly done a lot of groundwork," agreed Cliff.

"Yes, but most of the Pioneer Day committee has fizzled out now that I'm not heading it up anymore. I could make the necessary phone calls to get things moving again, but I can't go driving around talking to the merchants who want to participate as sponsors."

"Why don't you go ahead and make the phone calls, Elm? And give me this list of merchants you need to see and tell me what you need to talk to them about. I'll call on them. I usually have time left over after lunch."

"You'd do that?" Elm asked skeptically.

"I'd enjoy it," Cliff said.

"It's nice of you to help out," Charlotte told him.

"Pioneer Day sounds like one of the best small-town celebrations I've heard about. It would be a shame not to have it."

"Won't you have a sandwich, Cliff? We have an extra one," offered Charlotte.

Cliff ate half a sandwich with them, mostly to be polite, and because they seemed to crave company. Then he excused himself. He had to figure out how to approach Sarah.

Time hung heavy on Cliff's hands. Shortly after he got back to the inn, he decided to drive out to see Sarah, then he decided against it. Telephoning was out, since Marlene was on duty at the desk. He thought briefly about using the pay phone at the end of Main Street near the park, but decided that he'd have little privacy there, either.

Everyone in Curtisville was busy with family today. As much as he liked the town, it wasn't such a great place for a single person. Of course, if he had wanted to hang out with a singles crowd, he could have stayed in Wichita. Judging from what went on last night, there would be plenty of action left over for today.

Cliff didn't want action. What he wanted was something else. Peace and quiet, and happiness shining from a pair of velvety brown eyes. He didn't care what kind of mood Sarah was in, he had to see her today. And Ben. And Lucy.

On the ride out to the farm, he smiled to himself. It had only been a few days since he'd been there, since he'd seen Sarah, but it seemed like forever.

He felt as though he was coming home.

"BEN, GRAB HIM!"

"I can't, Mom!" hollered Ben.

"He's getting out that hole!"

"I've got him! Oops, he got away!"

Ben and Sarah were scrambling around the lambs' pen in chase of the bleating lambs. Sarah couldn't imagine how they had done it, but Tweedledum and Tweedledee had managed to butt a metal patch off the side of the corrugated metal barn and were trying their best to shove their way through the resulting hole.

Like a scene in a Three Stooges movie, Ben fell down in the sawdust on the floor, and just in time, Sarah managed to divert Tweedledee from trampling on his foot.

Ben lurched to his feet and brushed off his jeans. "We'll have to move the railing over, Mom," he said.

"You're right. Otherwise they'll just keep working at that hole until they get through it." She didn't know how to patch the hole herself. It was a job for Henry to do.

One of the lambs butted her playfully and waggled a tagged ear at her. Sarah would be heartily happy when the day arrived for Ben to sell these animals. She'd never liked sheep much.

"I've got some lumber over here," said Ben, dragging a board over.

"It shouldn't be too hard to do this," Sarah said, surveying the situation. "We'll attach the new boards to the old fence, and fortunately there's a support over there where we can nail the other side."

Ben went and got nails and a hammer, and Sarah brushed the hair out of her eyes. It was hot today, breathlessly hot. The leaves on the sycamore tree hung listlessly, weighted down with a coating of dust. Lucy remained inside the house, drawing crayon pictures of her visit to Medallion. They hadn't even eaten Sunday dinner, nor had they gone to church. It was too hot.

Ben stopped hammering. "I think I hear Cliff's car!" he exclaimed before throwing down the hammer and running out of the barn. Quilter, who had just settled down in a far corner of the barn to nurse her kittens, opened one startled green eye.

Sarah tested the railing they had built and decided it was steady enough to hold the lambs if they butted against it. Both Tweedledum and Tweedledee were standing in front of their trough, eyeing her with small enigmatic sheeps' smiles.

"Now don't you two try to get out of here," Sarah cautioned them. They merely stared at her.

Sarah massaged the aching small of her back for a moment before stepping outside. Cliff was getting out of his car, and Ben was excitedly relating the story of how the lambs almost got out of the barn.

Cliff smiled at Sarah over Ben's head. Tentatively she smiled back. She wasn't sure if he had gone to Wichita or not. She figured he probably had. She hadn't heard from him at all on Saturday, which was unusual. Of course, she hadn't been home all afternoon. He would have tried to find her, she thought, if he had been in town.

"I brought ice cream," he said. "Is anyone hungry?"

"You bet," said Ben, hopping up and down. Cliff reached into the car and brought out a gallon container of rapidly melting raspberry sherbet.

"Why don't you and Lucy get out the bowls and spoons," suggested Sarah. "Set them on the dining room table. We'll eat inside since it's so hot today."

"Okay," said Ben before racing toward the house carrying the sherbet.

Sarah and Cliff stared at each other. He noticed that the little wisps of hair around her face were stuck to her skin with perspiration. A wet stain between her shoulder blades spread across the back of her cotton shirt.

"I'm a mess," she apologized.

"You look fine to me," he replied.

"Tweedledum and Tweedledee almost got out."

"Ben told me."

"Yes, I heard him."

They stood staring at each other awkwardly, each wanting to ask the other certain questions.

Sarah wanted to ask Cliff, "Did you go to Wichita without me? Did you have a good time?" She hoped the answer was no on both counts.

Cliff wanted to ask Sarah, "Did you miss me? Did you wish you'd come with me? He hoped the answer was yes to both questions.

But neither of them asked these questions.

The heat out here was stifling, thought Sarah. The red geraniums in the planter on the porch drooped their heads, and the grass at the base of the sycamore tree was scorched and brown. The shrill of the cicadas in the shrubbery made her ears ache, and the dust of Cliff's arrival hung motionless in the air. Sarah sneezed.

"Gesundheit," said Cliff automatically, but it broke the silence.

Lucy appeared on the porch. The heat made her look wavy, like a reflection in a fun-house mirror.

"The ice cream is ready. I put it in the bowls."

"Good, Lucy," Sarah said automatically. She turned toward the house.

Lucy disappeared inside. The screen door slammed.

Cliff reached out and touched the back of Sarah's neck as they walked, the soft white part of it under her braid, and Sarah allowed this. Her hair there was damp, and it clung to his fingers. He disentangled them, letting his fingers move vertebra by vertebra down her spine. Sarah drew in her breath sharply, and while they were still hidden from the house by the broad trunk of the sycamore tree, he drifted his fingers all the way along her spine until he reached her waist.

Sarah stiffened, shot him an unfathomable look, and with a spurt of determination, moved quickly ahead.

Reluctantly he let his hand fall to his side, and then he followed her into the house.

Somewhere an owl cried a song of mourning. Sarah hung an electric lantern on a nail in the barn and shook the new railing in the lambs' pen.

"It looks like it will hold," Cliff said.

"I don't know," she said. "The lambs are pretty strong." There were deep shadows in the barn. The electric lantern threw their faces into sharp relief.

"I'll make sure that they can't possibly escape," Cliff said. He picked up the hammer and nails and, kneeling in the sawdust, hammered several nails. His muscles were well-defined beneath his white knit shirt, and they flexed with each blow of the hammer.

"There," Cliff said when he had finished. "They won't get out now."

"Thanks, Cliff," Sarah said.

He reached up and lifted the lantern off the nail. Sarah's face looked pinched and white. His heart warmed toward her.

"Come on," said Cliff. "We need to talk."

He stopped beneath the sycamore tree. Experimentally he propped the electric lantern against the trunk.

"Turn it off. The battery will only run down," Sarah said. Gracefully she folded her knees under her and sank into the purple shadows under the tree. Cliff sat beside her. They waited quietly, letting their eyes adjust to the darkness.

Sarah's hair gleamed in the moonlight. She had showered and changed clothes. She wore the same outfit she'd worn on the Fourth of July, the night they had first kissed.

"I went to Wichita," he began.

"You don't have to confess anything to me," Sarah interjected.

"I have nothing to confess, Sarah."

She tossed her head. She stared at the moon. It was so bright that she couldn't make out its features. It was so bright that it stung her eyes.

She tried to find an easy way to say the words that she wanted to say, but they didn't come naturally.

"Cliff, I—" She stopped, unable to go on.

"Is something wrong, Sarah?" He began to grow alarmed. She'd been acting strangely toward him all afternoon. Her smiles had been distracted and seemed forced.

"Oh," she said in a low tone, so low that he almost couldn't hear her.

"You can tell me, whatever it is," he told her.

Her eyes met his. They looked oddly defiant. He didn't know why.

"Cliff, I don't think we should see each other anymore."

He was so stunned that he couldn't speak. When he did, it was with all the incredulity that he felt at that moment.

"Just because I went to Wichita?"

Sarah shook her head. She stared at the ground for a moment, then blinked. "No, it isn't that."

"I had a terrible time, you know. It wasn't any fun without you. I met an actress who smoked brown cigarettes. I didn't like her. I—"

"It isn't going to work," Sarah said in despair. "I know it just isn't going to work."

"What?"

"You and me. Our relationship. You've already tired of our way of life here. You're used to big cities, fancy entertainment, sophisticated people. Your friend, the director of this play, for instance. I've never even met anyone who directs plays."

"What on earth does directing plays have to do with you and me? I love you, Sarah."

"Oh, I think that *you* think you love me. But maybe you *wanted* to be in love with someone after the disillusionment you went through after Devon. Here I was, ready, willing and able."

"Do you honestly believe that love is some kind of emotional aspirin?" he shot back at her with exasperation.

"Let me finish," she said. She looked him squarely in the eye. "Cliff, I love you more than I thought I could love anyone again. But we both know that love isn't going to be enough. What I want and what you want are two different things."

He tried to take her hand, but she pulled it away.

"Sarah, will you please listen to me?" he pleaded.

"There's no point in arguing. We're too different. What we expect from life is different—oh, I don't know, Cliff, explaining it is hard." Tears ran down her face now, and he moved to take her in his arms. She pulled away, but not completely. He held her by the upper arms, kneeling in the dried grass, smelling her Ivory-soap scent and wondering what to say to her. Apparently she had ideas about their relationship that she'd never revealed.

"I'm not enough for you, Cliff," she said. She started to sob, and watching her sadness crumble her face was too much for him. He released her arms, and she raised her hands to cover her face. He allowed her this privacy, his mind racing.

What did she mean, she wasn't enough for him? What did she mean, they were too different? Hadn't he taken her home to meet his parents so that she would see how similar their backgrounds were? Hadn't he made it clear how much he delighted in her company, how much he loved her?

"You're everything I ever wanted in a woman," he said firmly, knowing it to be true now more than ever before.

"I'm a *farmer*, Cliff," she said. "I get dirty and I ride a tractor, and I don't go to cocktail parties and I never will smoke brown cigarettes. I can't even manage time off to spend Saturday in Wichita. It's always going to be that way—I'll never change.''

"Thank God for that," Cliff said fervently.

Sarah wiped a tear trickling down her cheek.

"I can't face another abandonment. First Norrie and then James—yes, his death seemed like a kind of abandonment to me. Anyway, I've already made up my mind. I should never have become so attached to you. I should have known from the beginning that it wouldn't work."

"It worked pretty well up until a few days ago. You got your hackles up over nothing. I wouldn't have gone to Wichita if you hadn't been acting so standoffish," Cliff pointed out.

"Can't you see that going to Wichita doesn't have anything to do with this? What I'm saying is that I have to get out while I can. I have to put you out of my life now, while I still have the strength to do it." She drew a deep, trembling breath.

"Sarah, I love you, and I want you exactly as you are," Cliff said. "In fact, I want to marry you. If you'll have me, that is."

She stared at him. In the moonlight he could tell that all the color had drained from her face.

"Oh, Cliff," she said. "No. You don't mean that. You can't."

"Does that mean you will, or you won't?" He stared at her, wondering how things had gotten into this state of affairs.

"Cliff, I'm honored. But I see that it will never work. Never in a million years."

She had, in one fluid movement, risen to her feet.

"Sarah!"

She turned to him, and her eyes shone with unshed tears. "Cliff, I can't marry you. If we married, it would be for all the wrong reasons. I'm refusing for all the right ones. I really don't want to see you again." She wheeled and began to walk swiftly to the house. Her white trousers glowed blue in the moonlight.

Cliff steadied himself with one hand on the sycamore tree's trunk. Sarah disappeared into the house. The screen door closed with its familiar *thwump.*

He certainly hadn't known he was going to ask Sarah to marry him tonight.

And he certainly hadn't known she would refuse.

Chapter Seventeen

Cliff threw himself into his work. He had several farms to manage for absentee owners, and that took a lot of his time. He unsnarled the record books of a farmer in Marquette, and he advised a man near Lindsborg about an irrigation system. But through it all he wondered, *why?*

He loved Sarah. Sarah loved him. She had the peculiar idea that he didn't like living in Curtisville. True, there wasn't much to do in such a small town. But what there was to do, he liked. He achieved peace of mind when he worshipped in Sarah's church with its age-darkened walnut pews and glowing stained-glass windows. He enjoyed swimming in the old swimming hole at Windrush Valley Farm and paddling on the pond in the park in his rubber raft. He liked heading out across the fields on an ATV beside Ben. All these were fairly unsophisticated pleasures, and Cliff was initially amazed at how happy they made him at first. Now he had grown used to such simple gifts. They seemed altogether normal, natural and right.

Once in a while he'd like to take in a group like the Philip Pharr Dancers, but that wasn't a necessity. What was necessary to him was Sarah and her lively imagination, her dedication to home and family and her determination to make a go of Windrush Valley Farm all by herself. She was necessary, but she was out of reach.

He spent a lot of time in his room at the inn, brooding over what had gone wrong with Sarah. Once he drove out to the farm, past fields glowing with Sarah's bumper crop of sorghum. He saw her in the waving stalks of sorghum and in the fertile, well-managed soil. He imagined Sarah as the elemental earth mother. He had to see her, to talk some sense into her. At the farmhouse Lucy met him at the door and scampered off to tell Sarah that he was there. In a few minutes Lucy returned, dragging her feet, and told him in a quavery voice that her mother had a headache and didn't want to see him.

"Where's Ben?" he said, because he missed the little guy.

"He's visiting Grandma and Grandpa. He'll be sorry he missed you," Lucy said. She looked so woebegone that he wanted to pat her on the head and tell her not to worry, that everything would be all right. But all he did was turn around and walk back to his car, and he didn't think that everything would be all right at all.

Cliff filled lonely hours by helping Elm with his work for Pioneer Day. On his evening recreational walk, he often stopped by Elm and Charlotte's small house to use the telephone to call one person or another about preparations for the event, and soon Cliff had taken over the majority of Elm's committee work. This suited both of them. Elm could hang over Cliff's shoulder and supervise, but he didn't actually have the responsibility of pulling the festival together.

"Cliff, you seem to enjoy all this," said Charlotte one evening when Cliff and Elm had spread papers relating to Pioneer Day all over the small kitchen table.

"I do," said Cliff. "The people in Curtisville are so cooperative. Why, I asked the Supermart to donate ten dozen Popsicles, and all they wanted to know was, 'What flavor?'"

"That's the way people are around here. Everyone in the community loves Pioneer Day, and we look forward to it all year long," said Charlotte.

Cliff didn't know what Charlotte and Elm knew about his ruined relationship with their daughter. He never mentioned it. He was able to enjoy Charlotte and Elm for themselves. He wished things could be the way they used to be, however. He missed being part of their family.

Sometimes at night Cliff would get in his rubber raft and float out to the middle of the pond at the park, and he would lie back and stare at the vast sky full of stars, and he would ask out loud, "Why? Why doesn't she want to marry me?"

The stars never answered.

"I CAN'T BELIEVE you told him you didn't want to see him anymore," said Charlotte in dismay after Sarah confided what had happened.

"Don't run on and on about it, Mama," Sarah said.

"A nice man like that," huffed Charlotte, unable to resist making it clear exactly where she stood in the matter.

"I asked you not to talk about it," repeated Sarah, who was perilously close to tears.

"Somebody else might take a liking to Cliff," warned her mother before dropping the subject. After that, Charlotte seldom mentioned Cliff. In fact, she spoke of him so infrequently that Sarah grew curious to know what Cliff was doing.

"He stops by the house now and then," Charlotte said with obvious reluctance when Sarah asked, and then Charlotte said no more.

Sarah found an expensive gold Cross pen that she knew belonged to Cliff. It rolled out from under the television set at the farmhouse when she vacuumed. She gave the pen to Elm, who promised to return it to Cliff.

"Did you give Cliff his pen?" Sarah asked on her next visit to her parents.

"Oh, yes," Charlotte assured her.

"I suppose he was glad to have it back."

"I'm sure."

"What's Cliff been doing lately?" she asked. She concealed her almost morbid curiosity by bending over to retie her shoelace.

"I heard Ida Rae say that he went to Wichita again last weekend," volunteered Elm from behind the newspaper he was reading.

Sarah finished tying her shoelace and made her excuses to her parents. She didn't like to think about Cliff's going to Wichita.

"Why doesn't Cliff come over anymore?" asked Ben one day about a week later when she was helping him rearrange the toys on his bedroom shelf.

"He's very busy," Sarah said, paying inordinate interest to the placement of a Tonka jeep.

"Doesn't he like us?"

Sarah caught the anxiety in Ben's question. She sat down beside him on his bed and curved an arm around his shoulder.

"Of course Cliff likes us," she said.

"Then why doesn't he come over?" Ben's lower lip stuck out, and this made him look a lot like Elm. Sarah's heart went out to him.

She struggled for words to tell Ben what had happened.

"Sometimes, honey, adults find that they can't be friends anymore. Then they each go their own way. That's what happened to Cliff and me."

"I can still be friends with Cliff, can't I? We were going to mount the butterflies I've caught. He was teaching me how to throw a curveball. We were going to start a stamp collection this winter."

Heartsick, Sarah knew she should never have allowed Cliff to become so close to her children. At the time it had made sense. They lacked a real father figure in their lives, and Cliff liked them so much. But it had only caused heartbreak in the end.

"You can still be friends with Cliff," she told Ben.

"When will he come and see me?" Ben's eyes searched her face.

"I—I don't know," she said lamely. She could tell right away that this didn't satisfy Ben. He turned his back to her and stared at the wall.

"Ben, I—"

"It's okay, Mom," he said with a toneless finality that could only mean that it was not okay.

Sarah's hands fell to her sides. She wanted to cradle her son in her arms and tell him that she knew how much it hurt to be separated from someone you loved. She knew that better than anyone. But she also knew that Ben would only resent such a gesture, and maybe she couldn't blame him.

After this incident, she retreated to her bedroom where she lay down on her bed with a cool washcloth over her eyes. It was a Saturday afternoon, and the farm was quiet. Work and prayer, her sovereign remedies for everything, weren't helping her get over Cliff Oenbrink. Even spending extra time with her children palled after a while. They were good companions up to a point, but they weren't Cliff.

She was lulled by the gentle breeze blowing across her bed, and she fell into a doze. The next thing she knew, Lucy was tugging at her arm and saying urgently, "I can't find Ben, Mom."

"Maybe he's in the barn with Tweedledum and Tweedledee," mumbled Sarah as she shook Lucy's hand away.

"I looked there."

Sarah forced herself to come fully awake.

"Maybe he's out catching more butterflies," Sarah said, propping herself up on her elbows. She felt a twinge of worry, but she pushed it away. The wet washcloth fell on her forearm, and it felt wet and clammy. With an involuntary shiver, Sarah tossed the washcloth over the back of a nearby chair.

"I don't think he's looking for butterflies," Lucy said. "His specimen jar is on the sink."

Sarah stood up. Her head ached, and her back hurt. She didn't feel like coping with Ben now.

"Let's go look for him," she said nevertheless. Lucy slid her hand into Sarah's, and together they went downstairs.

"We were watching television together, and Ben went into the kitchen. I thought he went to get cookies, but he never came back. I looked everywhere for him, but I couldn't find him. Did I do the right thing to wake you up, Mom?" Lucy asked anxiously.

"Of course you did," Sarah reassured her. She held her aching head between both hands for a moment, trying to think of where Ben might be. She went into the downstairs bathroom and took an aspirin, hoping it would clear her head.

She walked out on the back porch and descended the porch stairs into a stifling hot day. Her eyelids felt as puffy as marshmallows. She peered under the porch. Maybe Ben was playing some solitary game there. He and Spanky used to spend a lot of time under the porch on hot days. But Ben wasn't there now.

She walked out to the barn with Lucy following along. Tweedledee and Tweedledum regarded her with bland expressions from their pen. Ben wasn't there, either.

Quilter shook off her nursing kittens and ran to greet Sarah. "Have you seen Ben, Quilter?" Sarah asked as she stooped to stroke the cat. Quilter only blinked.

It was then that Sarah noticed that one of the Honda all-terrain vehicles was missing. Her heart stilled in her chest.

"Lucy," said Sarah, trying to keep her voice casual. "Do you suppose Ben went riding on one of the ATVs?"

Lucy saw that one of them was missing. She lifted surprised eyes to Sarah's.

"I didn't hear him take it out," she said. "I think I would have heard him."

"Think hard, Lucy," said Sarah. "Did you hear any noise that might have been Ben taking that ATV out of the barn?"

Lucy considered this carefully. "I was watching *The Sound of Music* on television. I wasn't paying any attention to Ben, Mom. I *think* I would have heard him, but maybe I didn't."

Ben could have taken the ATV out of the barn without either of them hearing him if he wanted to. It wouldn't have been too hard for him to push it up the hill and then start it when he was over the hill and out of hearing distance of the house. Isn't that what Cliff used to do in his car when he sneaked out of his house to meet his girlfriend when he lived in Medallion? Sarah wondered if Cliff had ever told Ben that particular story. Cliff was such a hero to Ben.

"I'll have to go looking for him," Sarah said.

"You mean you're going to leave me here all alone?"

"Maybe I'd better take you over to the Vogels' house," Sarah told her.

"But Mom—"

"The Vogels are packing up this weekend, getting ready to move. Maybe you can help Mrs. Vogel."

"I like Mrs. Vogel, Mom, but what about Ben?"

"I'm going to find him," Sarah said with a certainty she didn't feel. Fighting panic, she shepherded Lucy into the pickup and drove the short distance to the Vogels' place. She told Mina that Ben was missing, and Mina agreed that Lucy could stay with her as long as she needed to. Sarah was back on her farm in less than seven minutes.

In the barn, she noticed that Ben had not worn either helmet or goggles. Both were hanging from their hooks. This only made her worry more. Ben never had liked to wear goggles or helmet, but on their tame forays around the farm during which Sarah was careful to stress safety, she had insisted.

With shaking fingers, Sarah lifted the keys from their nail, and with a sputter and a roar, she started up the remaining ATV. She turned sharply in the yard and gunned the motor all the way up the hill. As she drove it, she felt the tendency of the vehicle to lean backward. Without skillful driving, a three-wheeler like this one could tip backward on a hill and either crush or hurt the driver.

The vehicles might be unstable, but they were necessary to farm life. Because they were small, they could go places where a pickup truck or a tractor could not. ATVs possessed both power and maneuverability, making it easy to check on a crop in a far field. After James's accident Sarah had briefly considered getting rid of both ATVs. She hadn't, mainly because they were a convenience and because, to her, they were a fact of farm life. Now she almost wished she had sold both of them.

A brisk wind pushed her along as she roared toward the creek. The swimming hole was one place where she thought she might find Ben, but he wasn't there.

She wheeled the ATV around and set off toward the road. A too-sharp turn caused her to put down a foot to regain her balance. This again reminded Sarah how unstable this machine was. She tried to keep her feet on the pegs and to round curves by shifting her weight to the outside while leaning in slightly. She could only hope that Ben, too, would remember to observe all the safety rules.

Dust powdered the roadside weeds and swirled around her as she rode, all the while searching for a sight of Ben in the fields. There was no sign of him at the old fence by the highway where the rambling roses grew, nor was he in the orchard. She was beginning to feel desperate for a sight of his shaggy yellow hair, his patched blue jeans.

She swallowed, pushed up the windscreen on her helmet to wipe the perspiration from her forehead, and turned the ATV around. It was getting late in the day. She had no idea where Ben was, and in her present state of mind, she couldn't think of anyplace else to look. She'd have to get outside help. She headed back toward the house.

Afterward she didn't remember racing down the hill or dismounting from the ATV. She didn't remember how she got to the house. All she remembered was the icy fear in the pit of her stomach and the way her head throbbed so that she could barely think.

She paused for a moment, trying to decide who she should call. Henry? She dialed Henry's home number, and then she dialed his girlfriend's number. No one answered at either place. Frank Vogel—that was it. Frank would know what to do to find Ben.

"You mean you haven't found Ben yet?" said Mina Vogel, her voice sharp with alarm.

"No, and I—I'm so worried. Ben's never done anything like this before."

"Are you sure he took the ATV out?"

"I'm sure. It's missing, and there wasn't anyone else around the farm today who could have used it. And Ben does like to ride it, and he doesn't get to ride it often enough." Ben had pleaded only yesterday to ride the ATV, but Sarah had refused. He'd pleaded to go riding after dinner. Sarah had been exhausted from working in the fields since seven in the morning. Sarah's cheeks ached from held-back tears. Why, oh why hadn't she gone with him then?

"Frank has ridden to McPherson with Bernie to help Bernie move some used furniture he bought. I'm not sure when Frank will be back, Sarah, but he'll call you as soon as comes in."

"Thanks, Mina," Sarah said. When she hung up, she realized that, if she wanted immediate help, she had no choice but to call Cliff.

Cliff had often ridden with Ben on the ATVs. Maybe he knew of some particular place where Ben liked to go. She dialed the number of the Country Inn. Marlene answered, and Sarah tersely asked for Cliff.

"Why, I'll get him right now," Marlene said.

Cliff came to the phone immediately.

"Sarah?" he said, and she thought her heart would stop.

"Cliff, it's Ben," she said rapidly.

"Is anything wrong?" Cliff asked. He picked up on the apprehension in her voice right away.

"Oh, Cliff, Ben's taken the ATV out by himself, and I don't know where he is," she said, fighting tears.

"I'll be there right away," he said. "Do you want me to bring your parents out with me?" He knew Sarah needed all the moral support she could get, especially if something had happened to Ben.

"I don't want to upset Pop," Sarah said. She had a great fear of precipitating another heart attack.

"Elm's over at the Chatterbox. I just left him there. If you'd like, I'll swing by their house and pick up your mother. She can leave a note that she's gone to see you." They had done this once before, and Cliff knew that Charlotte's absence wouldn't worry Elm.

"All right. I'd like to have my mother here with me. Thank you, Cliff."

"We'll be there as soon as we can," Cliff promised.

Cliff stopped to pick up Charlotte, explaining briefly that Ben was missing. Charlotte, who managed crises well, stayed calm. They reached the farm in record time. When they reached the crest of Lornbacher Hill, they found Sarah pacing back and forth watching for Cliff's car.

"I've thought of every place I know where Ben might be," she said. "Cliff, when you ride with Ben, where do you go?"

"The swimming hole. Lucy's tree house, places like that," said Cliff.

"I didn't think of Lucy's tree house," Sarah said, wringing her hands.

"Let Cliff go and look for Ben," soothed Charlotte, slipping an arm around her tall daughter's waist.

"Cliff?" Sarah's eyes looked frantic.

"I'll ride down to the tree house on the ATV. Also, Ben might have gone over to the ridge on the Vogel farm. He likes the view from there."

"Sarah, how long has it been since you ate anything?" Charlotte didn't like the white pinched look around Sarah's eyes.

"I—oh, I don't know. At lunch I had a sandwich, but afterward I had a headache, and then I went upstairs to lie down. Oh, Mama, it's my fault! I should have talked with Ben more when he asked me about Cliff this afternoon." She watched as Cliff sped away on the ATV, wishing she could have gone with him. It was unsafe for two people to ride on one; otherwise she would have.

"There, there," said Charlotte, wondering what Sarah was talking about. "Come inside where it's cooler, and I'll fix you a glass of iced tea. No good will come of fretting. Ben will turn up safe and sound."

"Will he?" Sarah said distractedly. "Will he?"

"Of course," Charlotte said. She sat Sarah down on a kitchen chair and forced herself to keep a conversation going. Sarah needed to talk. Anyone could see that.

"So Ben asked about Cliff, did he?" Charlotte prompted.

Sarah sipped her tea. "Ben wanted to know why Cliff doesn't come over anymore. He misses Cliff so much, you know. I could have spent more time with Ben. I could have gone out on the ATVs with him today, but my head hurt, and I didn't like to think about Cliff never coming over anymore. And now Ben's gone, and I don't know where."

"Sarah, if you're thinking about James's accident, stop it right now."

"I can't help thinking about it," Sarah said brokenly.

"Well, don't. Ben's just indulging himself in a bit of boyish rebellion, and he'll turn up safe and sound."

"He didn't wear his helmet and goggles," murmured Sarah. "He should have worn his helmet and goggles."

"Still, Ben knows more than most kids about safe riding practices, because you taught him."

"He was too young to take the Kansas Farm Bureau's safety course, did you know that? I tried to get him in it, but you had to be thirteen."

They heard the roar of an ATV coming over Lornbacher Hill, and they both jumped to their feet. It was Cliff.

"He wasn't at the tree house or on the ridge," reported Cliff. He looked grim.

Sarah remembered something with a start. "I've just thought of one more place," she said excitedly. "There are some shallow caves far up Oley's Creek on the Wilsons' property. Ben's only been there once or twice, but he's always been curious about them. Maybe, just maybe, he decided to explore them."

"I don't know how to get there," Cliff said.

"The caves are reachable by car or truck," Sarah said. She lifted her keys off the ledge by the door and set off for the pickup at a near gallop with Cliff close on her heels.

"I'll stay here in case Ben comes home," Charlotte called after them, but by that time Sarah had started the motor of the pickup truck and Charlotte's last words were lost in the roar.

Sarah drove at breakneck speed, over the hill and down the other side. At a narrow dirt road, she turned right, bumping over gullies left by recent rains. Cliff glanced at her. The color had faded from her cheeks, and she had lost weight since he'd seen her.

"There's a narrow track through this grove of trees," Sarah said as she slowed the truck. "Help me look for it. There are overhanging branches concealing it.

"Is that the place?" Cliff pointed to a barely discernible trail.

"That's it," Sarah said. She turned the pickup abruptly.

"I could hold these branches aside," volunteered Cliff.

"That takes too much time," Sarah said through clenched teeth as she gunned the engine. The branches squealed across the top of the truck, and Cliff winced as one struck the windshield. Sarah kept driving, and he admired her grit.

She pulled the pickup to a stop in front of a flowering ash tree. Before Cliff could open his door, Sarah had leaped from her seat.

"We have to climb down a bank," she said, leading him through heavy undergrowth that ripped at their clothes.

"Wait," Cliff said suddenly. He had spied a glint of metal through the scrub. He bounded through the concealing vines and found the ATV three-wheeler.

"He's around here somewhere," Sarah said.

They scrambled down a muddy embankment.

"Ben?" called Sarah. "Ben?"

She thought she heard an answering cry, but she couldn't be sure. At the bottom of the embankment, she and Cliff fought their way through snarled shrubbery. Sarah spotted a small figure sprawled on the ground in front of the entrance to the caves. The red T-shirt was familiar, and so were the well-worn jeans.

"Ben!" She ran to him. He was lying on his stomach. And he was gazing with rapt attention at the scurryings of about five hundred ants beside an overturned rock.

"Ben!" she said again.

He barely looked up. "Hi, Mom! Look at these ants. Aren't they amazing?"

Sarah and Cliff exchanged incredulous glances. They had just spent the most nerve-racking hour of their lives searching for Ben, and Ben couldn't have cared less. Cliff's lips curved upward in a grin, and he rolled his eyes as if to say, "Boys will be boys."

"I turned over this rock and found all these ants under it," Ben explained, without looking up. "If I put the rock back very carefully, I won't even disturb their nest. Look how some of the ants carry those little white packages around. I think the white packages are ant larvae. Aren't they, Cliff?"

"You're probably right, Ben."

Sarah was weak with relief, but she was also outraged at the behavior of her son. "Benjamin Morrow, I certainly intend to have a word with you about taking that ATV out all by yourself. I've been worried sick about you, and so have a lot of other people."

For the first time since their arrival, Ben looked up with interest. "No kidding!" he exclaimed.

"No kidding," said Sarah. Cliff put an arm around her shoulders and hugged her to him. She smiled up at him gratefully.

"Let's put the rock back now, son, and get back to the house. It will soon be dark."

Ben let Cliff replace the rock over the ants' nest, and the three of them slowly climbed the embankment, easing their way by pulling themselves up with the aid of bushes and small saplings. Once they had reached the top, Cliff and Sarah lifted the ATV into the bed of the pickup truck, and the three of them rode up front in the cab with Cliff driving. Ben sat very quietly between Sarah and Cliff on the way back to the farm.

"What kind of trouble am I in, Mom?" he asked.

"Serious trouble. You took the ATV without my permission, you didn't wear either goggles or a helmet, and you frightened me to pieces. Why did you do it, Ben?"

"I was so mad," said Ben. "I just wanted to go away by myself."

"Angry at me?" asked Sarah.

"No, mad at Cliff. Because he doesn't come around anymore."

Cliff and Sarah exchanged a startled glance. The silence grew uncomfortable.

"I mean, it was like Cliff went away and left me flat," Ben said forlornly.

Sarah could certainly understand Ben's feelings. Norrie had gone away and left her flat, too, and she had only recently admitted to herself that she'd felt abandoned by James. One of the reasons she'd broken up with Cliff was her fear of abandonment.

"I think I know where you're coming from, Ben," she said slowly, keeping her eyes on the road ahead. "But it wasn't your fault that Cliff didn't come over anymore. He wasn't abandoning you."

Cliff cleared his throat. "That's right, Ben," he said. "I stayed away because your mother and I needed time to think things over."

"Well, have you thought things over?" Ben asked, looking hopefully from one to the other.

Cliff's eyes sought Sarah's. When he recognized the emotion in their depths, he said, "Yes, Ben. Yes, we have."

"Do I have to have a punishment, Mom?"

"Yes, I'm afraid so." But she put her arm around Ben, hugging him close.

Ben thought for a moment, and then he said with resignation, "That's fair, I guess. I'm sorry, Mom. But I had fun. And I sure do like those ants."

"For punishment, you can clean out the barn," Sarah said.

"Aw, Mom," said Ben, but that was all he said.

"Sometimes, if you'd like," said Cliff, "you and I could go visit your ants. We could take the ATVs. That is, if it's all right with your mother."

Her eyes met Cliff's over the top of Ben's head. There was a question in his, and she looked away in confusion. If there was a question, there should be an answer.

"Is that okay, Mom? If me and Cliff take the ATVs out together to see my ants?"

"Cliff and I," Sarah said automatically, and then, suddenly, she thought about how right those two words sounded together. "Cliff and I," she whispered again.

"I heard you the first time, Mom," said Ben. "But is it okay? Is it?"

"Yes," Sarah said, her heart lightening considerably. "Yes, Ben, I suppose it is."

When they reached the house, they got out of the pickup, and Charlotte hurried outside to embrace Ben.

Sarah and Cliff hung back, waiting beside the truck, and Cliff said, "Ben wouldn't have to miss me, Sarah. I could stick around, you know."

She had missed him terribly. After today, she didn't want to feel any more pain. She didn't want Ben to feel any more pain. She wanted all of them to be happy again, the way they had been happy when she and Cliff had been together.

"Well? Is it okay if I stay?" The way he looked at her was both touching and painful.

"Yes," she breathed, fitting her hand in his. "Yes. As long as you like."

Chapter Eighteen

"That doesn't look like a white elephant to me," Lucy observed with a look of puzzlement when she saw the old lamp Sarah carried into the dining room.

Sarah set the tarnished brass lamp on the dining-room table temporarily. "A white elephant, Lucy, is another name for something that someone doesn't want anymore. Lucky for us that Ben cleaned out the barn in time to find this old treasure. Maybe Cliff will get a good price for it at the white-elephant auction."

"Is it time to go?" Ben hollered from upstairs.

"Yes, Cliff's car is rolling down the hill right now," Sarah called back. She ran to smooth her hair with water. She was wearing it bouncing around her shoulders today because Cliff liked it that way, but it wouldn't lie smoothly on top.

"Is everyone ready for Pioneer Day?" boomed Cliff from the door.

"Yes, yes, we're coming," Sarah said as she emerged from the bathroom.

"It's awful early," Lucy said.

"Well, we have to be on time. As the new Pioneer Day chairman I want to be there when people start setting up their booths."

"Wasn't the Chautauqua good last night? I liked the guy who played General Custer the best," Ben said with relish.

"*I* liked Carry Nation the best. I'd like to have a hatchet like hers," Lucy said.

"You *would*," Sarah said, smothering a laugh.

Cliff dropped an appreciative kiss on Sarah's nose, and Lucy giggled. She seemed to love it when Cliff and Sarah showed their affection so openly.

"Come on, everybody, let's go," Cliff said, hurrying them all to his car. Lucy and Ben had a loud discussion about who was going to sit on the right side of the back seat, but Cliff recalled that it was Lucy's turn and said that Ben would sit on that side on the way home. They accepted this and piled in, and Sarah was once more thankful for Cliff's ability to handle her children. His presence took some of the pressure off her. She didn't have to be constantly firm and alert to Ben and Lucy's needs when Cliff was present.

Sarah and Cliff had reached an agreement on the day of Ben's unsanctioned ride on the ATV. For the time being, Sarah had shelved any worries she entertained about Cliff's unsuitability to remain in Curtisville. She was too busy loving him. It was enough to know that Cliff loved her now. She didn't want to worry about tomorrow.

Cliff glanced over at Sarah as he braked his car to a stop beneath the unfinished mural across the parking lot from the Chatterbox.

"Excuse me, Sarah, there's Lydia Claypool coming out of the restaurant. I need to ask her something about the parade floats." Cliff hurried off, and Sarah was immediately accosted by Ginnie Dubose.

"The Pioneer Ladies' balloon booth is in the worst place in the park, Sarah," she said. "We've got to move it, or Mrs. Ocher will have a fit."

"Well, I—"

"Anything wrong?" Cliff asked mildly as he returned.

"I was just telling Sarah about the Pioneer Ladies' balloon booth. Mrs. Ocher wants it behind the band shell where we'll have some protection from the wind."

"I'll take care of it," said Cliff with a wink at Sarah.

"Oh, and there's the problem about the ice," Ginnie remembered. "Janice Booth asked me to remind you that it hasn't been delivered yet."

"I'll handle that, too," Cliff said.

Sarah had to admire his grace under pressure.

"If I can help you, Cliff," Sarah began as Ginnie bustled in the direction of the park.

"How about mollifying the people who are running the soft-drink concession? They should have plenty of ice in about fifteen minutes."

They hurried toward the park, Lucy and Ben running ahead in their excitement. Sarah was surprised at how many people greeted Cliff.

"I didn't know you knew so many of us," she commented.

"Taking over the Pioneer Day committee helped me meet people," he said as he waved at a teenager who was setting out pots of flowers on a windowsill at the bank across the street.

"I still don't know how you managed to get so involved," she murmured.

Cliff laughed. "Every time I went in the Chatterbox, there was the committee in session. Somehow I got involved in their discussions in spite of myself. Then when Elm couldn't do everything by himself, I helped out. That's all."

"You're too modest, Cliff," she said seriously. "You've added your own touch to the festival. We've never had a white-elephant auction before. And I still don't understand why you won't tell anyone how the town intends to use the money raised by the auction."

"Yeah, Cliff, what's going to happen to all the money you make auctioning off people's old junk?" asked Ben as Sarah and Cliff caught up with him.

"Surprise," Cliff said, dodging a boy on a skateboard at the entrance to the park.

"Tell, tell!" Lucy demanded.

"No, not until after the auction," Cliff said mysteriously. He made a beeline for the Pioneer Ladies' balloon booth, leaving them all as baffled as ever.

Sarah spent time smoothing the feathers of the soft-drink concessionaires, and she watched Cliff as he talked earnestly with Janice Booth about the moving of the balloon booth. She noticed that several people came up to consult Cliff, and he dealt with all of their demands quickly and fairly. Her heart swelled with pride in him.

"Sarah, Sarah, the wind is whipping the Chautauqua tent," said Bernie Vogel as he ran by. Sarah and her brood followed at a run. Sure enough, some of the ropes had been freed from their moorings, and Sarah, Bernie and the kids held the ropes down until they could be fastened again.

There was a quiet moment afterward as Sarah and Bernie wandered back to the band shell together.

"Have you heard anything more from Tim?" Sarah asked hesitantly. She tried to check with the Vogels every couple of days to find out if there were any new developments, but she, like the Vogels, had almost given up hope that Tim would come home.

"No, I'm afraid we haven't heard a thing. Ma is still pretty torn up about what he did."

"I know. Maybe he'll be back in time for the farm auction. It's still set for next month, isn't it?"

"Yes. That's going to be an ordeal," Bernie said. He fixed his lips in a tight line.

"Does Tim know about it?"

"He knows, but don't count on him to come home for that. That's why he left in the first place," Bernie said. He sounded resigned to the fact that his brother would not be present.

Cliff rushed past. "I can't stop to talk—I've got a problem with the Future Farmers' float. I'll see you later," he called to Sarah.

She shot him a reassuring smile, and she left Bernie at the hot dog stand where he was going to sell hot dogs for his civic club.

People were beginning to fill the park. A high school group was offering rides in a covered wagon pulled by a bored-looking horse. A voice over the loudspeaker announced a sack race, and Ben and Lucy clamored to enter it. When Sarah gave her permission, they ran away through the trees to the playground. Sarah was hailed by Janice.

"Have you seen Cliff?" she asked Sarah.

Sarah gestured in the direction of the parade lineup. "He's dealing with a problem with one of the floats," she told her.

"I don't what we would have done without Cliff," Janice said. "He's been a godsend. A real lifesaver. If we couldn't have your father as head of the Pioneer Day committee, there's no one I'd rather have than Cliff Oenbrink." Janice disappeared into the crowd, leaving Sarah on her own.

What a good opinion everyone had of Cliff. How well he fit in here. Frankly it surprised her. And he seemed to take everything in his stride. If she hadn't known better, she would have thought that Cliff had been a community leader in Curtisville all his life.

The parade started in about an hour, and it was followed by a costume contest. After that, Lucy dragged Sarah to watch artists' demonstrations of making corn-husk dolls, and Sarah bought two handwoven willow baskets at the craft show. A box supper at twilight preceded the white-elephant auction.

Cliff was the auctioneer. The auction took place in the Chautauqua tent, with attendees seated on folding chairs in rows. Sarah was amused at the wholehearted way that Cliff entered into his auctioneer role. He had everyone laughing so hard when he described various white-elephant items that they were reluctant to settle down.

"I didn't know you knew how to do this," Sarah said, during a break.

"My uncle ran a livestock auction," he told her as he sipped water from a glass someone had shoved into his hand. That was all the explanation he had time to give before he had to rush back to the platform at the front of the tent.

The first item he held up this time was Sarah's old lamp. Cliff managed to get twenty dollars for it, which amazed Ben.

"Twenty dollars for that old thing?" he said. "We should have brought more of our old stuff."

"All we have at our house is old stuff, Ben," said Sarah.

"That's what I mean," Ben said seriously.

At the end of the auction, Janice, in her capacity as mayor, stepped up to the platform to announce that the auction had netted over five hundred dollars. A whisper of interest rippled throughout the crowd.

"Now," Janice said, her eyes brightening with glee, "I'll let Cliff Oenbrink, our hardworking chairman of the Pioneer Day committee, tell you exactly what the committee's plans are for this money."

Cliff took the microphone to a scattering of applause.

"I know a lot of you have been wondering why I've pushed this white-elephant auction so hard. I had a reason," he said. He paused. "When I first came to Curtisville a few months ago, I was curious about the unfinished mural on the side of the building across from the Chatterbox. I was told that the artist who started it left town before it could be finished. Your mayor informed me that the preliminary sketches were still floating around city hall somewhere, so I made it a point to take a look at them.

"I was impressed with the scope of the mural. It details a proud history, and I became convinced that the mural should— *must*—be finished. Curtisville needed money for our now-defunct Mural Fund, and I figured out a way to get that money.

"I suggested to the Pioneer Day committee that we sponsor a white-elephant auction. They agreed. Townspeople were more than happy to donate items to be auctioned tonight, and the bidders were generous, too. Ladies and gentlemen, I am pleased to announce that the five hundred dollars that you have bid on these white-elephant items will be spent to complete the Curtisville mural as soon as we can find a qualified artist. By the next Pioneer Day, you and I will watch together as the mural is finally unveiled!"

The crowd was silent for a moment, and then they were applauding and jumping to their feet. Someone whistled. Then many of the townpeople crowded around Cliff to shake his hand and to find out more about the mural.

Sarah was astonished. She'd had no idea that Cliff was planning to spearhead a drive to finish the mural. Nothing could have pleased the citizens of Curtisville more.

Cliff shouldered his way through the crowd. She reached out her hands, and his grip was strong. He was beaming happily. "Well?" he said. "Was it a good surprise?"

"It's wonderful, Cliff. The mural means a lot to people around here."

"It should. When it's finished, the downtown will be immeasurably brightened. Imagine being able to look out the windows of the Chatterbox or the Country Inn at such a beautiful painting."

More people gathered to shake Cliff's hand, and Sarah was separated from him in distance, but not in thought. For a moment, Sarah herself felt like the outsider, like the person who didn't belong here. She shook the feeling off. She would always belong here. She knew that. It was heartening to know that Cliff fit in here now, too.

"We want to go get ice cream," Lucy said, tugging at Sarah's arm.

"It's late, Lucy," she said.

"Oh, let them. Your mother and I will take them," said Elm behind her.

"Pop, I didn't see you," she said, turning and hugging first Elm, then Charlotte.

"We were here for the auction," Charlotte chimed in. "Isn't it lovely that the mural will be finished? Cliff's done such a good job as head of the Pioneer Day committee."

"We're planning to make him head of it again next year," Elm said.

"Next year? What if he isn't here?" Sarah said in surprise.

"Oh, he'll be here, all right. He's already promised me that," Elm assured her. "Come on, Lucy, Ben. You can pick up these youngsters at our house in an hour or so, Sarah."

Sarah watched Cliff's approach through the crowd. He had to stop to shake many hands, and she felt a burst of affection toward him. She realized that the way she felt about Cliff was the way so many other people in Curtisville felt. He wouldn't have been so readily accepted if he had come to town and sought to bowl everyone over with a hard sell of his expertise in farming. He'd known better than to do that. He had earned his place here. He had learned Curtisville ways and adopted Curtisville values. No, she corrected herself. He hadn't had to learn their values. He had grown up with similar ones, after all.

Cliff finally reached her. He touched her hand and smiled at her. "How about going for a walk with me down by the river," he suggested.

"Don't you have something you need to do?" Sarah asked.

"Probably, but I've delegated the clean-up chores to someone else. It's been a long day, and I'm entitled to a few minutes' rest."

Silently she nodded, and together they slipped away from the tent.

They strolled hand in hand toward the river. A strain of crickets shrilled at them from afar. A chill in the air made Sarah shiver. Cliff put his arm around her when they reached the path where he had first kissed her on the Fourth of July.

"Remember?" Cliff asked softly, and Sarah nodded.

The river sang a magical little tune as it tumbled over rocks. More rain this week had increased its flow, and it lapped at the edges of the path. Rocks along the bank that might have been fully exposed in a drier year were almost totally submerged now. The summer's heavy rainfall had been a blessing, for now Sarah was assured of having a good crop of sorghum. The farm's financial prospects were bright.

"Stop here," Cliff said, and he pulled her into his arms. He kissed her until her head spun. When he released her lips, she rested her head on his shoulder, wishing that she could prolong this romantic moment forever.

"Why wouldn't you marry me, Sarah, love, when I asked you?" he asked.

She lifted her head. His eyes glistened in the moonlight. They were wistful and full of love for her.

"I didn't think you would be happy in Curtisville for the rest of your life," she said truthfully. "I thought you would get tired of me. And the town."

"I would never get tired of you," he said. "As for Curtisville, I grew up in a place like this. After life on the fast track, Curtisville seems pleasantly normal. I've grown to like this town a lot, Sarah. I don't ever want to leave."

"You didn't like Medallion," she pointed out. "Almost every time you think about your hometown, you say something negative."

He stared at her. "But Medallion isn't anything like Curtisville," he said in bewilderment. "Did you think that just because I don't want to live in Medallion I wouldn't want to live here, either? All small towns aren't alike, you know."

"Aren't they? Certainly there are similarities."

"Oh, Sarah, let me tell you about my last year in Medallion. I was a Boy Scout and I was working toward Eagle Scout.

For my final Eagle Scout project I had to do something for community service, and I had an urge to use my organizational skills and organize some kind of festival like other small towns nearby had. Like Pioneer Day, in fact.''

"So did you organize one?"

"I certainly tried my hardest," Cliff said ruefully. "I went to business after business, trying to sell them on the idea that we needed our own unique celebration. I told them how it would benefit business. I attended a city council meeting and told the town leaders how much a festival would benefit civic pride. I got absolutely nowhere. No one wanted to do the work. No one wanted to donate any money to get it started. I ended up painting park benches for my Eagle Scout project when I could have done something more."

"The trouble you encountered in Medallion wouldn't happen in Curtisville. Everybody here is only too happy to help anyone or anything."

"That's what I found out when I began to work on the Pioneer Day committee. After my experience in Medallion, I couldn't believe the enthusiastic response of the community. It was a pleasure being Pioneer Day chairman. I'm looking forward to doing it again next year."

"That's what Pop said," Sarah murmured. She kissed his chin.

"So if you've been thinking that I'm going to disappear into the wilds of Wichita or Des Moines or Milwaukee, you've got another think coming. I'll be right here in Curtisville the rest of my life. I'll be coaching Little League teams and organizing Pioneer Day and hanging out at the Chatterbox, just like everyone else."

"Mmm," agreed Sarah.

"Which brings me back to the topic I wanted to discuss in the first place. Is there any reason now, Sarah Norquist Morrow, why you can't marry me?"

A whippoorwill cried in the distance, and Sarah focused on Cliff's dear face: his teeth that were slightly crooked; his nose that was a bit too sharp; his wide and expectant smile. She loved him. He had swept away all her reservations. They all seemed silly now.

"I can't think of any reason not to marry you, Cliff Oenbrink," she said.

"That's exactly what I thought," said Cliff with great satisfaction.

"Unless," she said suddenly, "you won't go into the delivery room with me when our children are born."

"Children? We already have two children," Cliff said.

"We'll want more," Sarah predicted.

"I guess I won't mind being in the delivery room with you," conceded Cliff. "After all, I did it for Quilter."

"What a lot we've shared in a few short months," Sarah said contentedly.

"What a lot we'll share for the rest of our lives," Cliff told her.

"Nothing could make me happier," Sarah replied, knowing at last that this was true. He tightened his arms around her, and she listened to the steady beat of his heart, wondering why it had been so hard to see that Cliff was the man for her. She had let things get so complicated, and she had almost lost him forever.

She loved him, and he loved her. Their love would go on forever, like the land. Like their faith. Like their shared values.

It was so simple, really.

Epilogue

In October

"I don't know if you should climb that hill, Elm," Charlotte fussed when Elm first proposed a walk up Lornbacher Hill, but he insisted that she humor him.

"I just want to walk slow and easy up the hill and slow and easy down the hill," he explained with elaborate patience, and Charlotte finally acquiesced. It was an October evening, and there would be frost on the fields tonight. But now, after supper, it was pleasantly cool.

After a small wedding in their church three days before, Sarah and Cliff had left for their honeymoon to an undisclosed destination. Charlotte and Elm had moved to the farm temporarily so that the children wouldn't be uprooted for the whole week.

Charlotte liked being back on the farm again, although she found that she didn't like it as much as she'd thought she would. Certain things seemed unfamiliar. For instance, it seemed like such a long walk up this hill. It hadn't always seemed so long.

"Sarah harvested a great crop of sorghum, didn't she?" Charlotte said in a conversational tone as they walked past a field of drying stalks.

"Are you needling me, Charlotte?" Elm looked down at her challengingly.

"Of course I'm not needling you," Charlotte said with irritation. "Still, I do think you ought to admit that Sarah was right."

"She's talking about buying cattle now," Elm said. "She says they can graze on the sorghum stalks after it's harvested. What would she want to go and buy cattle for?"

"Farming is different these days," Charlotte said.

"I'm not sure the change is for the better," Elm said testily.

"It's still the best way to live," Charlotte retorted.

"I don't know if it is or not."

"Oh, Elm, think what a thrill it is to look out over a field of wheat and realize that *you* grew that wheat, that *you* are the one who is going to feed the hungry people of the world! Why, how can you match that for satisfaction?"

"Charlotte, sometimes you sound like a damned poet. Anyway, it's not only wheat on Windrush Valley Farm nowadays. Your daughter sees to that."

"She's your daughter, too, Elmer Norquist. You should be proud of that."

They walked on for several steps, and Elm said softly, "I guess I am. I guess I am proud of Sarah."

"You should tell her so."

"I've never developed a taste for eating crow."

"Well, I think you'll have to in your old age. You're getting altogether too cantankerous for your own good. It would do you good to eat crow. Not the whole crow, perhaps, but a feather or two."

Elm chuckled. "Maybe you're right, Charlotte dear."

"It took you a long time to get around to admitting that, too. This is the first time you've admitted that I'm right in almost fifty years."

The moonlight made Charlotte's eyes sparkle behind her glasses, and Elm recalled the first time they'd walked up this hill. He'd just brought Charlotte to Windrush Valley Farm for the first time. Could it really have been almost fifty years ago?

"Fifty years," he mused. They stood at the top of the hill now.

"Just look, Elm," Charlotte said softly. The house lay below them, fringed with trees and mellow with the glow of lights shining from the windows. Even up here, they heard Lucy laugh. A tranquil wind soughed through the orchard, and Charlotte slipped her hand into Elm's.

"Now that's a pretty sight down there, isn't it?" Elm said, squeezing Charlotte's hand.

They stood and watched it for a while, remembering the house as it had been during the years they'd lived in it. First they'd lived with Elm's parents, then Duane was born. Duane and his attraction for kites, which he loved to fly over the fields of the farm. That love for things airborne had translated into a love for airplanes, and that was what had taken him into the Air Force at such an early age. They remembered with fondness Duane and his friend, Norrie Vogel, and Norrie's little brothers tramping in and out of the house at all hours of the day and night.

Then the arrival of the screaming bundle that had been Sarah, who protested most volubly her presence in the world until her colic abated. Sarah, her blond pigtails flying behind her as she raced out to the field to show Elm her certificate for being the top student in her class in the fourth grade.

Later, James had married Sarah and moved in, and Ben and Lucy had been born. Charlotte had held her first grandchild in her arms the night that Sarah brought him home from the hospital, moved to tears by the thought that this tiny morsel of humanity was to inherit what she and Elm and all the other Norquists for generations before them had spent their lifetimes building.

She felt a lump in her throat now, just thinking about it.

"It was all worth it," Charlotte whispered.

"What was that?" said Elm, turning his good ear toward her.

"The land. Worrying about it. Planting it. Harvesting the crop. Taking care of the land so it could be passed on to Sarah and Ben and Lucy. It was all worth it."

"You're not getting sentimental on me, are you, Charlotte?" demanded Elm. He was unsettled to see that her eyes shone with bright unshed tears.

"You loved it, too," she said. "You loved the land as much as I do."

"Ah, Charlotte," he said, settling his arm across her shoulders. "I still do. And I always will."

Charlotte brushed the tears from her eyes and pulled her light jacket more tightly around her.

"Come along, Elm," she said briskly. "It's time to go before we freeze out here."

"Not so fast," Elm said.

"It'll be a lot easier going down the hill than it was going up," Charlotte said, but she slowed her steps to match her husband's.

"You may be right about that, too," he said mildly, and he pulled her closer, glad for her warmth beside him.

At the bottom of the hill waited the house, full of memories, welcoming them home again.

PAMELA BROWNING

The HEARTLAND is its people.

It is families like the Morrows and the Vogels who have been neighbors and friends for generations. Together, they've celebrated births, mourned deaths, ploughed and harvested the land and raised their children to respect and love the rich soil with its bounty of golden wheat.

You've met Sarah Morrow and her family who have always owned Windrush Valley farm and you've seen her win the battle to save their heritage in #237 SIMPLE GIFTS. Be sure to join her neighbor, Tim Vogel, on his search for a new home and happiness as he leaves Curtisville and farming in #241 FLY AWAY (April). And don't miss #245 HARVEST HOME (May) when Mark Sherrod's troubled heart leads him on a search for his family and the home he's never known.

Experience the HEARTLAND stories of these people in #241 FLY AWAY (April) and #245 HARVEST HOME (May).

AR237-1

MAIL-IN-OFFER
OFFER CERTIFICATE ✂

I have enclosed the required number of proofs of purchase from any specially marked "Gifts From The Heart" Harlequin romance book, plus cash register receipts and a check or money order payable to Harlequin Gifts From The Heart Offer, to cover postage and handling.

002

CHECK ONE	ITEM	# OF PROOFS OF PURCHASE	POSTAGE & HANDLING FEE
	01 Brass Picture Frame	2	$ 1.00
	02 Heart-Shaped Candle Holders with Candles	3	$ 1.00
	03 Heart-Shaped Keepsake Box	4	$ 1.00
	04 Gold-Plated Heart Pendant	5	$ 1.00
	05 Collectors' Doll Limited quantities available	12	$ 2.75

NAME _____

STREET ADDRESS _____ APT. # _____

CITY _____ STATE _____ ZIP _____

Mail this certificate, designated number of proofs of purchase (inside back page) and check or money order for postage and handling to:

Gifts From The Heart, P.O. Box 4814
Reidsville, N. Carolina 27322-4814

NOTE THIS IMPORTANT OFFER'S TERMS

Requests must be postmarked by May 31, 1988. Only proofs of purchase from specially marked "Gifts From The Heart" Harlequin books will be accepted. This certificate plus cash register receipts and a check or money order to cover postage and handling must accompany your request and may not be reproduced in any manner. Offer void where prohibited, taxed or restricted by law. LIMIT ONE REQUEST PER NAME, FAMILY, GROUP, ORGANIZATION OR ADDRESS. Please allow up to 8 weeks after receipt of order for shipment. Offer only good in the U.S.A. Hurry—Limited quantities of collectors' doll available. Collectors' dolls will be mailed to first 15,000 qualifying submitters. All other submitters will receive 12 free previously unpublished Harlequin books and a postage & handling refund.

OFFER-1RR

GIFTS FROM THE HEART
from *Harlequin*

FREE BY MAIL With proofs of purchase
plus postage and handling

A. **Hand-polished solid brass picture frame 1-5/8″ × 1-3/8″ with 2 proofs of purchase.**

B. **Individually handworked, pair of heart-shaped glass candle holders (2″ diameter), 6″ candles included, with 3 proofs of purchase.**

C. **Heart-shaped porcelain keepsake box (1″ high) with delicate flower motif with 4 proofs of purchase.**

D. **Radiant gold-plated heart pendant on 16″ chain with complimentary satin pouch with 5 proofs of purchase.**

E. **Beautiful collectors' doll with genuine porcelain face, hands and feet, and a charming heart appliqué on dress with 12 proofs of purchase. Limited quantities available. See offer terms.**

HERE IS HOW TO GET YOUR FREE GIFTS

Send us the required number of proofs of purchase (below) of specially marked ''Gifts From The Heart'' Harlequin books and cash register receipts with the Offer Certificate (available in the back pages) properly completed, plus a check or money order (do not send cash) payable to Harlequin Gifts From The Heart Offer. We'll RUSH you your specified gift. Hurry—Limited quantities of collectors' doll available. See offer terms.

402R

GIFTS FROM THE HEART
ONE PROOF
OF PURCHASE

To collect your free gift by mail you must include the necessary number of proofs of purchase with order certificate.